D0503215

GENERATION WONDER

GENERATION WONDER

THE NEW AGE OF HEROES

Edited by Barry Lyga

With illustrations by Colleen Doran

AMULET BOOKS • NEW YORK

PUBLISHER'S NOTE: This is a work of fiction. Names, characters, places, and incidents are either the product of the authors' imagination or used fictitiously, and any resemblance to actual persons, living or dead, business establishments, events, or locales is entirely coincidental.

Cataloging-in-Publication Data has been applied for and may be obtained from the Library of Congress.

ISBN 978-1-4197-5446-3

"Love to Hate" © 2022 Lamar Giles
"Fire That Lasts" © 2022 Sarah Trabucchi
"Ordinary Kid" © 2022 Joseph Bruchac
"Fly, Lions, Fly" © 2022 Morgan Baden
"My Life as a Houseplant" © 2022 Matthew Phillion
"Aubrey vs. the Ninth Circle of Hell (aka Prom)" © 2022 Elizabeth Eulberg Inc.
"Something Borrowed, or The Costume" © 2022 Danielle Paige
"The Knight's Gambit" © 2022 Varian Johnson
"The Night I Caught a Bullet" © 2022 Sterling Gates
"Mecha Girl" © 2022 Axie Oh
"Queeroes and Villains" © 2022 Anna-Marie McLemore
Foreword and "Power Baby Blue Grows Up" © 2022 Barry Lyga
"Bumped!" © 2022 Mercer Street Creative, Inc.
Illustrations © 2022 Colleen Doran
Book design by Hana Anouk Nakamura and Brenda E. Angelilli

Published in 2022 by Amulet Books, an imprint of ABRAMS. All rights reserved. No portion of this book may be reproduced, stored in a retrieval system, or transmitted in any form or by any means, mechanical, electronic, photocopying, recording, or otherwise, without written permission from the publisher.

Printed and bound in U.S.A.
10 9 8 7 6 5 4 3 2 1

Amulet Books® is a registered trademark of Harry N. Abrams, Inc.

ABRAMS The Art of Books
195 Broadway, New York, NY 10007
abramsbooks.com

CONTENTS

PAGE vi: Foreword

PAGE 1: *"Love to Hate"* by Lamar Giles

PAGE 29: *"Fire That Lasts"* by Sarah MacLean

PAGE 63: *"Ordinary Kid"* by Joseph Bruchac

PAGE 93: *"Fly, Lions, Fly"* by Morgan Baden

PAGE 125: *"My Life as a Houseplant"* by Matthew Phillion

PAGE 149: *"Aubrey vs. the Ninth Circle of Hell (aka Prom)"* by Elizabeth Eulberg

PAGE 181: *"Something Borrowed, or The Costume"* by Danielle Paige

PAGE 205: *"The Knight's Gambit"* by Varian Johnson

PAGE 225: *"The Night I Caught a Bullet"* by Sterling Gates

PAGE 263: *"Mecha Girl"* by Axie Oh

PAGE 285: *"Queeroes and Villains"* by Anna-Marie McLemore

PAGE 301: *"Power Baby Blue Grows Up"* by Barry Lyga

PAGE 335: *"Bumped!"* by Paul Levitz

PAGE 352: About the Authors

FOREWORD

By BARRY LYGA

SUPERHEROES. IT'S NO SECRET THAT I LOVE THEM.

It's beyond love, actually. I think there is a very real possibility that a lifetime of reading about, thinking about, and writing about superheroes has altered my DNA to the point that my alleles generate four-color inks and old newsprint.

My dad introduced me to superhero stories when I was a child, reading me the old Spider-Man comic strips and buying me Legion of Super-Heroes comics to keep me quiet on the six-hour drives to visit his parents. My mouth closed; my mind opened.

Triumph. Tragedy. The empyreal. The infernal. Even the mundane, filtered through the fantastical. Superhero stories are, appropriately enough, a sort of super-genre, encompassing all other narrative types: romance, thriller, mystery, horror, coming-of-age. I could go on, but you know them as well as I do. No matter what kind of story you're telling, there's a way to tell it with a superhero. Superheroes are flexible (and I'm not just talking about Plastic Man). You can wrap a superhero around any kind of tale, as you will see in the worlds our contributors have conjured for you.

Island private school for the future's elite? Check!

A girl who understands love in a world where emotions have been made illegal? Check!

A kid who just wants to use his powers to become rich and famous on the basketball court . . . only to have a pesky murder attempt get in the way? Check!

These stories and ten more await you in this, an anthology that gives a big bear hug to the history of superheroes while at the same time looking forward into a world that is more equitable, more diverse, and more heroic than ever.

Superheroes must strike that nigh-impossible balance of being both timely and timeless. Look at Superman: In 1938, when he was introduced, the audience understood intuitively that his costume, with its red shorts over a blue leotard, was meant to evoke circus strongmen and similar performers of the day. That aesthetic lasted almost eighty years before DC Comics—presumably tired of our too-hip modern age's "hilarious" snark about wearing underwear on the outside—deep-sixed the red trunks.

Funny thing, though—within a few years, everyone agreed that it just looked wrong to see Superman without those red trunks over his tights. DC brought back the trunks, as is right, and those who think it's the height of comedy to joke about wearing one's underwear on the outside should ponder the stratospheric success of Madonna or Lady Gaga for a moment and then shut up.

Superheroes simultaneously provide wish fulfillment and wish destruction. At their very best, they perform a truly amazing trick, showing us what we should aspire to while at the same time acknowledging that no, you're never really going to fly, because you aren't from the doomed planet Krypton. Like the rest of us, you were born to a very boring human being.*

You're never gonna fly.

But . . .

But it's good to dream of flying.

It's good to aspire to things we can't necessarily achieve. Because along the path to that impossible dream lie thousands of opportunities we'd never see if we hadn't set out on the journey in the first place.

And all of us—*all* of us—can always be better. Do better.

Why do I love superheroes? It's not the action poses, the capes, or the laser breath. It's knowing that we poor, pathetic, earthbound humans have the capacity to envision and create something better than us, and then strive to achieve that goal every day.

(And also the action poses, the capes, and the laser breath.)

When I look at the superhero landscape at the dawn of the third decade of this terrorism-born, fascism-resurgent, pandemic-ravaged millennium, I see a (long-overdue) attempt at diversity and inclusion, which I applaud.

But in many cases, it's the same old costumes with new faces under the masks. The same old ideas dressed up in diversity chic.

---

* And for the love of Zeus, spare me the nonsense about "Batman is better than Superman because anyone can be Batman!" Yeah, anyone born into a billion-dollar fortune with a genetic predisposition for great abs can be Batman. Oh, and you get to watch your parents gunned down in front of you. Does that sound like fun?

The superhero has been with us since 1938. (Some argue it's been even longer, but let's not get into that now.) The last truly new, truly radical character was probably Wolverine.

Who was introduced in 1974.

So let's see what we can do about that. Maybe we can reimagine the superhero from the ground up, a creation for the age of Obama and Trump, not Herbert Hoover or Richard Nixon. New powers. New motivations. New perspectives. New worlds.

A new age of heroes for an age that sorely needs them.

Tie your towel around your neck, and don't let your parents catch you jumping off the deck. We're about to fly.

—Barry Lyga
April 2021

LOVE TO HATE

by LAMAR GILES

FRIDAY

TY REVELL KNOWS HE'S THE KIND OF HOOPER

you love to hate.

It's the first game of the year. The Warton High Trojans are playing in the local university's sold-out, ten thousand–seat indoor stadium because . . . well, because when you attract fans the way future NBA lottery pick Ty Revell does, that's what's necessary.

It's all too easy for him. Left-right crossover, spin move, toss ball between the frozen defender's legs, retrieve ball in paint, windmill slam.

The crowd goes absolutely bananas. *"Re-vell! Re-vell!"*

That's highlight number six.

He's not worried about his points, rebounds, assists, or steals. Those are money automatically. These days he's more concerned with how many options the local news has for their "Revell Reel."

This is a blowout game, though. Coach will probably sit him and the other starters for the fourth, give the bench some playing time. Ty loves doing his job well enough that those guys get the spotlight for a while. Makes him feel like less of a . . . a cheat?

The thing he's heard his whole life—from coaches, from teachers, from pastors preaching the gospel truth—is that success comes from hard work. Overcoming daily struggles, making tough decisions, and striving for incremental improvement is what makes you a winner. Supposedly, excellence requires sacrifice.

From the time Ty was five years old, first glimpsed the secret colors of the world around him, and felt the spectacular way his body reacted, he's been excellent at pretty much everything. Effortlessly.

The other team inbounds the ball. Ty backs off the baseline, gives the dude room to get it in. He sees how the pass will happen a second before it leaves his opponent's hands. He knows the ball's spin and speed and who's gonna catch it, even though that guy's nowhere near Ty's line of sight. He sees it in the minor twitches of muscles, the way the currents of air circulate in a spectrum of colors invisible to everyone but Ty. The signals, impressions, premonitions—whatever you want to call them—make his muscles tingle, and it's only a conscious decision to slow down, to *play normal*, that prevents his hand from snapping to the ball the way a frog's tongue snaps to a fly, then zooming to the basket for another soaring dunk. Highlight number seven.

Instead, he *allows* the small forward to catch the ball and break for a hole in Warton's defense. Ty stays a step behind, making a good show of going for the block, smacking the backboard a microsecond after the ball touches it and spins through the hoop. Scouts have been dinging him for his defense all year. Irritating, because he can stop any offensive play anytime he wants, but more flaws in his game mean less suspicion.

The next play, Ty hits a three to close the quarter and trots to the bench while waving at the crowd cheering him on. He's come to expect the standing ovations. Would probably feel weird if they *didn't* jump to their feet and scream his name, like maybe he's holding back *too* much. The electricity in the air is mostly the kind he's grown used to. But there's something else crackling.

Something he doesn't like the taste of (oily), the smell of (old firecrackers), or the feel of (pinpricks, heat, aggression).

There's a guy standing in the bleachers, but he ain't clapping.

Not totally unusual—if Ty did that spin move between-the-legs shit to the team you root for, would you clap? But, like, this dude isn't even watching the court. He's turned all the way around, facing the crowd, looking for someone. Also, through Ty's special perception, dude's stained red, like the girl in that movie with the prom and the pig's blood.

"Revell!" Coach barks. He wants Ty with the team.

When the fourth quarter starts and the crowd's seated, Ty's the weirdo not paying attention to the game. Because he's watching that guy. As Ty twists in his folding chair to see what he's doing, Mr. Red turns away, still searching.

Ty senses movement—feels a pull—from ten rows up. A woman stands with an empty soda cup, excuses herself as she moves toward the stairs. Perhaps on her way to concessions for a refill or the bathroom. Mr. Red isn't going to give her the chance.

Dude spots the woman a second after Ty does and explodes out of his seat, bumping outstretched knees and toppling half-full popcorn buckets with no concern. The people he knocks into voice their displeasure. They grow alarmingly silent when Mr. Red pulls the pistol from inside his jacket.

A lot happens between the moment that gun appears and someone screams.

Mr. Red makes it to the aisle; the bloody sheen through which Ty perceives him *blazes*. The woman, whoever she is to Mr. Red, can't possibly see him; she's looking the other way. Yet she goes still in her tracks, maybe sensing the danger that's smacking Ty in the face in a *regular* human instinct kinda way. The gut punch that warns you about the bad thing coming, but maybe not in time to save you.

She faces the man, recognition and some grim history hardening her features. The normal spectrum of colors in which Ty sees her shifts to the same crimson as Mr. Red's aura. Still, no one screams. It's all happening that fast.

Ty sees it the way he sees things on the court. The infinitesimal muscle twitches. The currents in the air. Mr. Red's gun has a seven-pound pull, and he's exerting five and a half pounds already. No one's going to stop him. No one *has* to stop him.

Ty almost does what he's perfected on the court: hold back. He almost makes himself look at the play Warton's running while bracing for the sound of the pistol and hoping Mr. Red has terrible aim.

But if he misses her, who else will get hit? That gun's got fifteen rounds—a count that pops into Ty's head, though he knows very little about firearms. What if Mr. Red squeezes that trigger over and over and over? Even if it's just one perfect shot, what would that mean? Letting that woman die because Ty doesn't want to be that other kind of hero?

That's not reason enough.

Mr. Red is exerting six pounds of pressure on his seven-pound trigger when Ty *moves*.

The world slows, then stops. If there were time, Ty would hold back a little. There's not, so this is what it feels like to slice between seconds and breaths and the shift from six pounds of pressure to six and a half. He plants one foot on the scorer's table and propels himself forward with such force the wood splinters. He sails over the heads of the people Mr. Red terrorized while stalking his target, clearing thirty-five feet, landing beside the gunman with a *whoosh!* before snatching the pistol with his right hand, mangling Mr. Red's trigger finger in the process, then planting the meaty edge of his left hand firmly against Mr. Red's sternum. Ty's intent is to shove the man to the ground, where others might jump in and restrain him.

He's not holding back, though. First time in a long time.

The force of his shove is the same force he's just exerted to make a world-record-breaking long jump. That force *lifts* Mr. Red and propels him a long way—to center court.

The crunch when the man lands stops play as effectively as a referee's whistle.

No one understands at first. Did a crazy fan run onto the court? That doesn't make sense, because he didn't run—he flew. And the way his legs are angled, like a difficult geometry problem, he may never run again.

"Hey! Hey!" someone yells, pointing.

Recognition—muscles, air, color—reminds Ty that there's still a gun in his hand, and that can be a whole other problem for a Black boy like him, so in a motion that would look like a glitch in reality to anyone who's quick enough to catch it, he disassembles the gun and drops the pieces.

Everyone's staring, something he usually welcomes. No cheers this time. Only a stadium's worth of silence.

Until Mr. Red's pained wailing shreds the air and begins the work of tearing Ty's life apart.

QBC News at Six, sports segment:

"In local news, Warton High School's nationally recognized basketball team is under investigation in an alleged cheating scandal. Cell phone footage from a recent game appears to show the school's star player displaying preternatural abilities, something long banned in amateur and professional sports. Pending further investigation, consequences for the lauded program could include—"

MONDAY

"Jesus!" Coach drops his satchel and clutches his chest.

For a nightmarish second, Ty fears he's driven the man to a heart attack, but his senses confirm Coach's heart is strong and beating normally. Though his spiking adrenaline has the air tasting like a storm cloud. Ty shifts uncomfortably in the office chair.

"How did you—?" Coach looks to the open window behind his desk. They are on the third floor.

"I didn't feel like walking past everyone," Ty says. Coach has never been concerned about *how* Ty got into his office before. He probably has a lot of questions now. Who wouldn't? Ty says, "I tried to text you this weekend."

Coach gathers his bag, then makes his way to the high-backed chair behind his desk. "My phone got broken during all the commotion on Friday."

His heart skips. So that's a lie.

"Oh," Ty says. "I'm sorry. About your phone."

"Is there something you need?"

"I thought you might want to talk about . . . it. What happened."

So many conversations in this office over the last three years. Everything from advice about girls to their favorite movies. Rarely do they discuss basketball, because Ty has all the stuff on the court handled. In this office, they relax. Ty says things he can't say to his dad. Coach has said Ty reminds him of his son, who's grown up and works in a big city a few hours north.

If Coach is disappointed, Ty can take it. He just wishes Coach would say that. Ty wants them to talk again.

Coach rotates his chair halfway, facing the trophies and plaques along the far wall. "I've been advised by the district's legal counsel not to discuss the incident that occurred on Friday night."

"Legal counsel?"

Coach spins toward Ty again. His face is stone. "You should tell your parents in case they want to hire someone."

Hire someone? For what? Ty blurts, "I'm sorry. OK? I'm sorry."

Coach grinds his teeth, his jaw pulsing bright purple in Ty's spectral vision.

Ty rises. It's too soon, that's all. "I'll see you in practice later."

"Don't you dare set foot on my court again. You hear me?"

Ty doesn't feel pain and had only the loosest concept of what it even was until this moment. Those words *hurt*.

"Coach, I . . . I . . ."

"They want to vacate our championships. The State Athletic League wants to *destroy us* because of what you've done."

"They can't," Ty says, knowing no such thing. His only experience with the League was a dude in a suit handing him an MVP trophy and shaking his hand while cameras flashed. Will they take that, too? "Can I talk to them? Explain that I've always held back on the court? I'm really good about not doing extra stuff when—"

"Son," Coach says, "don't tell me any more about what you can do. I'm trying to salvage our program for all the other kids. Your teammates. Someone has to look out for them. The less I know, the better. Now, go to class."

Coach doesn't tell Ty to get out of his sight, but the way he spins his chair so he's looking at those trophies that might not mean anything soon, Ty reads the room without the use of a single superpower.

The time between classes is different from usual. He's used to stares and side-eyes, so that's not the change. Before, it was this wild mix ranging from love to envy. Even people who "didn't like him" really meant they didn't like that they weren't him. With his Spectral Sense, walking past mildly jealous classmates (and teachers) was like pushing through the thinnest green spiderweb. Not pleasant, but bearable. Before.

Now the dynamic is different. There's absolutely no green in the spectrum of colors and intentions overlaying every person and thing around him. No one is jealous. There are strands of red (anger), flashes of umber (disgust), a lot of yellow (fear). It's second block before Ty sees a few of his teammates in the hall. He tips his chin toward the ceiling—their signature *what up, though* nod—but his point guard, power forward, and center don't return the gesture. They turn away.

It stops him cold, and a small underclassman collides with him. The kid bounces off Ty like a tennis ball off a brick wall.

Ty spins, stuttering an apology and offering a hand, but the little dude crab walks backward, terrified. A teacher (one known for strong strands of envy, when that was a thing) yells, "God, Ty's attacking him!"

Students scuttle away, though not too far. As afraid as they are, Ty's still the best show around. The school resource officer rounds the corner with his baton drawn, and more people than Ty can count are recording with their phones. The emotional spectrum shifts rapidly, filling his head with enough panic noise and color to nearly overwhelm him, when a delicate hand alights on his shoulder.

Ty's puzzled about who—or what—could possibly have gotten so close without his knowledge.

"Enough," this new person says.

The shifting spectrum of colors and intentions through which he sees the world becomes stained glass. Frozen. Everything except Ty and . . .

"Who the fuck are you?" He flinches away from her.

She's short, like five two. Dark brown skin. Denim outfit. Hair blown out, framing her face like a black halo. Beneath her jacket, a T-shirt with an old-school Nintendo controller and the words **CLASSICALLY TRAINED**.

"You're a gamer?" he says, then feels immediately silly since time's frozen all around them and that's probably more important than whether she's played the new *Zelda*.

She shakes her head. "You seem like you pick things up quickly, so I'm giving you a small do-over. Get through that, then come find me in the basement."

"The basement? Is that code?"

"Maybe you're not so quick." She pinches the bridge of her nose like she's fighting a headache. "Meet me in the area of the school beneath the first floor. Got it?"

She slaps his shoulder again, and the world skips backward, rewinding in jerky, unnatural motions, everyone moving like the demon-possessed in a broad-daylight horror movie until—

It's second block before Ty sees a few of his teammates in the hall. He tips his chin toward the ceiling—their signature what up, though nod—but his point guard, power forward, and center don't return the gesture. They turn away.

It stops him cold, and—

Ty steps aside, allowing the tiny underclassman who's been walking too closely behind him to pass. The rest of his classmates keep it moving, and he's no longer concerned with the rainbow waves of fear, anger, and disappointment pulsing off them.

He's too busy looking for the stairs to the basement.

The class bell is a distant sound from the gloomy corridors beneath the school. The basement utilizes the building's entire footprint, a dark mirror of the bustling corridors he's left above.

"Hey! I'm here," he calls, feeling the unease you feel before the obligatory jump scare in a spooky movie.

Reaching with all his senses, he tries to detect the girl, but . . . nothing. He doesn't believe he could've beaten her here, which ramps up his discomfort. What *is* she that she doesn't register like every other physical thing in the building?

A voice calls back, "Down the hall, last door on your right."

Walking the corridor, Ty passes rooms that could be (were?) whole classrooms. They're filled with boxes and file cabinets and assorted whatever. An entire floor of the school converted into a junk drawer. When he reaches that last door, he finds the girl with her feet kicked up on a desk and a controller in her hand—PlayStation 2, not Nintendo. The console's hooked to a janky TV, and the game's one he kind of recognizes. At least the character she's playing looks familiar.

"What is that?" he says.

"*God of War II.*"

"Ohhhhh. I played the one from a couple of years back, where the dude's got a kid. It was fire."

She pauses the game and places her feet back on the floor, facing him. "Yup. That one was good. This one's my favorite, though." He expects her to elaborate, but instead, she says, "I'm Dana."

"Ty."

"I know. Have you wondered why I'm the only person even attempting to have a real conversation with you after Friday?"

Ty's stomach churns, and he looks at anything but her. This room is less cluttered than the ones he passed. The stuffed boxes are relegated to a far corner, giving him a better sense of what used to go on here. There are faded posters on the wall, declaring things like **THE PRESS IS THE FOURTH ESTATE** and **THE FIRST AMENDMENT IS MY JAM**. An old journalism room? When was the last time this school even had a newspaper? Not since he's been here. They definitely would've interviewed him.

"All of your former admirers have moved on, Ty," Dana says.

His focus snaps back. Harshly. "Do you even go here?"

"No."

"Knew it!" he says, more to himself than her, grasping for something to feel OK about. "I would've noticed you."

"No, you wouldn't. Maybe if I were six inches taller, two shades lighter, and lived in a bikini. I've seen what you be liking on the Gram."

He feels *attacked* but hides it well.

She says, "You're not special—"

He takes two steps toward her—not quite in her personal space, but aggressive enough so she hears him. "Thirty-one points per game. Sixty-three percent from the field. A state championship three-peat. Who's hooping more special than that?"

Dana's face remains emotionless. "I mean your *scandal* isn't special. A lot of athletes have enhanced abilities, high school to pro, so many that everyone agrees to turn a blind eye unless something happens that they can't unsee. If you're not Super-Shot punching Doctor Demon through a skyscraper in New York City or the Peace Platoon smashing terrorists in some desert, most folks are happy to pretend there aren't people in their neighborhoods who can do what we do."

"What exactly do *you* do? What was that you pulled upstairs?"

Dana's head tilts sympathetically. She unpauses her game and continues to fight mythical monsters onscreen. "You've shown all the people you thought loved you something they can't unsee. It's going to get worse. Then it's going to be nothing. No one's going to care about where you are a month from now, let alone in ten years. No NBA. No shoe deal. No dating those IG models you waste so much time dreaming about."

"This is bullshit. I'm out." Ty makes for the door.

"I like *God of War II* best because the final boss fight takes you back to a moment from the first game. That's *my* sweet spot: do-overs. But, you kinda deduced that already, didn't you? Call me if you decide to exercise your options. My number's in your jacket pocket."

He's about to tell her to fuck all the way off, but the world does another weird backward skip. Not so extreme as when she did it upstairs, but enough for her chair to be empty and

God of War II to be back on the start menu, ready for him to play.

If he wants.

━━━━━━━━━━━━━━━━━━━━━━━

The tardy bell is ringing when he emerges from the basement. So he's late for social studies.

He enters the room, apologizing to Mr. Duncan, not even thinking he'll need more than words, because part of him is still stuck in the old days—just three days ago—when teachers let him get away with whatever. But the teacher/usually exuberant basketball fan sends Ty to the principal's office on sight. The principal then advises Ty to leave school grounds. Not a suspension, mind you. A "cooling off" period.

No one's going to care about where you are a month from now.

Ty sprints home, wondering if Dana's estimated timing is too generous.

━━━━━━━━━━━━━━━━━━━━━━━

Dad's on the phone. Upstairs. With the door closed. No abilities necessary to suss it all; Dad's just loud.

"—take it back? How you gonna take back money you weren't supposed to give us in the first place? Tell me that. Look . . . *look*! When all this blows over and the country's best basketball player is at Kentucky instead of your shithole school, remember this conversation, you son of a bitch!"

Then a crash—the phone flung against Dad's door.

Ty's still in the foyer, afraid to go farther.

"What are you doing home?" Mom shuffles out of the kitchen in her bathrobe, gripping a coffee mug. There's not even a little bit of coffee in that cup. The spectral spokes shooting from the bourbon feel like sharp medicine.

"They sent me home."

Mom takes a big gulp, chuckles. "Happy Monday, then. I'm going to lie down, sweetie. OK?"

"Sure, Mom." Ty climbs the stairs while Mom burrows between the big decorative pillows on the couch. Sneaking past Dad's office doesn't work because the old man is waiting in the doorway.

"Come here, Ty." Dad waves him inside.

They sit, a solid minute goes by before they speak. And when they do . . .

"Son," Dad starts, "I've been on calls all morning. Your recruiters aren't reacting well to the events that transpired."

"Did I hear you say someone gave you money? And they want it back?"

"That's nothing you should concern yourself with. I'm worried about *you*, son."

Ty sags in his chair, holding back hot tears. It's the first time since Friday that anyone's expressed any concern for *his* well-being.

Then Dad says, "We may need to put some serious thought into you playing overseas."

"Huh?"

Dad produces his iPad and presents a website. "Bahrain doesn't really care about players being . . . enhanced. Not the most lavish accommodations in the world, but several of their league's coaches love the mixtape I sent them. The best part is they'll take real good care of you, so you won't have hardly any living expenses while you're there."

No more hot tears. Just heat. Anger. "What about you and Mom?"

"To keep expenses low, we'll stay here, managing your money until you're ready to— Ty? Ty, where are you going?"

Ty is downstairs and outside fast enough to suck air from Dad's office, leaving the old man gasping.

A couple of minutes later and a few miles away, Ty stops running. Not because he's tired. Because he's lost.

When he left his house, he wasn't thinking. When he doesn't think, something like instinct takes over. It's like how if he misplaces his keys or his phone, he can close his eyes and just move, navigating doorways and avoiding furniture without incident. Within a few steps, he's always found what he's looking for.

So what's he looking for now?

He's on a cracked sidewalk with weeds crawling from the splits in the concrete. Those snaking tendrils are pretty much the only greenery around, a jarring contrast to the tree-lined streets and manicured lawns in his neighborhood. Here the buildings are short and made of faded brick. The asphalt is ashy. The *sky* is ashy with streaky gray mist that's more like factory smoke than clouds. The craziest part is he's almost certain the day was bright and sunny back at his house. What a difference a few miles makes.

Now that he's out of his head and absorbing all the details around him, Ty still doesn't know where he's going. So he strolls, his hands stuffed in his pockets, passing an open pawn shop. An out-of-business soul food spot. A boarded-up, graffiti-scrawled doorway with an awning sheltering a dozing homeless man.

Ty slow walks a block or three, contemplating a return home, when he hears a familiar sound: a bouncing ball.

It's faint, but he tracks the sound to the end of the block, then rounds the corner. It's loud now, and so are the voices. Someone yells, "I'm open!"

Ty's close enough to hear what sounds like a quiet wish at this distance. *"Kobe!"*

The next sound will be a swish—if there's even a net on the rim—or a *bonk!* if the shot's a brick.

It's a *bonk!* and that's OK.

Ty's at the chain-link fence now with his eyes on the game. It's a small public play area with only two half-courts side by side. A kid's park. No real runs here, then. Just fun. That's also OK.

It's a loose three-on-three between what looks to be a group of ten-year-olds. At a glance, Ty can tell the casual players from the more advanced ones. There's a taller, lankier kid who keeps his head up when he dribbles and attempts a step-back three that ain't quite James Harden but might be damn close in a couple of years.

The other standout impresses him with a mean handle. When the lanky boy's step-back hits rim and bounces out to her, the kid instantly pulls off an in-and-out dribble that shakes her defender before she slides along the baseline for a silky finger roll. All with her off hand encased in a cast and fastened to her chest by a sling. (Well, Ty assumes the hand in the cast is her off hand, because if she's dribbling like that with her *actual* off hand . . . whoa!)

All the kids cheer the highlight-worthy move, and it's enough to make Ty pass through the gate for a better look at the game.

He's barely two steps inside the perimeter before a woman says, "What the hell are you doing here? Are you following me?"

She's talking to someone else, he thinks. Has to be. Except his Spectral Sense kicks in, and he *feels* the confusion (orange and pulsing), fear (yellow and clenched), and . . . anger? Anger is red. Always red. When he faces her, it's like getting splashed in the face with warm arterial spray.

Ty stumbles backward, almost loses his balance. He's that startled.

The raging blood clot of a person retreats slightly, too. Ty blinks rapidly, forcing his eyes to focus on a more normal spectrum so he can see her real face. His breath catches. "You?"

It's the woman. From the stadium. The one he saved.

No. Wait. No. No. No.

He understands, though, deep down. When he left his house, he wasn't thinking. The compass in his head switched to autopilot and led him toward what he wanted to find: her.

There she is. Shuffling sideways so she's between him and the basketball court, almost in a fighting stance. Her purse clutched in one hand while she roots in it with the other.

"Hold on, lady. Hold on. I—" Ty says, not knowing how to finish. He can't even explain why he's there to himself.

She retrieves her cell from her bag and holds it like a weapon. "Leave now! I won't call the cops if you do."

Now the red is strong. Inside Ty, too. His rage bubbles. "You're going to call the cops? For what? I saved you, lady."

He can't tell if what she says next is her comeback or if she didn't hear him in the midst of her panic. It doesn't really matter. "You people think you can do anything you want and you're better than us—"

"You people?"

"Flying around and throwing whole cars and bursting into flame. It's crazy. Reggie might never walk again 'cause of what you done to him."

"Reggie?" She can't mean Mr. Red. But she does. Scattered portions of her aura shift to dark green-purple bruises. A mix of fear and shame. The color of damage.

"We oughtta sue your ass. And—and press charges."

Ty's quiet when he says, "Reggie is the man who was going to shoot you."

"I—I ain't see no gun." A lie. More shame splotches appear.

Her mouth opens to say more, probably to threaten him with the police again, but he doesn't give her the chance. Ty's gone in a breath, a new destination firmly fixed in his mind.

Rushing up the sidewalk in a better and brighter neighborhood, dodging folks out for strolls and walking their dogs, he nimbly fishes his phone from one pocket and Dana's scribbled number from another. His hastily typed text:

I'm in

They meet at the university stadium where he played that last game, the sun squatting on the horizon. Loose groups of students flit by while Ty half-heartedly swipes through pics and videos on his phone—better times. When he glances up, she's there.

Dana says, "I didn't startle you this time. Losing my touch."

There's little humor in her tone, and Ty's not in a joking mood, so he gets down to it. "Can you really give me a do-over? Like back in the hallway?"

"Yes and no. It won't be like the hallway. This is a bigger leap. It's subject to less precision."

He stands, alarmed. "Hold up. How much less precise? I ain't trying to be fighting dinosaurs."

"Minutes. Hours, sometimes. That's why I asked you to come back to the stadium. My aim's a little better when I don't have to deal with space *and* time. If we're off by an hour, you're still in the vicinity of where you need to be."

"Question." He feels silly, but . . . "Do I need to avoid running into myself? I saw this movie where a guy went back in time and got shoved into his past self, and they melted into goo."

"That one's *Timecop*, and it's just a movie. I'm sending your *consciousness* back. I'm inserting *current* you into *old* you. Like overwriting a file."

"Is that safe?"

"Do you care?"

No. Not now.

"That's what I thought," she says. "What changed your mind, anyway?"

Ty almost says *everything*. There's maybe some truth to that. But . . . "For real, what I did . . . did it even matter? No one even seemed to care that I saved that lady's life. Not even the lady."

Dana's face is flat, expressionless. Judgment-free. Or so Ty tells himself.

"Hang on, this will be . . . disorienting." She grabs his shoulder, squeezes, and . . .

. . . Ty shoots like a bullet through a kaleidoscope barrel the length of the universe. He tries to scream, but he has no mouth. By the time the horror of being a disembodied consciousness creeps in, it's . . .

FRIDAY (AGAIN)

He's outside the stadium where he'd been standing with Dana a moment ago and three days in the future. He stumbles into his point guard, who does this sort of heroic hug-catch thing to keep Ty from tumbling down the school bus steps.

"You OK, Ty?" His voice is thick with concern.

They get off the bus together, and the rest of the team forms a cocoon around a woozy, unstable Ty. Coach pushes through. "Son! Son, are you all right?"

Coach presses his hands to Ty's cheeks like a grandma checking for fever. Ty remembers the man almost throwing him from his office three days from now and lies, "I'm fine."

Physically, it's the truth. His legs are activating again. All of his many senses are processing information at an exceptional rate, but he also can't stop thinking about how many people who are so concerned with his well-being now won't want to utter a word to him in less than seventy-two hours.

If he doesn't do what needs to be done.

People form a path from the bus to the stadium entrance on either side of him. Hoop fans wanting an up close and personal with the future superstar.

Ty's motions are mechanical at this point. Scribbling an autograph on a jersey, a T-shirt, a mini Warton High basketball. The same way it happened the first time, when the only future he'd considered involved the Los Angeles Lakers or whatever other team got lucky enough to snatch him up.

"Ty, Ty! Over here!"

The little girl's left arm is in a blue cast and a sling. She offers him a silver Sharpie with her good hand, the same hand she'll use for a sick in-and-out dribble to get free for a baseline drive and a finger roll in a few days. What the hell?

He kneels so he's at the kid's level, knowing she's not a ghost but feeling the same sort of fright. Shaky, he says, "What up, little baller."

A nasty bruise surrounds the girl's left eye. A blood blossom stains half her cornea. Was she in a car accident or something?

"Will you sign my cast?" The child beams. There are noticeable gaps in her smile. Maybe those teeth fell out naturally. Maybe.

Ty forces himself to grab the kid's Sharpie, starts to squiggle his usual nonsense signature when a woman presses up behind the kid and Ty's lungs stop working.

It's her. The woman who would've died. Who will die. The woman who'll threaten to call the cops on him just for being in the same park as her and her kid. The woman who will never make it to that park because *he's going to let her die.*

Up close, with no rage aura obscuring his view, he sees her bruises, too. Sees how skittish she is, scanning every which way. When she's convinced they're safe, she speaks. "My Reesie loves you."

"Reesie?"

"That's me." The little bruised and beaten kid grins. "I like Theresa better, though! Will you score thirty for me tonight?"

"Reesie," her mom scolds. "You can't expect people to do your bidding."

"Naw," Ty says, numb. "I can definitely do that for her." He's pretty sure he had at least forty the first time around. Least he can do is reassure the kid, since he's come back to let her mother get murdered.

Ty returns the Sharpie. Reesie—*Theresa*—says, "Thank you sooo much!"

She and her mother wave goodbye and fade into the crowd, though Ty doesn't move. His inaction goes on long enough for Coach to come over.

"What are you doing, Revell? Game time."

"Yeah. I know."

At the end of the third, when he's on his way to the bench, Ty spots all the players in this particular drama. The woman, far up in the bleachers, seated next to Theresa. The girl slurps the last dregs of her soda.

Reggie, the man with the gun—Theresa's father, the mother's boyfriend, someone else entirely, who knows?—is close to finding her in the crowd. Ty moves into the huddle, not hearing a word Coach says, then takes a seat on the bench, bracing himself to do nothing.

The crowd is a low buzz behind him. He stares straight ahead, not needing his eyes to sense it all unfolding again. Theresa's mom taking her soda cup, standing up. Reggie moving toward the aisle.

All Ty has to do is sit, and he'll keep all he's worked for. All he's earned. What he deserves. A promising basketball career. Coach's admiration. His teammates' love. Mom and Dad's pride.

So long as he doesn't mess it up again with some other misstep. Some impulsive thing that screws up all of *their* plans.

Ty's always been told excellence requires sacrifice. Is this what everyone meant? Sacrifice Reesie's mom to be a perfect basketball-playing, money-making machine who knows everyone in his life could turn on him in the time it takes to exert seven pounds of pressure on a trigger? A lot of people could probably live with paying for a bright and comfortable future with someone else's blood.

But he can't.

Ty Revell, former future basketball star, rises off the bench, eyes the man aiming a gun at a defenseless mother, and he *moves* . . .

"Just get out of here," Coach orders, staving off members of the press. "Go with your mom and dad."

Ty welcomes Coach's distraction, pushing into the corridors of the stadium, but instead of taking a right to meet his parents, he takes a left toward Dana. She motions him into a room used to store concession supplies—candy, carbonation tanks for soda fountains, cases of popcorn. She's munching on some Gummi Bears when he shuts the door behind them.

"Bravo," she says. "I was hoping you'd do the right thing. I'm proud of you."

He wonders if she might be the first person in his life to truly mean those words.

"What if I hadn't saved her?"

"I would have. And you never would've seen me again. I would've let you have the life you chose. I doubt you would've enjoyed it much. You were dealing with some monkey's paw shit there."

He doesn't quite get the reference, but context clues . . .

She says, "Doing the things that are most right won't earn you many trophies, Ty."

"Trophies are overrated. So, now what?"

"You like movies? Well, I've always wanted to say this." She pulls a business card from her jacket pocket and hands it over. All it says is:

DANA DAWN
AKA
TIMELINE

"Ty, I'm putting a crew together."

He takes her hand, and she whisks them away.

FIRE THAT LASTS

by SARAH MacLEAN

1

THE FIRST TIME IT HAPPENED, I WAS IN HUMAN
physiology.

My small group was huddled around a little aluminum tray. Sofia Ortiz and Laura Michaels were discussing who should be the one to slice open the frog in front of us.

"Everyone knows you're gonna puke, Sofia."

"I am not."

"You turned green when we had to dissect a *worm*. Give me the knife."

Unable to argue with facts, Sofia passed the blade to Laura, but not without an irritated, "It's *called* a *scalpel*."

Laura had just turned to her green-gray victim when we heard the bell. Not the high, shrill mechanical ring that indicated the end of class—the other one. Low and rich, a hum that had, at some point in the past, been chosen to calm us.

After all, it was supposed to keep us from anger.

My back was to the room, but I turned, like we all did, trying to swallow the fear that came in the echo of the sound. The panic that tightened my throat. Swelled my tongue.

I looked down at my wrist, just like we all did. Touched the blank black screen on the cuff I wore, just like we all did. Hated the still-unfamiliar feel of it, just like we all did.

We'd all heard the bells before, but no one was more unsettled by them—by what they meant—than a roomful of year tens. I'd been wearing my cuff for only three weeks. Sofia had turned sixteen three days earlier. I could practically hear her scratching at the strap of hers.

I wondered if it felt too tight, like mine.

"Stay calm," Mr. Kim said, low and soothing. Trained. Prepared. "Deep breaths."

A sign above the doorway blinked slowly in blue: RELAX.

I took a deep breath, just like we all did.

But I saw something the others didn't.

In the hallway outside the door, a shimmering, blinding light, white, like a lightning bolt, so bright that it blocked out everything else. The pop of Mark Lavoie's gum. The twitching hum of the halogen bulb in the corner of the room. The nauseating scent of formaldehyde, made worse now that it was mixed with the body spray Will Jenkins bathed in every day.

The fact that I could no longer smell that body spray was proof that something extremely serious was happening.

If I'd been another kid, I might not have understood. I might have thought it was a trick of the light—the sun refracting through the window. Molly Thibeaux, whom I sat next to for a while during algebra in year seven, had these weird headaches that started with a zigzagging light across her field of vision.

If only I'd been Molly, I would've raised my hand and escaped to the nurse.

Except it wasn't the sun, and it wasn't a headache.

"Do you see that?" I asked Sofia quietly.

"See what?" she replied, her thick dark hair falling like a curtain in front of her face, hiding everything but her fingers, playing with her cuff.

"The light in the hallway."

Please say yes. Let it be some new technology. Some new warning.

She lifted her head. Looked to the door. "What light?"

The light that crackled and shimmered in the hallway beyond, dancing in bright, impossible white that only I could see.

I was named Ember for a poem by someone named Emily Dickinson, which had always seemed weird to me, considering how little poetry we were allowed to read. When I was little, my mom used to recite her poems to me again and again.

I'm Nobody! Who are you?

They all seemed silly at the time.

I know better now.

2

No one ever went toward the bells. Parents drilled that rule into children. Teachers, too. It was among the first things we learned, like not running into the street, or not petting strange dogs.

Stay clear of the bells.

Especially when they were close. You didn't want to be taken by accident.

But that day in human physiology, while Sofia and Lauren and Mark and Will all watched the door, frozen, I walked toward it.

"Ember." Mr. Kim spoke as my hand touched the doorknob, his voice firm and steady. Meant to hold me back. To keep me safe.

Just me, though. Just those of us in the room. Whoever was outside? They had to fend for themselves.

In the hallway, the bell chimed, slow and incessant, in time with the lazy blink of a massive sign that hung from the ceiling: **CALM IS BALM**.

How many times had I rolled my eyes at that rhyme in the years before I got my cuff? They couldn't think of anything better? It was so uninspired.

But now, as it flashed in slow, cerulean rhythm, I realized it didn't have to be inspired.

Beneath the sign, two white boys faced off, breathing heavily. One had a bloody nose, the other a split lip. But they weren't fighting . . . not anymore. Whatever anger they'd had was gone, replaced by something else as they stared each other down. Fear. Not the nervousness that had closed the throats of the others in my class, but actual fear. The kind that released adrenaline. The kind that raised heart rates.

They'd been altered.

High on the walls around us, screens—the Company's monitors—glowed red. On the boys' wrists, smaller versions of those damning screens did the same. They would stay red until the Mediators came. They would be all the proof the Mediators needed.

Surrounding the boys, arcing between them, was a circle of crackling light, bright and white, unpleasant to look at. And still, I walked toward it.

No one ever went toward the bells. And absolutely no one ever went toward the altered.

That's what the boys were now: mistakes to be corrected.

Except they weren't mistakes. Mistakes could be erased and rewritten. Given a second chance. These two would be erased, but there would be no rewriting. No second chances.

Their eyes went wide as I approached.

"Shit," whispered the boy with the bloody nose. I'd never seen him before—I'd have remembered his orange hair and pale, freckled face—but I didn't like the way he looked at me, wary and unpleasant.

He knew I wasn't a Mediator. I didn't wear the white suit. I wasn't holding the black bag. I was a kid, like them.

But he knew I wasn't normal.

He looked around, then down at his cuff, knowing that if he ran, he'd still be caught. Knowing that he'd be Reformed and Returned. Brought back different. Brought back calm.

"Don't run," I said, not knowing why.

He shook his head. "Fuck that." He took off, the lightning arcing above him following him. Shifting. Going from white to yellow. From anger to fear.

"You shouldn't be here," said the boy who stayed—the one who'd done the most damage. I knew him. Or I'd *noticed* him. It was impossible not to notice Aidan Wright. He was a head taller than the rest of the school, long and lanky, like he'd been given extra bones at birth. I was surprised to see him here, wrapped up in this. He was usually quiet, keeping to the edges of hallways and rooms, hunched over, his curly brown hair flopping over his face as though, if he tried hard enough, he might be able to avoid notice. He wasn't the kind of guy who set off the monitors.

At least, he hadn't been. Before now.

"*Hey*," he said, louder than before. Trying for my attention. "Listen. If you get near me—"

"I know."

They'd think I'd been altered, and even though my monitor was blank, I'd be taken away.

Reformed and Returned. Empty.

I reached for him anyway, and he narrowed his eyes, skeptical. The light above him shimmered. Bright white. Rich gold. I could hear his heartbeat and his heavy breaths. "What are you doing?"

I didn't know what I was doing. More importantly, I didn't know *why I was doing it*. "Can you see it?"

"See what?"

"The light."

His brow furrowed. "What light?"

There was no denying it. What I could see. What I could *do*. "Give me your hand."

He didn't hesitate. He should have, but instead, he did as I asked. His palm slid against mine, warm and rough and sure, like he knew what was going to happen.

The arc of light twisted as I touched him, and I gasped, my heart pounding as his emotion poured into me—ribbons of bitter anger followed by fiery frustration and then terror and desperation, harsh and wild with the knowledge of what would happen when they came. And finally, something else. Something like wonder. A taste of it. Brighter than the rest. Green and lush.

His monitor blinked.

The red disappeared. The screens in the hallway flipped off.

"Holy shit." Skepticism turned to reverence. "You stopped it."

I looked up at him, and he held my gaze with his.

The light arcing above us disappeared.

He released a long breath, and I let him go. Or I tried to, until I looked into his gray eyes and saw that there was more. Something else. Something I couldn't recognize, arcing between us. His heart beat a heavy rhythm, steady . . . but already beginning to pick up speed.

Light sizzled, sandwiched in the space between our palms.

RELAX blinked on a screen in the distance, behind his head, and I grabbed hold of him again. Protecting him again. "You'll trigger them."

"You're—"

I cut him off. "Shh. Breathe. Count."

The beginning of the nonsensical lessons they'd drilled into all of us when we were too young to understand what might happen if we didn't learn them. Before we had emotion monitors.

More stupid rhymes.

Breathe. Count. In. Out.

One. Two. Shake it through.

Ridiculous lessons. No one ever told us that in the moment, as the bells chimed and the monitors flashed, we'd never be able to stop the fear from coming.

"You reversed it," he said.

The truth shattered through me.

"Who are you?"

I'm Nobody!

I wasn't supposed to be able to do it. Nobody was supposed to be able to do it.

"You're the—"

"No." I cut him off before he could finish the thought. It was a legend. A myth. "*No.*" I shook my head, wild panic flaring, throat tight. Heart pounding.

I couldn't be.

It was just a story.

His hand shifted in mine until I wasn't holding him anymore. He was holding me. Tight, firm. Steady. "Don't panic. The monitors."

I looked back toward the classroom where I'd been minutes earlier, the narrow rectangle of glass in the door now filled with faces. My friends. My teacher.

A different kind of monitor. A dozen of them.

"Hey." That word again, soft, sure. I tore my gaze away and looked down at where we touched—another thing that wasn't allowed. Not when the monitors were so new.

Time slowed as I stared at our hands, palm to palm, his long fingers, bronzed as though he spent time in the sun, wrapped tightly around mine. His knuckles were pink and raw from the fight, and I wondered if they were sore. If they weren't, they would be.

He was so warm. Steady. Calm. And on his wrist, his monitor was black again. Blank.

It was lying.

The monitor might not detect his emotions, but I could feel them hot inside me.

Wonder. Hope. Relief. And there, underneath the rest, fear. Not the kind I'd felt in him before. This was broader. Sadder.

This was fear for me.

And somehow, without him even speaking, I heard his quiet whisper. *You're the Remedy.*

I met his eyes, like storm clouds, full of revelation. My throat went tight and painful. "I have to . . ."

He nodded and let me go. And my hand, suddenly free of him, felt empty. Like I'd lost something before I'd found it.

"You have to disappear, Ember."

3

The first thing they took from us was love.

Well, not *us*. They took it from our parents and our parents' parents, and our parents' parents' parents, and so on . . . until they didn't have to take it from us, because by the time we came along, it didn't exist anymore. They'd burned the books, destroyed the art, and banned the old movies that even hinted at it. All the music, too. Once, in year five, I'd found a picture in an old book—two skeletons entwined in a grave. When I asked my teacher about it, she'd immediately confiscated the material and reported it to the Company. They'd sent it for burning.

Fondness was allowed, but not love.

Melancholy was allowed, but not grief.

Happiness was allowed, but not joy.

Irritation was allowed, but not rage.

And so on. They knew they could not prevent our instant biological responses. But they also knew that if they prohibited intense emotions, they could ensure that the rules would be followed. Proper paths would be walked. The species would survive.

Whatever survival meant.

So they banned the emotions, and with them, their memory. If we didn't know they'd ever existed, the theory went, we would be less likely to feel them.

To be altered.

And for a long time, for me, that was true.

I still thought about those skeletons, though.

I still wondered.

4

My mother met me at the door that afternoon, and I knew something was wrong. She was a doctor and worked for the Company, and she was never home after school, definitely never looking like this, fear behind her eyes. Doctors who worked for the Company rarely looked moved by anything. It was part of the job. My mother wasn't a Reformer—at least, she'd never admitted she was. But even doctors who didn't treat ALTERS (Amygdaloid-Limbic-Temporal Emotional Recall Syndrome) saw what was done to the people who set off the bells.

Calm was how they survived what they witnessed.

But my mother didn't look calm when she came out onto the porch that afternoon, her blond hair pulled into an efficient ponytail and her normally pink skin somehow pale in the bright sun. Her gaze fell to my wrist, where my cuff lay heavy and quiet. "Let's take a walk."

Behind our house there was a perfectly manicured

sloping green hill that ended in a narrow, twisting river that had once been so wild and rushing that it had cut itself into the earth as the city had grown up around it. Now, it was at perpetual low tide, and though the water still rushed, it just churned up mud and silt—a constant reminder of what was beneath its surface.

That afternoon, my mother and I walked along the river, like we had a thousand times before, but this time, something was different. This time, she wasn't relaxed. (It didn't matter that we passed at least four RELAX signs). She wasn't altered enough to trigger her monitor, but I could tell.

I could see the panic shimmering around her.

I ignored the emotion, afraid of what it might do to me. Afraid I might not be able to control it the way she did. Instead, I concentrated on my shoes—worn at the toe and the heel, no longer the pristine white they'd been when I'd bought them. Why did I always buy white shoes, anyway? They never stayed clean.

And still, I did it. As though someday I might be the kind of person who avoided mess.

Too late for that.

"Do you want to talk about it?"

I really didn't. If she knew, she'd be in huge trouble. The Company had whole groups of people whose job it was to root out abnormal activity. And they didn't like disloyalty. Even among parents.

Especially among them.

"Talk about what?"

She didn't look at me. Instead, she looked down at her

own shoes—the black ankle boots she'd worn every day of my life, always in pristine condition. I wondered if she had other shoes.

It seemed like something a girl should know about her mom.

"The school called. Told me the bells rang today."

I shrugged, leaning down to pick up a smooth, flat stone from the dirt path.

"They said you went toward them." When I didn't respond, she added, "They said there was a boy who seemed altered."

"He wasn't," I said urgently. Even when I'd touched him, while the monitors had been blinking and the bells had been ringing and my class had been staring—even as I'd felt his emotions, a wild confusion of thoughts—he hadn't seemed altered. He'd seemed . . . *right*.

I didn't say any of that to my mom, but her eyebrows were raised as though she understood it all anyway. "I had to go toward them," I said softly. "I couldn't let . . ."

I trailed off. She worked for the Company. However I finished my sentence, it could get her into trouble.

We were beneath a small bridge, one I'd walked over a thousand times. One I'd stood and screamed under as a child, reveling in the sound echoing around me, until my mom decided that bridge-screaming might someday bring me too close to anger and put a stop to it.

I threw the smooth stone in my hand into the water.

"What did you see?"

I looked at her and heard the understanding in the question. She knew.

She passed me, her steps even, those boots with their black heels somehow sturdy even here, on the uneven bank of this river that was no longer a river.

My steps weren't even, though.

She knew.

And she was home early.

Which meant someone else knew, too. Someone had sent her.

I stopped, the water below echoing beneath the bridge, louder and louder until it sounded like rage. "Mom?"

She heard me somehow. Turned back.

Later, I would remember the shiny black toes of her boots, the dirty white toes of my sneakers. Later, I would remember the way my heart began to pound in my chest. Hard and fast and unfamiliar.

And I would never forget the bell that rang there beneath that bridge, the low timbre of it echoing all around us. Designed decades ago to calm us. To keep us from anger.

Now, all I felt was a straight shot of fear.

I looked up. Met the clear blue of my mother's eyes, so different from my own. They were full of tears. Harsh, angry light arced above her.

My fear became panic.

The bell rang again.

The light grew brighter, blindingly white.

My throat was tight. I looked down at my wrist, where I expected to find my emotion monitor red and angry.

I'd rung the bells, after all.

Except I hadn't. She had. It was her monitor that was red,

hers that was angry. I reached for her, and she stepped away, quickly turning. Crouching.

"You have to go, Ember."

"Mom—"

She moved a clump of weeds away from the bridge, revealing a place where it had crumbled. She reached into the hole and pulled out a backpack.

Thrust it into my hands.

It was heavy. Like her sadness. Like mine.

"How did you know?" I whispered, urgent. "How did you know to pack this?"

"It doesn't matter. You have to go now."

"No. Explain it to me. How did you know I was the Remedy?"

"*Are*." She looked at me then, her beautiful eyes full of truth. "You *are* the Remedy." The bells chimed incessantly, and her wrist monitor began to pulse along with her heartbeat, faster and faster. She was getting more emotional. "Ember. *Now*."

The lightning around her shimmered. White. Yellow. Blue. Red. Too bright.

She was panicking.

"Mom." I reached for her. "You have to calm down. The Mediators." She stepped away, the light coming between us, making it hard to see her. "Please . . . Mom! Let me . . ." I lunged, grabbing for her fingers. "I can make it stop."

"No." She pulled away from me, and later, I would hate them most for that—for taking away that last touch. For stealing the warm softness of her skin. The last touch of my mother before she was altered. "Listen to me, Ember. *There's a pair of you.*"

She looked over my shoulder, toward our house, and a deep, cold dread rioted through me.

"They're here." I didn't have to say it. She didn't have to confirm it.

The Company.

They were coming.

To save me, she was letting herself feel. Panic. Devastation. Frustration. Rage.

All of it.

There was so much she'd never said.

I didn't stay to watch them take her. If I had, I'm not sure I would have been able to go on. I'm not sure I would have discovered the truth:

That my anger didn't trigger the monitors. Maybe that was because my anger was not anger at all. It was not simple and could not be defined or quantified. It was not off the charts. It did not require blinking neon signs or deep breathing. It was not abnormal.

It was my normal.

5

Long before we lived in that house on the river—before we lived anywhere—someone had placed life-size sculptures of humans at even intervals in the water. There were twenty of them, each slightly different than the next, spread across two miles or so, leading from our house through the center of the city. When I was little, it had been a game to find the differences between them.

That one had its arms raised.

That one's head was turned.

That one looked like it was walking.

The bodies were beautiful, all angles and muscle. Perfect specimens. Except they didn't have faces.

Faces were less than perfect, I supposed.

Faces were what got you into trouble.

Are you—Nobody—too?

But beneath the bridge where I had screamed and where my mother had stored the bag that held money and food and a change of clothes for me, there was a statue that was different from all the rest. It was my favorite when I was young and we'd played the game and everything had seemed normal . . . everything, that was, except that statue.

Because that statue did have a face.

It was turned downward, as though it was looking at something in its hands, except there was nothing there. Long ago, before we'd lived there, whatever it held had been removed. What was left were the scars, chunks of stonework that no one had taken the time to chisel away.

The jagged pieces might have been smoothed if the river had kept its height instead of simply churning up the muck and carrying leaves and sticks along, leaving them tangled in the sculpture's legs, as though trying to hold it back. To keep it from chasing after whatever had been stolen from it.

To keep it from acting on what could not be stolen from its face.

That thing I could see but could not feel.

Not until that day.

Two years had passed since that day my mother let herself be altered and the Company had taken her. Perhaps it was best that she never came back. Those who were Reformed were returned less than themselves, unable to feel even those feelings that were allowed. The ones that had not been linked to rage. Amusement. Contentment. Distaste. Gratitude.

I didn't feel them, either.

They hadn't caught me, and still, I was Reformed.

Emotion was my enemy, and I fought it as plainly as I fought the Company, the memory of that day on a loop in my mind. Aidan, and the way he'd stared at me, full of revelation. My mother, and the way she'd stared at me, full of understanding.

The words they'd both said. *You're the Remedy.*

And then, once I'd moved past the loss, the understanding that I was alone in the world and able to fight, I spent my nights running toward the bells. Toward the fights. The violence. The anger. The hurt.

And when I found it, I took it. Silenced the monitors and left.

As though Nobody had been there to begin with.

But soon, I was no longer Nobody. Because people started talking about me. They called me the Remedy, because even in a world that had been stripped of emotion and taught to fear it, people looked to legend for explanations.

I spent my days searching for everything I could find about the Remedy.

We'd never learned about it in school, but every once in a while, a kid mentioned it in passing.

Wouldn't it be great if there was a Remedy?

Any time it was invoked, it was with a half laugh, awkward and halting, as though whoever was speaking knew they shouldn't. That at best, it was a tall tale. And at worst, if it was real, it was dangerous.

Then we wouldn't need the Mediators.

We wouldn't need the monitors.

We wouldn't need the Company.

No one ever said the last one out loud.

There was talk of the way information had spread before the Company took it all over, claimed the wires and the tubes and the pathways made for it and then took over the places that were supposed to act as hubs for it. Schools. Libraries. Museums. Bookstores. It barely took a generation before the Company controlled all of it.

And once it controlled both information and emotion, people simply . . . accepted the rules. Maybe because it was impossible to fight. Maybe because it was easier not to.

Finding places to ask questions about the Remedy—about *me*—was difficult. But I learned quickly to ask for information that didn't seem suspicious. The pathology of ALTERS. The technology of the monitors. How the Mediators operated, and the Reformers.

I found a few places where people told stories.

Legends.

I lived in a small room above a shop that sold obscure antiques, owned by an older woman with brown skin and kind eyes who was a natural storyteller. Padma hadn't blinked when I'd turned up in the shop after seeing the **ROOM FOR RENT** sign in her window the morning after I'd lost everything. I was wet and dirty, and my eyes were puffy from crying, but she hadn't asked where I'd come from. Or who I was.

She never did, not even when I started asking questions of my own. About the items in the shop. The books behind the counter. The paintings in the long, narrow drawers that remained locked most days.

But she seemed to know what stories I wanted to hear.

Stories about the Remedy.

Legends that there'd been one before. Maybe more.

Whispers that there might be one again.

Maybe more.

I was there in the city, however, able to disappear into a crowd with no fear of my monitor ever triggering the sensors and summoning the Mediators, and I made legend real, even though I didn't understand it. Even though I had a thousand questions that no one, not even my sage landlady, could answer.

Questions I didn't know how to ask.

So I spent the days searching. Wondering. And trying not to let my mother's last words echo too loud in my mind.

There's a pair of you.

The memory of that promise was sharp and painful, and when I let myself remember what it was like to be part of a pair—to be touched, to be held, to be carried, to be cared for—it was acute. Enough that I imagined one day it would activate my cuff. Bring the Mediators.

So I did everything I could to forget the promise. To ignore the memory.

To reform myself.

In the beginning, the nights were short and the bells uncommon. Maybe they'd ring twice, one always far enough away that I wouldn't have heard it if not for the light that drew me to the feelings. That lit up those who felt.

But slowly, over time, the bells began to ring more frequently. Night after night. Hour after hour. And the anger . . . it became more palpable. The rage more frustrated. The terror more intense.

Later, I would understand why.

Later, I would understand that I was a part of the reason.

I stopped sleeping at night, because the emotions seemed to be worse in the dark, and if I couldn't get to the bells in time, the Mediators would.

I learned fast to get to the bells in time.

I was half myth, half mystery. Some swore I was a middle-aged man with muscles for days (such a cliché); others were certain they'd seen a girl who could fly (I wish—I was just great at jumping between rooftops); still others claimed I was a witch (I didn't know a single spell).

Once, in the winter, I wore a fuzzy hat in the shape of a raccoon head as I siphoned the energy from a drunken brawl, and for weeks there were rumors that I was a bear-shifter. More than a few people didn't believe I existed at all. They thought the Company technology was just breaking down.

And then there was him.

6

That night, I saw the light before I heard the bells. I was already running toward it when the low chime began, a promise that I had mere minutes before the Mediators arrived. Over the rooftops, down a fire escape, and into a dark alleyway—it was always a dark alleyway, I'd learned—where I found a cluster of people piled atop each other, clearly having tumbled out the side entrance of the kind of place that made it too easy to lose your temper.

A ball of lightning encircled them, a riot of colors.

The bells were ringing, and emotion monitors installed high on the exterior walls of the buildings all around us were flashing red. A massive neon sign shone a bright blue RELAX into the night.

It wasn't doing the trick.

I approached in the darkness, counting the limbs and the varied cadence of the squeaks and grunts. Six people. Maybe seven.

Not one of them worried about the bells.

Usually by the time I arrived, the shimmering white of rage had faded to the yellow of fear, the people who had been altered having forgotten whatever the fight was about. But something had set this group off, and nothing was going to stop them unless I jumped into the fray.

A woman—young and slight—was tossed from the pile, and I watched as she tucked her knees and rolled onto her side, facing away from the fight. I started with her, crouching low, reaching out.

The red light of her emotion monitor cast an ominous glow on her pale skin. When she spoke, her words were harsh and angry. "Who are you?"

I kept my hood up, hiding my eyes. "Nobody."

"No," she said, shaking her head, even as she let me set my fingers on her skin. "You're the Remedy."

And then it was my turn to be shocked, because she pushed me away. "Don't touch me."

The bells rang louder.

"I have to," I said. "If I don't, they'll come for you."

She pushed herself to her feet. Raised a proud chin. "Let them come."

"You don't mean that," I said, standing, trying to reason with her. "They'll take you. They'll Reform you."

"And what will *you* do?"

The words rioted through me. "I'll turn off the monitor. I'll make you calm."

"You mean *you'll* Reform me," she said, the words full of certainty. "You're just like them."

I reeled back at the accusation. "What? No!"

A seed of something woke in me. Something that was not calm.

The neon overhead blinked, slow and steady.

RELAX.

I turned to the group of people who'd been fighting—six more, besides the woman—each one with an emotion monitor blinking their fury. Each one with recognition in their eyes. They knew who I was. What I could do.

But they didn't want it.

They didn't want calm.

My frustration grew, hot and angry in my belly, rising through me, roaring alongside the bells all around us.

"They're coming," I said, desperation twisting through me. Didn't they see? Lightning arced all around them, angry and bright and powerful.

But they weren't angry at each other. They were angry *at me*. *You're just like them.*

Something cracked inside me. Altered. I looked down at my cuff. I wouldn't be able to escape if it activated. I had to calm down. I had to breathe. To count.

Breathe. Count. In. Out.

The stupid poem didn't work. It never worked.

The bells rang louder. More shimmering light filled the alley, no longer dark. At least, no longer dark for me. I couldn't see anything but light. Sheer and white. My cuff blinked on. Brilliant and bold and impossible to ignore.

From a distance, I heard the Mediators. And panic joined the other emotions, my own heart beginning to pound, fast and terrifying.

They were coming for us all.

RELAX.

The Mediators were closing in, turning down the alleyway, their heavy footsteps loud and even like the bells that summoned them.

And I couldn't save anyone. Not even myself.

We ran. Down the alleyway and around the back of the

building, hoping we wouldn't get trapped there in some dead end. The path twisted and turned, people peeling off through doors and into even smaller, narrower passageways. It didn't matter. As long as their monitors glowed, the Mediators would find them.

Just like they would find me.

And then *he* found me, a hand snaking out of the darkness, grabbing my sleeve, pulling me against a broad, warm body before tugging me down a half dozen steps and into a short, shadowed walkway.

"Let me go!" I hissed, pushing against his grip, fear spiking for a moment before he spoke.

"Shh." His whisper was low, so soft in my ear that it was breath rather than sound. "They'll hear you."

I held up my wrist, where the small square glowed crimson. "I'm already theirs."

"No. I won't let that happen," he said, the words harsh and firm, like a command. And I believed him, impossibly, as he pulled me through two low doorways to a ladder that shot straight into the sky. "Up."

I climbed, emotions rioting around me. When I reached the top, my guide immediately behind me, a terrified scream sounded in the distance. I turned, my heart pounding, to see lightning spark red in the night and then disappear. Someone had been found.

"They took one of them." I turned back toward the ladder. "I have to go. I have to help." I could see the lightning, bright and terrifying, streaking across the sky, marking everyone's hiding places. Yellow now with the fear that came with being hunted. "They'll let me help them now."

"No," he said, catching me again, pulling me across the roof even as I struggled against his grip.

"I have to."

"No. If you go back, they'll take you."

"They haven't for two years," I countered as a second shout sounded in the darkness. I couldn't stop them if I was here. I couldn't fight them if I was here.

But I could fight *him*. I rounded on him, my fist already flying. He backed away, and my bare knuckles grazed his jaw, not enough to strike, but enough to touch him. To feel his frustration. His desperation. His wonder. His relief.

Familiar.

There wasn't time to think about it. His grip loosened enough for me to pull away, my own emotions unfamiliar.

Anger. Frustration. Desperation. Fear. For myself. For those people.

The monitors blinking everywhere.

And those bells, louder with every second.

"This isn't how it ends," I said, backing away toward the edge of the roof as he straightened. "I'm all there is between us and them, and I'm not going down without a fight."

Another shout in the distance. Another yellow light turned red, then extinguished.

Another *life* extinguished.

I turned toward it and ran for the edge of the roof. One of them wasn't far.

RELAX.

I paused, looking down into the alleyway below, toward the street in the distance where another van full of Mediators pulled to a stop. They were coming for me. It was only a matter of time.

And then he spoke again, and I didn't have to look to know he was panicked. "Ember. Please."

My name. He knew my name.

There's a pair of you.

7

I hadn't heard anyone speak it in two years.

I couldn't help myself. I looked back as he stepped into the glow of one of the monitors, his tan skin blinking red in the light.

Recognition flared. "Aidan."

"Yes." He smiled, easy and calm, like he'd been waiting his whole life for this moment. To find me. Like he'd been searching since the moment I'd taken his anger that day two years ago outside of human physiology and everything had changed. He put his hand to his chest. "Aidan. You remember."

Of course I did. I remembered him. I'd remembered him so many times that the past didn't seem the right place for him. "I remember you."

He nodded, approaching. "Good. I remember you, too."

"You're . . ." I trailed off. "Bigger." His muscles had caught up with all those bones. He was stronger now.

Sturdier.

I shook my head. "How did you . . ." How did he find me? "How?"

"You saved my life." He came toward me, slow and steady, arms spread, like he was afraid I might bolt. "I've been looking for you every day since then. How could I do anything else?" He reached for me. Said the words I'd said to him two years earlier. "Breathe. Count."

"It's bullshit; it doesn't work."

He laughed. Like we weren't on a rooftop running from Mediators. Like I hadn't been altered. "No, it doesn't."

I'd been altered.

I was being altered.

I looked at his hand, large and steady. And for a wild moment, I wondered what would happen if I slipped my hand into it. It was so tempting. So terrifying.

He watched me. "What happens to it?"

"To what?"

"To the emotion. When you take it."

"Nothing." Like an enemy, once vanquished, I left it where it fell.

He shook his head, looking down at the light in my hands. "Not possible."

"It's been two years since I siphoned my first feeling."

"*My* first feeling," he said softly, like it meant something. Like I should remember the way his anger had felt. His fear. And the rest.

As if I could forget.

"I've never been able to do anything but take emotion away. Nothing happens to it. It just . . . disappears."

One side of his mouth kicked up in a smile. "No. Nothing that powerful just disappears."

If it didn't disappear, what did that mean? Who was I if all that emotion remained inside me? What would I become?

What would I be able to do?

"Ember," he whispered. "You're holding it all. Alone."

Alone.

So many emotions. So much anger and pain and frustration. And I'd been taking it all, holding it all, making space for it all. And instead of being soothed, people had found more. Each one had a limitless capacity for emotion.

And my capacity? Was it limitless too?

Tears came, hot and unexpected. "There is so much."

He nodded. "I know. I've been looking for you." The words were a gift. A promise. He'd been looking for me, and he'd found me, and now I wasn't alone.

There's a pair of you.

That hand, still outstretched. Still steady. "If I touch you while I'm like this, I don't know what will happen." I had never set off the monitors before. What if I made him a target, too? I'd felt so much earlier, just brushing my skin against his. If I let myself really touch him . . . what would come of it?

He seemed to understand. "Let's find out."

I reached for him, full of fear and excitement and something else. Something more dangerous than every emotion I'd ever siphoned. Hope.

I hadn't even touched him yet when it happened—when the light arced between our hands. He exhaled harshly, surprised, and I snapped my gaze to his. "Can you see it?"

He nodded. "Hard to miss it."

The light was focused for the first time since I'd discovered I was the Remedy. Except now, it didn't feel like what I was doing before had been the Remedy.

This was the Remedy.

I brought my other hand to the arc of energy humming between us, and he did the same. And we stayed like that as I poured everything I had into it—all the anger and fear and panic and loss and sorrow. And it vibrated with color and light, there between us.

And he stood with me, beside me, helping me hold it.

Beautiful.

Not like the enemy.

Like *power*.

I looked into his eyes—those gray eyes, impossibly familiar, that looked the same as they had that day in the hallway, full of recognition and admiration and revelation. And for a moment, I let myself feel those things, too.

I let myself remember them.

"A few months ago, I found something beautiful," I whispered, suddenly wanting desperately to tell the story. To share it with someone.

There was no time, but still I wanted him to know.

Aidan replied, slow and easy, like we had our whole lives ahead of us. "Tell me."

I swallowed. "The bells rang, and I went toward them, expecting to find what I always do."

"A fight."

I nodded. "Anger. Pain."

"And that night?"

I smiled, remembering it. "It was something else. It was . . ." I searched for the word. That word no one had ever taught me. "It was beautiful."

He leaned forward, like he knew what I'd seen. Like he could name it. "Tell me."

"They were so happy," I whispered, tears in my eyes as I remembered the couple, entwined. "I've never seen anything like it." The colors had been so rich, like jewels.

No wonder they'd taken it from us.

When they'd heard the bells, they'd stayed locked together, entwined, like the skeletons in the book the Company had burned when I was young.

"I took it from them," I said. "I took it, because I wanted to save them." Sadness coursed through me. It had been so beautiful. And when I'd finished and the monitors had blinked off, I'd seen the loss in their eyes. "I thought I was saving them . . . but I stole it."

He nodded toward the glowing orb between us, the one I held with ease. "Give it back."

I did. The memory of that emotion surfaced, and I pushed it into the orb, along with the hope I felt tonight. The wonder. The pride.

When we couldn't hold it anymore, we released it, and it grew larger and larger until we were inside it, and it shimmered all around us.

"Holy shit," he said, his eyes bright with the reflection of the enormous dome of light. With his emotions. With mine. "I told you they didn't just disappear."

Whether it was joy or delight or desire or all three, Aidan reached for me then—or I reached for him. All that mattered was that his lips were on mine, and we were kissing, and my fingers were tangling in his hair as his hands stroked down my back and pulled me tight to him.

Or maybe I was pressing tight to him. It didn't matter. All that mattered was that we had found each other, and that we weren't afraid, and that we weren't going to go quietly.

I sighed into his mouth, and he slid his tongue against mine, and I memorized him—the fresh scent of his soap and the barely there mint on his breath and the warmth. He was so *warm*, like the best kind of promise. The one you never doubt.

When he broke the kiss, his hands came to cradle my face as he stared at me, studying me like he wanted to remember this moment forever, and I forgot to breathe. "I knew it," he whispered. "I knew it the moment you touched me that first time. Ember. For the fire in your eyes when you came for me. For the fire you left with me when you disappeared."

I grabbed his hands at my cheeks and went up on my toes and kissed him again, and he groaned low in his throat, kissing me back for a long, delicious moment before he stopped me again.

"Ember," he whispered, and he smiled at me—that bright, beautiful smile that lived in my memories. Not anymore, though. Now, that smile that tempted me with something that felt like more than *like*. That smile that felt like hope. Like joy. Like something I'd never felt before.

A shout sounded in the distance, and we turned toward

it. They'd found us. Of course they had. The orb of light in the night was difficult to miss.

The bells were ringing louder than I'd ever heard them. Louder than anyone had, because they were ringing all around us.

A trio of Mediators stood outside the orb, eyes wide and uncertain, their legendary calm suddenly in chaos.

RELAX, blinked the neon sign behind them.

Not anymore.

Aidan reached for my hand, lacing his fingers through mine, sure and strong, and I took a deep breath, ready to fight, the truth rioting through me.

Anger, hope, joy, grief . . . love. They were no longer the enemy.

They are the revolution.

And it starts now.

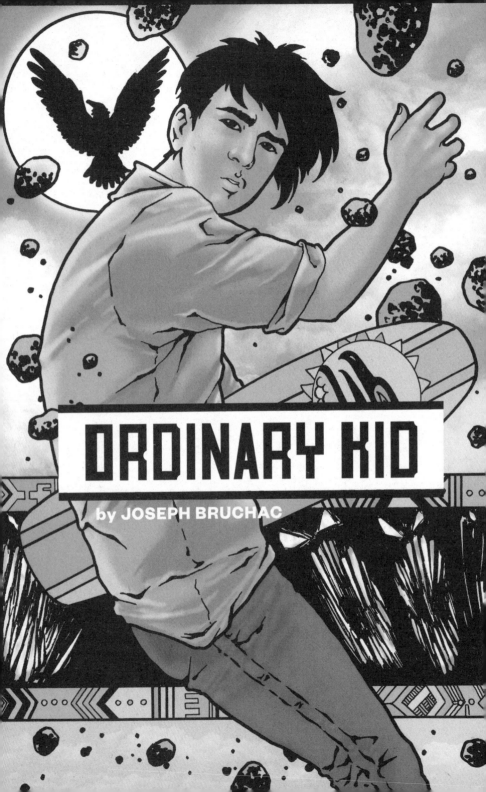

ORDINARY KID

by JOSEPH BRUCHAC

"I'M STILL JUST AN ORDINARY KID," LEONARD
Skye said.

"Tell that to him," Crow replied, looking up.

Leonard followed his feathered friend's gaze.

Thirty feet up in the ash tree, his arms wrapped around the trunk and a very confused look on his face, sat Billy Ray Jones.

He'd been placed there gently, aside from the brief time when he'd been turned upside down and twirled before being set down on that high branch.

He had no idea how he had gotten there, and he certainly had no idea that Leonard had anything to do with it.

No one ever seemed to see what Leonard was able to do lately, just as no one else ever saw Crow, even when he was perched on Leonard's left shoulder. So Billy Ray would not remember the way Leonard had pointed at him, twirled his finger around three times, and then gestured at the tree.

What Billy Ray would remember was that something had happened just as he was about to grab Mary Big Tree's shoulder and make his usual demand that she give him her lunch money. It would probably take him the rest of the recess to recover enough to climb back down and make his way to his sixth-period class.

Lesson learned? Leonard thought.

"Maybe," Crow said, reading his mind as usual.

It had worked last week with Custer Phillips, the other chief bully at Winnebonka High School. Custer—named for his father's favorite military figure—had the habit of shooting spitballs at the few Indian kids in second-period math. So it went every day, with the teacher, who belonged to the same gun cub as Custer's dad, totally ignoring it. Until last Wednesday, when one of those spitballs had reversed course in midair and sped back to smack Custer in the nose.

From his seat two rows away, Leonard had watched as Custer looked cross-eyed at the tip of his own nose, wiped away the drop of water with his finger, and then shook his head. As unwilling as his namesake had been to accept that proceeding further might be unwise, he'd formed another spitball and inserted it into the thick plastic straw he used as a blowgun.

A spitball, though, was too easy. So when he'd sent that spitball back, he'd made it grow so big it exploded like a water balloon, soaking Custer from head to toe. *How was I able to do that?* Leonard had wondered then. And why was it that now he somehow knew about . . . things. Things that were about to happen, or maybe not happen, if he had anything to do with it.

How did I get to be this way? Leonard thought.

"You know how," Crow answered, yet again reading his mind.

Leonard nodded. Until a few weeks ago, he had been an average tenth-grade Native American kid trapped in a largely white school along with a few dozen of his fellow Sokokis. If there was such a thing as an average Native American kid in a mostly white school like Winnebonka High.

It wasn't that everyone treated him badly. Some, like Olivia Hamilton, whom he'd helped by letting her interview him for an essay she'd written about, of all things, the Bureau of Indian Affairs, actually used to smile at him from time to time. Though she stayed with her clique of other good-looking, trendy senior girls, the Emmas. Although now that he thought about it, she hadn't smiled at him or anyone lately. In fact, she and the other Emmas all had been looking sad and distracted since the latest disappearance.

And that really bothered him—both the disappearances and the fact that there seemed to be nothing he could do about it. Even though Aunt Marilyn told him the opposite, that there was always something you could do, even if it was only keeping your eyes open when everyone else wasn't even trying to look.

Speaking of looking, most people, including the few other Indian kids, almost never looked at Leonard. They just ignored him, as there was nothing special about him. He was small—small enough that he could have hidden by making himself smaller, like a rabbit in the undergrowth. Except something in him couldn't accept that. Which was why his glasses were always cracked, his lip or his nose usually bleeding by the end of the day. It was only the fact that he was so easy to dismiss—easy as swatting a gnat—that kept him from attracting even more punishment. It was no challenge to beat up the crazy little Indian kid who actually dared to stand up for people who didn't really care if Leonard lived or died.

Sometimes Leonard wondered why he was even still alive. How could anyone think of high school as a happy-go-lucky place, like in some of the old movies? It wasn't just the bullies. The road to happiness was studded with speed bumps every way you turned.

There was, for example, the party crew—the Cool Car Crew, as they called themselves. Junior and senior guys from well-off families who had their own expensive vehicles and too much freedom. They hosted weekend drinking parties at the house of whoever's parents were away for a night or two. If you were a pretty girl and had any smarts, you never accepted an invitation to one of those parties. No Emma ever went to one, for example. The thought of those parties and what might happen to girls at them really bugged Leonard, too. Another thing he couldn't do anything about.

Then there were the top predators on the food chain: the ones who controlled the flow of drugs. Those ranged from opioids lifted from parents' medicine cabinets to pot and X to stuff whose code names changed from year to year. Somehow, none of those guys ever got caught.

It was like being shot in the heart every time Leonard heard about some kid overdosing and almost dying or he saw some freshman girl who'd been invited to a party and now looked like her whole world had crashed and burned. He wished he *could* do something. He even looked at the moon, which his old people called the Night Guardian, some nights when her face was so full she seemed to be listening and whispered, "Grandmother, what can I do? Help me, please."

Then, as he was walking across the field on his way home one day, that thing had come hurtling out of the sky. At first, he'd thought it was a meteorite streaking straight toward him.

Leonard knew a lot about meteorites, just as he knew every episode of *Star Trek* and could quote every memorable line from not only the TV shows but also the movies. According to his aunt, though he was not always sure of her veracity, he'd been named after Leonard Nimoy. One of his greatest disappointments in fourth grade had been finding out that the Vulcan neck pinch did not work outside of the confines of the TV screen. He'd tried it on Custer Phillips, who was in the process of punching Billy Yee, whose father worked at the new computer chip factory and had just moved to the area. The ineffectiveness of the technique hurt more than the bloody lip he was given in exchange for his admittedly successful attempt at securing Billy's escape.

Getting back to his encounter with what he'd assumed was a bit of interplanetary debris pulled in by the gravity of the Earth and flaming brilliantly as a result of its sudden encounter with atmospheric friction, Leonard was both thrilled and concerned about the fact that it was heading straight toward him. Most meteors never reach the surface of the earth. They burn up before they exit the stratosphere. As far as he knew, people actually getting hit by meteorites was about a one-in-a-billion event.

His apprehension about being eighty-sixed by a small remnant of what might once have been a planet quickly changed when that meteorite suddenly stopped in midair just before reaching him. It rotated twice, then dropped with a soft feathery thud onto the ground in front of him.

"Ah, perfect," a voice said—not so much from the direction of the flaming ball at his feet as from inside his own head.

Then, as the flames were sucked inside the object and it turned black as coal, something else happened. Wings unfolded from the midnight-black former shooting star. And there it was—a jumbo-size crow looking up at him. As Leonard stared open-mouthed, it cocked its head and winked.

"What's up, Doc?" the birdlike being said in a voice exactly like that of Bugs Bunny.

Leonard had always loved Bugs Bunny. Almost as much as Wile E. Coyote in those old cartoons. In part, it was because of what Aunt Marilyn had told him one day when she happened to glance over his shoulder while he was watching Bugs outwit Elmer Fudd once again.

"Straight out of old Indian stories," his aunt had said. "Classic trickster. And that Fudd person with his gun is just like a white Indian agent."

Bugs Bunny voice or not, Leonard still didn't answer the crow being's query—if it was that—right away.

"Hmm," it said, its voice sort of echoing, as if it was coming from the creature's beak and from somewhere inside Leonard's head at the same time.

"Take me to your leader, Earth man!" it demanded in a distinctly mechanical voice.

"I don't know our leader," Leonard said, "if you mean the president. Plus, I don't really think of him as *our* leader, anyhow."

The crow started laughing. "Good one," it said in a voice that somehow seemed more normal for a talking black bird. "Seems to me like this is going to be the beginning of a beautiful friendship." It chuckled. "You can call me Crow."

"Crow?" Leonard said.

"You got it," Crow replied.

"Why are you here?" Leonard asked.

"Because I'm not anyplace else."

"Seriously, why here?"

"You want my help?"

"Maybe," Leonard said. In movies and books, he'd encountered more than one story of supernatural beings offering deals to mortals, usually in exchange for their souls or a number of nonexpendable body parts. "Depends on what it'll cost me."

Crow chuckled. "Good answer. Would you believe me if I told you that what I have for you is free of charge, just as long as I get to stick around and see where it gets you?"

"I might," Leonard said. "Believe you, I mean."

"OK," Crow replied. "That's an even better answer. But first, you got any questions?"

"Why did you choose me?"

"Because," Crow said, cocking its head a second time before suddenly digging its head under its wing and coming out with what looked like an oversize flea. "Soooo?" it said out of the corner of its beak.

Leonard sighed. He knew what was going to happen. He would say yes, and then all sorts of problems would come into his life. But then again, he already had plenty of problems. Like being an orphan, his mom and dad having died in that house fire on the rez when he was six.

Which was how he'd ended up in the slipshod care of an elderly aunt who lived in a trailer park. Aunt Marilyn. His only relative, who was more interested in soap operas than actual life, his or her own. She didn't seem to notice when he came home bleeding or bruised, though she regularly restocked the first aid kit in the bathroom. And she replaced his glasses when the cracks got too numerous for him to see well.

To her credit, she had gotten him a library card, which had been a major lifeline. Being able to lose himself in the books he borrowed and devoured like some kids ate French fries gave him food for his mind.

And speaking of food, Aunt Marilyn did feed him—most nights, at least. And she spent just enough of her social security and her late husband's pension on clothes to keep him from looking like a refugee from a Goodwill store.

And now and then, she uttered something interesting, like that remark about there always being something a person could do. Or that observation about Bugs Bunny being in the trickster lineage of Rabbit and Coyote. "That Coyote—no matter how many times he gets beat up, he always bounces back, don't he?" But then, just when Leonard thought they were going to have a real talk, she'd turn back to *General Hospital*.

His aunt had not gotten him the iPhone he used to watch old TV shows and movies. He'd bought that himself, using money earned from the odd jobs he started doing when he was a fifth grader. He didn't take it with him to school. That way, it wouldn't get stolen on his way home by the gang of eighth-grade kids who hung out together, the ones who later became dealers. After losing his watch and his first phone to them, he'd learned to not carry anything he wasn't ready to lose. That was why he always kept his cash under the insole of his right shoe and carried only change in his pockets. Just enough for them to leave him alone after taking it—and maybe hitting him a few times.

Back then, he'd dreamed about growing and no longer being an easy target. But that had not happened. By tenth grade, instead of being six two and muscled like the Rock, he was still a skinny, undersize, powerless Indian kid. So far at the bottom of the school food chain that he'd need a ladder to reach ankle level. What made it worse was his own overdeveloped moral compass. Try as he might to control himself, it was impossible for him to observe wrongdoing without wanting to step in. It didn't matter if it was a school bully picking on someone or a teacher saying something—usually about Native Americans—that was untrue or vaguely racist. As a result, he was always nursing bruises or spending time in detention. He already had a vision of what his life would be like as a frustrated, overly moral adult. How it would probably end with him being shanked as he tried to stop a mugger from stealing an old lady's purse or shot by a cop while protesting whatever the latest racial or social injustice might be when he was a grown-up. If he lived that long.

"Still waiting," Crow said.

"OK," Leonard said.

Which was when Crow opened its beak, and what had looked like an oversized flea started blowing itself up like a balloon until it was at least ten feet tall with a big mouth studded with shark teeth. At which point it opened that mouth and swallowed Leonard whole, and he found himself sloshing around in its belly, every inch of his body burning as if he'd been dropped into a bath filled with acid.

"Oh sh—" he'd started to say. But before that second word could leave his mouth, he'd found himself standing there just as he had been before suffering the world's worst flea bite, the pain gone. He was filled with the strangest feeling he'd ever felt. It took him a minute to realize what it was. Then the word, unaccustomed as he was to it, came to him: confidence. Not only that—his vision had gotten better. His nearsightedness was gone. He took off his taped-together glasses and looked at them.

"All right," Crow said. "You can toss those specs. Ha! That was an easy one. Guess you were meant for this."

"Easy?" Leonard said, remembering the feeling of having his skin and flesh burned down to the bone.

Crow nodded. "Yup. Easy-peasy."

"What's it like when it's not easy?"

"You do not want to know."

And now, here he was, your smaller-than-average Native American teenager . . . with superpowers. Thus far, those powers included the ability to move objects—and people—without touching them and the uncanny ability to sense when someone was picking on someone else.

He'd discovered that there was a small price to pay whenever he did something telekinetic. It made him a little tired and a lot hungry when he moved something. But he recovered quicker each time.

"So my superpower is being an anti-bully?" he'd asked Crow after his first week of exploring his abilities.

"Maybe," Crow had answered. He was good at one-word answers that didn't really answer anything.

"So I'm not going to save the world from evil, or defeat supervillains, or prevent alien monsters from destroying major cities?"

"Could be," Crow said. Two whole words this time, but not any more helpful.

Leonard looked up at the Jones kid, who was shaking his head and starting to climb down the tree.

Well, Leonard thought, *at least it's better than not being able to do anything.* Which had been the case before Crow entered his life.

Was it time to go back inside?

He looked at his watch—the watch that was still on his wrist, unlike the Timex with the expansion band that had been taken from him when he was a freshman by a senior burnout named RJ, who had pawned it to buy cigarettes.

His days of being pushed around were over. True, he was still the shortest kid in his class and unlikely to ever become a basketball star. But he was no longer the easy target he had been. And he was helping other kids as well, even if they never knew it.

Despite the fact that their reservation was only ten miles from the town, it was as though the Sokoki kids were immigrants at Winnebonka High—which was far from Native-friendly, despite its phony Indian name. If you were an athlete of any color—especially a football or basketball player—then you were sort of accepted. And if you were one of the smartest kids in the school, it was hard for people to put you down or ignore you, even if your skin was brown. But if you were just an average kid like Leonard, and not a jock or a brainiac at all, you'd usually find yourself either ignored or picked on.

The town had always been a tough place for skins. That

was probably why so many of them tended to vanish as soon as they hit their teenage years—catch a bus, hitchhike out of town, whatever. Girls more than boys. And none of them ever returned or even sent an email to their relatives.

It was, Leonard supposed, better than the alternative he'd heard happened a lot on other reservations—suicide. Sometimes half a dozen kids who had all palled around together since they were little, first one kid and then another. It hurt his head to think about it.

It still bothered him. Not just the suicides, but the way kids his age had regularly disappeared the whole time he'd been living with his aunt, all of them young teens. Maybe one every three months. There were rumors that they weren't just running away. That maybe they were being taken to some city as slaves.

He'd been so troubled by the possibility that he'd even asked Aunt Marilyn about it a year ago. He'd expected no real response. But that had been another time she'd surprised him, turning off the TV and turning to look at him in a way that made her look a whole lot younger than the more than eighty years he knew she had on her bones.

"Listen," she'd said. "There's some things still out there. Old things wearing our bodies like old clothes. But you're not ready to do anything about that—right now, at least. You hear me?"

And then she'd turned back to the TV, but not before a picture came into Leonard's mind, as if he were seeing what his aunt was thinking. It was a picture of a big black van with opaque windows.

Remembering that, Leonard thought about how he'd been changed. He thought about how it had happened. About the flea engulfing him. About what Crow had done next. Which was to was flap up onto his shoulder, lean close to his ear, and say, "Here."

Leonard had heard a buzzing like that of a sweat bee, but that was it. No big deal. No flashing lights, no sudden surge of power, no feeling of invincibility. Just a little bee buzz. But it had worked, like turning on a light switch.

"Try moving that rock," Crow had said, nodding toward what had to be a hundred-pound boulder.

Leonard had taken one step toward it before Crow said, "No."

"No?"

"No. Just point at it and tell it to move, but without saying it out loud."

"*Move*," Leonard had thought, pointing at it with one finger. And just like that, the rock shook and then rolled over as if a pry bar had been shoved under it.

"Telekinesis?"

"Yup."

"So, aside from moving rocks, what else can I do?"

"You'll see."

Over the three months since he'd gotten his new powers, Leonard had seen. He'd learned a lot about what he could do. He'd discovered he could move just about anything as long as it weighed less than half a ton. So pianos, maybe, but not pickup trucks. He'd also discovered that physical gestures like pointing, the way he had just done with Billy Ray, helped him focus, sort of fine-tune his aim.

Over the course of the last few weeks, using his abilities, he had managed to put a serious dent in the drug trade at Winnebonka. Or at least driven it underground rather than out in the open in the hallways, the locker rooms, and the north exit, where the bigger deals had been taking place. If you looked up at the ceiling of the boys' locker room, you could see embedded up there the hundred or so white pills that had rocketed up out of the bottle Whit Rogers (whose specialty was opioids) had been offering to one of the football players. As well as the larger dent Whit's head made when he'd rocketed up there, hit, then floated back down.

Leonard had looked at the finger he'd just used to levitate the dealer and his drugs, blown on the end of it like it was a .45, and thought, *I could do this all day!*

Leonard had also ruined the weekends of the Cool Car Crew. It had been surprisingly rewarding to stand at the edge of the parking lot each Friday, spin his index finger in a small circle, and watch all the valve stems in their tires—including the spares—unscrew themselves and jet off like tiny hummingbirds.

He felt pretty good about it. Actually, more than pretty good. He felt . . . empowered, both figuratively and literally. And it had only taken half a dozen double cheeseburgers and three strawberry milkshakes for him to get back to full strength after the flat tire trick—less than he'd needed for each drug deal he'd prevented.

Today, though, he had a new idea. Something he had to do after school, just to make sure, before he moved on to the next thing that he sensed was on its way, even if he didn't know what it was yet.

"You sure about this?" Crow said, hearing the thought in Leonard's mind before he voiced it.

"Pretty sure."

The bell rang, and Leonard joined the throng of kids heading back inside for afternoon classes.

Leonard did not move the numerals of the digital clock in the classroom ahead. It had worked the first few times he'd tried, resulting in an early dismissal. But today, he stayed patient, thinking. When the bell rang, though, he was the first person out the door of the classroom. He zipped down the hall and out the main doors. He'd discovered that, though it wasn't exactly flying, he was able to move faster than others, sort of think himself forward.

But if he really wanted to go fast, he had an even better way to do that. Before anyone else was out of the building, he gestured toward the hedge around the school.

"Hey, Wiggie," he said. "Here, boy!"

The leaves shook, and then his Golden Dragon skateboard came rocketing out of the hedge and landed in front of him. In the weeks he'd owned it, Leonard had customized its paint job. It was now emblazoned with double curve designs of the sort that used to be etched into the birch bark of canoes and wigwams. There were birds with wide wings and curling arches and lines that created symbols for protecting your home and drawing on your mind for strength. Wigwaol was the old name for a canoe, so he'd named it Wiggie.

He hopped on, bent low, and pointed straight ahead, and Wiggie took off as if it were rocket-propelled.

The gun club was at the edge of town. You could see it from a mile away because of the massive American flag flying at the front gate from a pole that was at least ninety feet tall.

Leonard stopped Wiggie in front of the gate. He could see half a dozen cars parked in the lot inside, next to the stations where members could set up for target practice. He could also see the targets downrange in front of the eighteen-foot-tall earthen backstop. They were not your standard bull's-eyes. Instead, they were a mix of stuffed dummies and pictures. All of them were Arab, Mexican, or Asian men. Leering, threatening, brown-skinned caricatures, all holding weapons.

The first time Leonard had walked by the gun club, which was only half a mile from his trailer park, he'd been a fifth grader. It had shocked him so much that he'd mentioned it to his aunt. He'd expected her to say no more than her usual "uh-huh" without looking away from the screen. But that day, Aunt Marilyn had surprised him by turning off the set and taking him by the arm.

"Listen, you," she'd said, "stay away from there. You

hear me? When I was your age, you know what they had on those targets?"

Then, without waiting for him to respond, she'd answered her own question.

"Indians."

Then, before he could say anything, she'd let go of his arm. "Dinner's in the fridge," she'd said, then turned *The Young and the Restless* back on.

Leonard stepped off his board and pointed at a patch of blackberries. "Hide, boy," he said. Like an obedient dog, Wiggie wiggled back and forth and then wheeled itself into the thick undergrowth.

"You really gonna do this?" Crow said.

Leonard walked up to the gate and swung his hand to the left. The gate opened, then closed behind him after he walked through.

No one came out of the guard shack. It was as if he were as invisible as Crow. Which was, he'd recently discovered, pretty much the case. If he didn't want to be seen, he wasn't noticed. He knew he wasn't actually invisible, since he still cast a shadow. But he was a walking blind spot in everyone else's vision, unless he wanted to be seen.

The first station of the gun range was occupied by none other than Lee Phillips, Custer's uncle. The Confederate flag decal on the back window of his truck was a hint as to where

his first name came from. He was member of the local Loyal
Boys, who viewed the Second Amendment as the only part of
the Constitution anyone needed to know, and he was foreman
of the town road crew. He was supposed to be at work now,
but no one was about to tell him that practicing his marks-
manship was less important than filling potholes. Lee was six
foot two, a barroom brawler, and a man who kept bad company. It was not just a rumor that the high school dealers re-
lied on him for some of their product. RJ—the same RJ who
had stolen Leonard's watch two years ago, still in town and
still a burnout—was their major source for pot. But it was Lee
who, by the way of his nephew Custer and Custer's best buddy,
Whit Rogers, was a dependable deliverer of Adderall and its
speedy cousins. Jelly babies, lid poppers, and the like, as kids
called them.

On his visit to the town garage two days ago, Leonard—
standing in plain sight and totally unseen—had watched Lee
Phillips hand a bottle of amphetamines to another member of
the town crew who had to stay awake for a night shift.

Leonard walked up to Lee's left side as he took careful aim
with his .30–06. He waited till the big man was about to pull
the trigger, then flicked his finger.

BLAM! A hole appeared in the belly of the knife-wielding
jihadi target fifty yards to the left of his.

"HEY!" yelled the man at that station. "Shoot your own
dang A-rab!"

"Sorry, Wash!" Lee Phillips yelled back as he began looking
at his gun, trying to figure out what had gone haywire.

"Satisfied?" Crow said as he flapped up off Leonard's shoulder and landed on the roof of the shooting station.

Once again, Leonard didn't answer. Instead, he walked past the firing line ten paces downrange, stopping directly in front of the long gun Lee Phillips was once again aiming at the target, carefully checking his line of sight. Then Leonard turned and held up his right hand.

"Dumb idea," Crow said. "As if you're going to listen to me."

BLAM!

Leonard lowered his hand and began juggling the hot slug he'd just caught from one palm to the other. He felt hungry enough to eat not just a buffalo burger but a whole buffalo. But despite the slight weakness in his knees, he felt great!

"Hey," he said, "look!" He held up the lead slug between his thumb and index finger. "It worked."

"Lucky for both of us," Crow said. "Satisfied now?"

Leonard walked back up to where Lee Phillips stood shaking his head as he looked down the breech of his .30–06. Leonard reached out and dropped the still-warm slug onto the metal table in front of the big man, where it landed with a loud *plunk!*

It startled Lee Phillips so much that he stumbled back, dropping his rifle on the ground as he tripped over a shooting stand and went rolling backward down the berm.

"Satisfied," Leonard said to Crow as he turned and began walking toward the exit.

And ready, he thought. The image of a black van had just come into his mind, as well as a few other pictures.

"Ready for tonight," he said out loud.

"Guess you are," Crow replied, flapping down to land on his shoulder. "After dinner."

Leonard looked at himself in the bathroom mirror. Although it might not have been absolutely necessary, he had dressed entirely in black, including a ski mask. True, he was able to make himself unseen, but the outfit still felt appropriate. *To get myself in the right mood*, he thought.

Despite having said he was ready for what he was about to do, he still felt a certain amount of uncertainty. After all, not that long ago, he'd been one step below dweeb-hood. Transitioning to superhero status felt more believable if he had some sort of costume.

"Plus, we are now twinsies," Crow said, bringing a smile to Leonard's face as he left the bathroom and closed the door as quietly as possible so as not to distract his aunt from her incessant TV watching.

As if she'd even notice me, he thought. And then immediately revised that thought as he turned around, because Aunt Marilyn was standing six feet away and looking straight at him.

Not only that—she was looking at Crow, too. As if she could see him.

"I can," she said.

"Yup," Crow agreed. "She can."

Leonard looked at Crow. Then he looked at Aunt Marilyn. Then he looked at Crow again. Somehow, even though one was avian and the other human, they seemed to be wearing the same expression.

"It runs in the family," Aunt Marilyn said.

"So to speak," Crow agreed.

"What?" Leonard said. He was so far at sea in this conversation that he felt as if he were about to drown.

"Mteowlin," Aunt Marilyn said.

And then Leonard understood. Maybe not completely, but enough.

Mteowlin—a person of power, according to their oldest Wabanaki traditions.

Aunt Marilyn nodded. "Yup," she said. "You got it."

To become a mteowlin, you needed a spirit helper. Some kind of being that chose you, bestowed upon you certain gifts. Like Crow.

But wasn't it said, Leonard thought, *that . . .*

"It runs in the blood," Aunt Marilyn said, completing his thought. "Now, I don't have much of it, but I can see some things. I could tell that you might be one who would get it all. It's not something you can teach. It just has to come to you. And telling you about it before it happened, before you really had it, could have confused things. So what I've been doing is just staying out of your way until the time was right."

It was the longest speech Leonard had ever heard from her.

"So the time is right now?"

Aunt Marilyn nodded, and so did Crow.

"So you aren't from outer space?" Leonard said to Crow.

"Depends on how you define outer space," Crow replied.

Leonard shook his head and sighed. It was confusing, but he didn't feel confused. He felt OK with it, even though he knew he'd have more questions.

"But not now," Crow said.

"Go save your girlfriend," Aunt Marilyn said. Then she immediately raised her hand and smiled. "Getting ahead of myself," she said.

She handed him a bag. "You'll need these."

Leonard looked inside it. It held a dozen of his favorite chocolate high-energy protein bars.

It was almost Halloween. As Leonard coasted along on Wiggie toward the school gym at thirty miles an hour, he passed carved pumpkins on front porches and larger-than-life blow-up skeletons, witches, monsters, and goblins of all kinds. As if there wasn't enough real scary stuff to worry about in the world—most of it their own doing—white folks had to put those exaggerated nightmarish figures out on their neatly manicured lawns. Even though it was only six p.m., most of those grotesque cartoon caricatures of danger were already lit up by little spotlights since it was already past twilight.

The time when the monsters come out, Leonard thought.

"Yup," Crow said into Leonard's left ear, his claws digging a little deeper into Leonard's shoulder as he dipped and coasted into the turn onto Winnebonka Drive. "They are coming for sure."

Six p.m. The time when the girls' cross country team would be in the locker room, changing back into street clothes after practice. They'd be coming out the side door of the gym in little groups, some of them to walk a few blocks home, some to be picked up by parents. One or two might be met by boyfriends in the Cool Car Crew. The ones in groups would be safe. So would the ones getting in cars driven by moms or dads or maybe older brothers or sisters. And the ones being picked up by boyfriends—though how safe that was depended on which boyfriend it was.

It was the stragglers who'd be truly vulnerable. Especially the last one out.

And tonight, though Leonard didn't know how he knew it, the last one out of the gym, unaccompanied by any of the other Emmas, would be Olivia Hammond.

He leaned against the streetlight that illuminated the lot, watching unseen as carefree kids came walking out of the school, faces still flushed from their workout, gym bags in their hands or packs on their backs. Passing him in groups, climbing into cars.

Then they were all gone, and the lot was empty. Almost.

He felt the van coming before he saw it or heard it.

As it glided up and stopped beside the building, just around the corner from the gym's side exit, Leonard could see inside it. Not through the black windows or the unopened doors, but another way, with his mind. He saw the three large men wearing black from their sneakers to the ski masks hiding everything but their eyes and mouths.

One to drive. Two to grab.

And even with a ski mask, he recognized the biggest of the three.

It was Lee Phillips. Apparently, drug dealing didn't bring all of his extra revenue.

Leonard also saw what else was in that van. The duct tape. The zip ties. The roll of nylon cord.

The front window of the van rolled down, and the barrel of an air rifle appeared and fired a second later. The streetlight above Leonard shattered and went dark, as did most of the parking lot, especially the part near the side door.

The gym door opened and Olivia Hammond stepped out. Her long dark hair hung loose over the left side of her face, but it didn't cover the smile that was usually there. The same smile she used to give Leonard when they passed in the halls. He'd always wished he could get up the courage to do more than nod back.

The door to the van began to slide open and a gloved hand appeared holding a white cloth. Soaked with chloroform, Leonard guessed. Then a dark-sneakered foot slowly emerged. Olivia was unaware of the van or the men in it. She took one graceful step and then another as the gym door automatically closed behind her.

It was all happening faster than Leonard had expected.

"Well?" Crow cawed in his ear.

"Right!" Leonard said. He lifted his right hand and swung it to the side. The half-open van door slammed shut on both the foot and the gloved hand with a crunching thud, followed by a scream that was more angry than agonized.

Leonard flew forward. Now he was standing next to Olivia, his hand on her arm, between her and the black van, which she was looking at over his shoulder.

"Run," he said. "Go straight home. Don't look back. And call 911."

Her eyes focused on his, stayed there for a split second, as if she were really seeing him for the first time. Then she turned and started running.

He hadn't expected her to obey him. Or had he? He'd felt himself sort of put something into his voice as he spoke.

He turned toward the van.

The door was open again, and someone was being pushed out of it. A large man who fell to the ground moaning, his right leg twisted, his gloved and equally twisted right hand clutched to his chest. Lee Phillips.

The driver's door opened. Someone stepped out. Except maybe "someone" wasn't the right word for him or for the other figure that came out of the back of the van at the same time. Not some*ones*. Some*things*. It seemed that the company Lee Phillips kept was more than just bad. What was concealed by those ski masks might not be human faces. And maybe the kids they'd abducted in the past—something Leonard was certain had happened—had not been taken for the white slave trade but for something even darker.

And Leonard understood what Aunt Marilyn had warned him about that one time. *Old things wearing our bodies.* She'd warned him then because he was not ready. But was he ready now?

The first figure that had climbed out of the van stopped and looked at him. More than looked—its eyes were twin red flames. And as it stared at Leonard, it opened its mouth in a wide grin. OK, way too wide. Just as the teeth were way too big. Long and sharp as the teeth of a kiwakw, one of those cannibal monsters in old Penacook stories.

Wake up!

Crow's voice echoed inside Leonard's head at the same time as his talons dug into his shoulder, probably hard enough to draw blood.

Which was what he needed, seeing as how that first black-clad figure had somehow—without Leonard noticing—crossed from the van to where Leonard was standing. The kiwakw, or whatever it was, was less than an arm's length away. Reaching for him.

Leonard reacted the way someone would if they suddenly realized a hornet was diving at their head. He ducked, swatting violently with one hand as he fell backward.

Swatted maybe more violently than was needed, seeing as how that hand gesture not only lifted the kiwakw off its feet, it also hurled it back so hard it could have covered twenty times the distance from Leonard to the black van. Would have, had the solid brick wall of the gym not terminated its flight. When it hit, it came apart with a loud splat, big black globs like ink flying off in all directions and then dissipating into smoke.

Leonard only saw that out of the corner of his eye. No longer semi-hypnotized, he was aware of the second black being coming at him from the van's sliding door. And his reaction to it was already underway before monster number one had hit the wall.

"*Wiggie!*" he shouted, halfway through falling backward.

The Golden Dragon skateboard shot past Leonard, lifting itself off the ground like a rocket. It struck the black figure in the chest, tearing through it as if it were made of cardboard. It spun in midair through the resultant cloud of black smoke, landed back on its wheels, and whirred over to nudge Leonard's side as he lay on the asphalt.

Crow was sitting on Leonard's chest. He picked at Leonard's shoulder with his beak.

"You OK, boss?" Crow asked.

Leonard took a deep breath. He'd skinned his elbows when he fell and hit the back of his head. But other than that, he seemed to be intact. And the part of him that was accepting his new role in life was already figuring out what his next moves would be.

Get up and go over to the van. Use some of those zip ties to secure Lee Phillips. Tell the police—who would soon arrive, from the sound of distant sirens he was hearing—how he'd been skateboarding in the lot. Then, when he'd seen someone coming out of that van, how he had slammed the door shut on him. Accept the fact that, for a while at least, he might go from being a zero to a hero. Then go home to tell Aunt Marilyn about the events of the night and talk with her, really talk, about a lot of things.

But right now?

Leonard looked at Crow.

"I really need that bag of energy bars I left over by the streetlight," he said.

FLY, LIONS, FLY

by **MORGAN BADEN**

THE ZIP CODE WAS NEW, BUT CECE FELT NOTHING but old. Another school, another cheerleading squad, and yet another time she'd have to work her way up from the bottom of the cheerleading hierarchy. Now, she worried her body was growing tired. Spent. And at fifteen, she'd never be this young again.

She held out a leg, stretching her hamstring. As if to prove her point, her hip popped.

When Cece opened her locker—if she was counting correctly, this was the sixth locker she'd had since elementary school, all of them with the same smell—her bright blue pom-poms tumbled out, landing on her fresh white sneakers.

"Go, Lions!" someone shouted. Behind her, the hallway was a living organism, seething with movement, teeming with misdirected energy. Cece didn't turn around and instead kept digging for her gym bag. She'd learned a few schools back that there was only one group of kids she cared about getting to know: the cheerleading squad. Her teammates. The Pinewood Lions were the best in the nation, and as of a few weeks ago, she was officially one of them.

Now she just needed to get them to actually like her.

Cece followed the squeaks and grunts coming from the practice gym and painted on a smile before pulling open the double doors. A flash of gold caught her eye: Maisie, their captain, soaring up to the rafters, her yellow practice uniform a spot of sun against the gray ceiling. Captains earned special pom-poms, and Maisie's golden pair glinted under the fluorescent lights. She kicked her legs, arched her back. Then gravity beckoned, and Maisie fell from the sky. Her bases—Greta and

Hope and Hazel—caught her almost silently. A flawless basket toss.

Twelve girls clad in stretchy miniskirts and tanks, thigh muscles like you wouldn't believe and fire in their bellies that only seemed to light up more on the mat. The Lions cheerleaders were legendary, and Cece felt lucky to have joined them. She just hated that they didn't seem to feel the same way.

It wasn't that her skills were a problem—she was a stunning athlete, powerful and daring—but there was something keeping the rest of the squad from letting her in fully. It had been nearly a month since she'd joined them, and still, she just couldn't find her way inside.

She needed time, she knew. *They* needed time.

She cleared her throat, sent a wish to the universe that her tight hamstrings wouldn't hold her back, and entered the gym, ready to warm up alone. As usual.

"OK, everyone!" Maisie's voice cut through the chatter, the squeaks of shoes on the shiny floor, and the low music playing from an old stereo in the corner. She clapped her hands. Immediately, the squad fell into place, lining up to face their captain. Cece stood next to Alex, a girl she knew from Spanish class. Cece smiled hopefully at her, but Alex quickly averted her eyes, shifted her hips, and turned her attention back to Maisie.

Cece tried to pretend her cheeks weren't burning with shame at being slighted yet again by one of her teammates. But this time, in a flash, her embarrassment turned to anger. Cece wasn't just a good cheerleader; she was a *great* one. She'd elevated the cheer program at every school she'd enrolled in and had been a star flyer—one of the girls at the top of every stunt, who had the control and flexibility to soar through the air—for years. So why did the Lions make her feel like some kind of second-rate has-been?

"We have a mere eight weeks until Nationals," Maisie announced, her glittery pom-poms stationed on her hips.

"Eight weeks until we reclaim our title!" Alex blurted. Cece winced—but to her surprise, the rest of the squad hooted and hollered.

She narrowed her eyes and studied her teammates to see if their faces revealed any truths, any buried secrets, about what had happened at last year's National competition. It was a mystery to everyone in the cheer industry. Even the insider blogs that Cece inhaled whenever she could hadn't been able to figure out what had caused the world-famous Pinewood Lions to forfeit the biggest, most important competition of the year. After winning every event along the way, the Lions had simply . . . failed to show up.

And still, no one at Pinewood City High School talked about it.

Cece couldn't really blame them. Imagine being the talk of the cheer industry, the absolute favorites to win, and then skipping out on the whole thing. Imagine passing the trophy case in the front hall of Pinewood City High every day, taunted by the empty space in the front that had been meant for your big triumph.

Cece's eyes landed back on her captain. Maisie was stoic, dramatic. She met each girl's eye, lingering on Cece's longest.

"Every one of those weeks will require absolute commitment from each of you. Total dedication and sacrifice."

They all nodded. Even Cece, whose hamstrings tightened. She imagined she could pluck them like guitar strings. Cece knew dedication. She understood commitment. Her mother was active military—hence all the moving—and she didn't take promises lightly. She was a Lion, and she was ready for everything that entailed.

She just needed to prove it to her squad.

What Cece loved best about cheerleading was the surprise of it all.

The first time her father had witnessed one of her competitions, she'd been worried he would stop breathing. By the time the event was over, he'd turned a sickly shade of gray, and he'd downed three glasses of his favorite whiskey that night, shaking his head between every sip and whispering, "My god. Those stunts."

Most people only saw cheerleaders on the sidelines at football and basketball games, leading chants with rhyming words, occasionally throwing a small basket toss to amp up the crowd. But the real sport of cheerleading happened way off the field in gyms across the nation, where hordes of teams gathered to compete, the air practically shimmering with energy. With heat. Everyone waiting to see who could dance, who could choreograph, who could tumble, and most importantly, who could perfect the wildest, most dangerous stunts.

To see who could *fly*.

Cece lived for it. The adrenaline, the endorphins, the way nearly anything could happen on the mat—how the cleanest tumblers could trip, the smoothest dancers could stumble, the easiest stunts could collapse.

Back in the practice gym, Maisie called a huddle. Today's experiment was risky, and Cece felt a thick rope of jealousy snake around her heart. *I bet I could do this stunt better than anyone*, she found herself thinking.

But there was no time to brood. She was new. She had to pay her dues. Joining the circle, clapping and hooting, she understood why Maisie hadn't chosen her to fly. But that didn't make it any easier to watch Mina do it.

Someone started a steady drumbeat with her feet, a backbeat that filled the gym with a hum of energy that soon began to crackle like it was rising from the mats. Three bases on the ground, two standing on their shoulders, and Mina way up top, stretching toward the rafters. Cece watched as Mina climbed and flew, her face grim with determination. Up, up, up she went. Tiny but packed with strength, Mina was the Lions' star, the girl who always got to soar.

"Li-ons, Li-ons, Li-ons," Cece and her teammates chanted. Mina was close to the top; the stunt was nearly perfect.

But Cece saw something on Mina's face—a flash of pain, maybe, or surprise—and all at once, it went wrong.

It happened in an instant: Mina, about to leap off her base's shoulders and dive toward the floor, instead crumpled a little, her body folding in on itself. When she was supposed to be in the shape of an upside-down V, she was tucked into a loose ball. Her ankle hit Vivi in the face. Shocked by the force of it, Vivi fumbled, her own foot digging too deeply into Alex's neck—Alex, who was holding up the whole stunt from the bottom—then faltered, her knees buckling.

And Mina just . . . fell.

She landed on the mat hard, a pile of limbs, a shout of pain. The girls who were supposed to catch her—whose sole job, in fact, was to serve as a soft place to land—looked stunned. Confused.

And then, furious.

"Are you OK?" Cece dashed to Mina, whose eyes were dazed. She blinked, and her expression turned to terror.

"Um," she said weakly.

Maisie stomped over. "What the hell happened?!"

"I don't know," Mina protested. "I wasn't . . . someone . . ."

Maisie clapped her hands to get the team's attention. "Unacceptable!" she screeched.

Her rage had distorted her face, and as Cece stared, speechless—she'd never seen a captain get so *mad* about a simple stunt fall, especially when, to Cece's trained eye, it had seemed like a true accident—a flurry of conversation erupted around them. Greta pointed angrily at Alex; Hazel and June both shook their heads, pink blotches of fury climbing up their necks. Crumpled on the floor, Mina, too, was angry.

In an instant, Cece learned something new about the Lions: They weren't good at failing. Their picture-perfect veneer cracked, and out seeped chaos.

Cece refocused on Mina, who was rubbing her ankle. "Do you need some ice? Maybe we should find the trainer?"

"No," Mina said quickly. "No! I'm fine. Just a little shaken."

"Same," Maisie snapped. Arms crossed, she glared at every member of the squad in turn. Except, Cece noticed, her.

Cece had been involved in stunts gone wrong before. Every cheerleader had! But she had never seen a squad rush to blame someone for a simple fall so quickly, especially one where no one had had any visible bruises or broken bones. Mina was going to be fine, to Cece's surprise. So why was everyone so pissed?

As Mina straightened up, testing out her ankle, Maisie evened her breath and ferociously fixed her ponytail. "I'll remind everyone that coordination and trust are what make us successful," she said witheringly. She waited a beat, and in her pause, Cece saw a flash of something new on her face.

Fear.

So much fear, it took Cece's breath away.

"If we can't coordinate, we will fail," Maisie continued. "Do you understand? And we cannot—must not—fail."

Silently, the rest of the squad nodded, a sense of humble determination settling over them. And Cece felt it again, that unmistakable certainty that she was missing something. That her teammates were having a conversation without her, even though she was standing right there.

Maisie sucked in a breath, her golden poms at her hips. "Let's do it again. Now."

Practice ended early and abruptly. When the squad departed in a flurry of whispers, leaving Cece to roll up the mats by

herself, she assumed they were all off to do something excit-
ing without her. Mina's fall seemed to have been forgotten,
including by Mina herself, but the feeling that she had missed
some crucial lesson about the Lions hung around Cece long
after she'd left the quiet, darkened gym.

At home in the kitchen, her dad was baking his famous
chocolate chip cookies while her mom thumbed through a
cookbook. "Hey, sweets," she said. "Any thoughts for dinner?"

"Pizza?" she said eagerly. Her mom's face fell, her finger
hovering over a dog-eared page.

Cece shrugged and dragged her pom-poms and gym bag
to her bedroom. On the way, the television in the living room
caught her attention, a "breaking news" chyron at the bottom
of the screen. It was the local evening news, and a reporter
stood in front of a messy scene; debris littered the sidewalk
outside an abandoned-looking building, and fear was etched
into the lines of the reporter's face.

"If you're just joining us, we're bringing you breaking news
from Avenue M in the business district, where another small
explosion has rocked the area," the reporter said, gripping her
microphone. "Eyewitnesses claim to have heard several loud
noises, followed by an explosion that ripped the roof off of
this unoccupied building and shattered windows up and down
the block."

Cece stared. A tiny pinch of tension took root in her
stomach.

"This is the fifth instance in recent weeks of unexplained
property damage, and while we can clearly see that something

unexpected has occurred"—the reporter gestured behind her, to where shards of glass glinted on the sidewalk and a small but dark plume of smoke was rising from the back of the building—"police continue to refuse to answer questions about this latest in what appears to be a series of similar incidents. They are withholding information about any potential victims or suspects, claiming that releasing that information would hinder their investigation."

She blinked a few times, waiting for the station to cut back to the anchor, and Cece's eyes panned over the scene. A flash of gold sparked, crackling just at the border of the camera's range. It caught Cece's attention, but before her eyes could focus on it, it was gone, and the broadcast switched back to the on-air hosts in the studio. Why was it, Cece wondered, that all local news broadcasters looked like they were related?

In the studio, a salt-and-pepper-haired man who could have been eighty or not a day over thirty-five blinked seriously at Cece. "Thanks for that report from the scene, Liz." Abruptly, he turned to his coanchor. "Gladys, what do you think?"

Gladys eyed the camera. "Well, Al, I think it's superher—"

"Let's move on to the weather!" Al frantically gestured to someone off camera before a map of Pinewood City lit up the screen.

"Whoa!"

Cece jumped, her heart leaping right along with her. "Dad! Warn a girl when you're creeping up behind her, would ya?"

He pointed at the screen. "Did she just say what I think she said? Superheroes? In Pinewood City?"

Cece considered the idea. It was strange, thinking maybe there were some circling around them right now, perched in the trees dotting their backyard . . .

Before Cece was even born, superheroes and villains had been famous (and infamous) for their epic battles around the globe; they'd been as much a part of the landscape as the weather. But eventually, the collateral damage from their clashes had forced the world's leading governments to work together on a joint set of superhero restrictions. Since those mandates had been established—Cece's history teachers had always called them "peace accords," even though the villains had objected to the term—superhero and villain activity had dwindled. The really bad villains had been vanquished; the really good superheroes had retired. To Cece, it all felt like kid stuff, and imaginary, distant history. Superheroes had become symbols of the past, as antiquated as the old-fashioned answering machines Cece had seen in movies.

"There can't be any superheroes here," Cece said. "What about the peace accords?"

Cece's dad had been a history teacher before she came along. She braced herself for a litany of dates and names and backstories about various government resolutions. She wished she'd grabbed one of the cookies he'd baked for sustenance.

"For starters, I'm pleased to hear you're learning stuff in history class," he chuckled. But then his face grew serious, his gaze distant. "After the Villain Uprising of ninety-nine, when the villains were mostly destroyed, the Superhero Alliance could tell they were falling out of favor. They agreed to back off for a while . . . but it's been twenty years, Cees. And rumors of villains have been rising in the past year or so, especially in the big cities." He met Cece's eyes. "As history shows us time and again, peace never lasts. Maybe the villains *and* the superheroes are getting restless."

"So you think . . ." Cece struggled to get the words out. Because if he was right, and if the news anchor had really been about to say what it sounded like she was going to say, there were bad guys hanging around Pinewood City.

"I think . . ." His voice trailed off. He stared at the screen until it cut to commercial, and then he added grimly, "I think you should stay away from the business district for now."

After dinner—she'd been able to convince her mom that pizza was the right answer—she spent the night watching old clips of the Lions at past competitions. (It wasn't the first time she'd eschewed any kind of attempt at a social life in favor of improving her craft, and she knew it wouldn't be the last.) She thought she'd study their cohesion and see if there was some secret to how they all worked together—some insight into how they moved on the mat, how she could mimic them in order to be more accepted. Maybe then she'd finally become a flyer, like Mina.

Because all Cece really wanted to do was fly.

Reviewing the clips was a curious exercise. The squad's routines were impeccable. The cheerleaders performed like mirror images of each other, each girl anticipating the moves of the one next to her. Cece yawned as she clicked around, scrolling until she landed on last year's regional competition, the one right before the big national event where the Lions had been expected to win. She hungrily clicked play.

She watched it over and over: the Lions' pom-poms sparkling in the lights, their choreography flawless, their stunts powerful, Maisie's golden hands directing the crowd's attention. Then Cece clicked over to the awards ceremony. In it, all the competing squads lined the stage, drumming the mat with their poms. Poms that, Cece realized, were noticeably not blue or gold.

Because last year, the Lions had skipped out on the awards ceremony—arguably the best part of the whole thing, in Cece's opinion.

The judges had called their name—"And now, in first place, earning the highest marks ever achieved in a regional competition in this state and setting a new record, the Pinewood Lions!"—and then . . . the mat remained empty. Cece could see the confusion on the judges' faces and hear the whispers of the crowd as the Lions failed to materialize.

It was odd, Cece thought, how the Lions appeared to have a habit of not sticking around.

She kept looking.

Everyone knew about last year's Nationals, of course. But as Cece dove deeper into the abyss of old cheerleading videos, she discovered there was so much more to the story. The Lions cheerleading squad was missing about a quarter of the time they were meant to be on the mat, or even on the field. From competitions to awards ceremonies to football and basketball halftimes, the squad couldn't seem to consistently show up where they were expected. Only their incredible performances in the rest of the competitions kept them in the running.

Cece sat up in bed, mind racing. Outside, a branch tapped on her window.

She knew, suddenly, how to fit in with the Lions.

All she had to do was figure out where they kept going, then meet them there.

That weekend, Cece went undercover—or as undercover as a five-foot-six, sharp-angled athlete with streaming red hair and absolutely no sense of direction in a new town could be—on a mission to figure out the squad's secrets.

She stalked their social media accounts on Saturday morning, which led her to an organic café around the corner from Maisie's house. Inside, sunlight fell over the squad's seniors, Maisie and June and Aesha and Quinn, their heads bowed toward the center of their table as they talked and laughed. From her perch on a bench across the street, her gray hoodie pulled tight over her hair, Cece eventually admitted to herself that there was absolutely nothing scandalous or mysterious about their omelets. Her stomach growled.

When the seniors dispersed, Cece discovered that Alex and Mina had tagged photos of themselves in some of the shops downtown, so she jogged the mile and change and managed to duck behind a delivery van just as Mina's tiny head popped out of a jewelry shop. Cece used the van's mirrors to follow their movements. Alex carried a couple of shopping bags, Mina an iced coffee, but then someone who looked like Mina's mom pulled up on the corner, and both girls hopped in, disappearing into weekend traffic.

The whole day followed in a similar fashion. Every time Cece thought she was on to something, the Lions cheerleaders turned out to be doing regular, normal things. Yoga classes. (Her own hamstring ached at the sight.) A matinee. Manicures. A furtive make-out session in the tree-lined, shaded section of the town's largest park.

It was at that moment when Cece saw Greta and Hope clinging to each other in the shadows that she realized her plan wasn't working. She'd wasted an entire day stalking the Lions rather than doing something useful like, oh, trying to actually befriend them. Brooding, she began walking home, barely noticing which streets she was turning down, wondering if she was making Something out of Nothing, if maybe it was *her* that was off, not the rest of the squad. Maybe she'd been reading the situation all wrong.

Clearly, the Lions cheerleaders were always disappearing for the simplest of reasons: because they'd been invited somewhere else more important.

Just as the sky was fading into the soft blue color of her favorite jeans, Cece crossed at a light and took a real look around at where she was. She'd been wandering a bit aimlessly, assuming she was headed in the direction of home, but she suddenly realized she had ended up in the business district, which now, on a Saturday evening, felt deserted and a tinge scary.

Tall office buildings loomed over her, their shadows darkening the spots the sun could no longer reach; the sandwich shops and cafés were closed.

Cece shivered. Just down the block was where last night's accident, the one she'd seen on the news, had happened. Police tape was still wrapped around the street signs, cordoning off the middle of the block; the windows of the nearby buildings were shattered. A whiff of smoke, of burned wood and plastic, lingered in the air, which whirled about her with increased velocity. A storm was blowing in.

Cece stepped closer to the crime scene. Even traffic was quiet in this area on weekends, and she suddenly felt keenly aware of how alone she was.

Still, she crept forward.

Debris littered the sidewalk, and she peered at it. She wasn't sure what she was searching for; she just knew something was tugging at her insides, and all she could think to do was look for something that would make it stop.

Cigarette butts. Squashed soda cans. A lone sandwich wrapper floating around her feet on a renewed gust of wind. Glass shards left over from the explosion lighting up the sidewalk.

A blast of air whipped around the corner, careening toward her.

It carried a piece of gold with it.

Automatically, reflexively, Cece held out her hand. Not to *stop* the thing that was aiming straight for her, but to catch it.

The wind delivered the gold right into her open palm.

Her fingers gripped it. Her brain registered the sensation: paper-thin but hefty, smooth but crinkly.

She squeezed her eyes closed, holding the gold tight in her hand. Whatever it was, it nearly singed her palm. A buzz of heat, of energy, crackled, then burst up her arm, following her bloodstream, making her toes tingle, her hair practically stand on end.

For a second, with her eyes closed and her feet planted firmly on the ground, Cece would have sworn she was flying.

Almost immediately, her body acclimated to the rush the gold had given her. She opened her eyes. She felt like herself, only . . . more.

Blinking away her confusion, Cece glanced at her hand. Slowly, her brain told her fingers to peel back, one by one.

"What the . . ." she muttered.

A single strand of a sparkly gold pom-pom sat innocently against her skin.

Maisie's pom-pom.

Cece spent the rest of the weekend staring at the sparkly gold pom-pom strand as much as possible while also trying to hide it from her parents, who were on a cleaning tear.

"I can't wait until cheerleading ends," her dad moaned over the drone of the vacuum. "Your poms keep getting caught in this thing."

But cheerleading would never end for Cece, she knew. High school, then college, then a pro team, and then probably coaching as a career. What part of "cheerleading is life" did her parents not understand?

In her room, she studied the gold strand. She'd carried it home in her pocket the night before, trying to convince herself she was imagining the heat she felt against her hip. Then she'd carefully tucked it into a plastic snack bag, labeled it **DO NOT DISTURB** in Sharpie (see: parents' cleaning tear), and propped it up on her nightstand.

Every hour on the hour during the night, she'd awoken to check on it. Predictably, it didn't move or anything. It didn't sprout eyes or legs; it didn't change color. It looked just like all the other parts of Maisie's pom-poms.

Which of course made a new question tickle the back of Cece's brain: If one single strand could make Cece feel the way she did when she held it . . . what must it feel like to hold hundreds of strands?

She sighed. She scratched her cheek. Brushed her hair. Stared.

Last week in chemistry, they'd done their first lab experiment. She had liked the whole process—forming a hypothesis, observing the results. It was time for an at-home experiment, she decided. Because maybe she'd imagined the whole thing. Right?

So sometime in the afternoon, when her parents were out grocery shopping and she was supposed to be doing homework, she braced herself. She did a few jumping jacks to work out her nerves, had the last-minute genius idea of turning her phone's video recorder on, and then—slowly, steadily—reached out to the sealed baggie.

She opened it and, in one fast breath, dumped the sparkly strand onto her palm.

The damn thing nearly burned her hand off.

Exhaustion turned into a low-grade lethargy by Monday, combined with a pounding headache from staying up way too late, trying to research her way out of her confusion. Perhaps unsurprisingly, "magic pom-pom" and "hot pom-pom that burns hand" and "what are pom-poms made of and why did I nearly catch fire" didn't turn up any useful answers on the Internet.

She hadn't been able to decide if it was safer to bring the baggie with her to school or to leave it at home. In the end, she'd secured it safely inside the (locked) front zipper pocket of her backpack and toted it with her to every class, not daring to leave it in her locker unattended. The small of her back grew hotter and itchier with every passing class.

Finally, it was time for practice. Cece gulped a soda for a sugar-and-caffeine hit and met her teammates in the practice gym. She was nervous, restless. Her hamstrings pulsed again. She eyed Maisie carefully. And visibly. For the entire two hours.

By the end of practice, Maisie had had it. She snapped at her, "Can I help you with something, Cece?"

A hush settled over the gym as every member of the squad turned to see Cece's response.

Cece was so tired, she didn't have the energy to lie. She decided to just go for it. "Actually, yeah."

Maisie raised an eyebrow. The girls began to close ranks, circling around their captain, until Cece was facing the entire squad.

Cece cleared her throat. She suddenly knew what she had to do. "Can I borrow your pom-poms for a sec?"

The gym was silent. Cece could hear her own heartbeat. She almost thought she could hear a sound coming from her backpack, which was across the gym on the bottom bleacher, lying with all the other backpacks and duffel bags and water bottles the squad lugged around each day. Like the sparkly gold strand was calling her name.

Ceeee-ceeee, it whispered.

Cece swallowed. Was she having some kind of cheerleading-induced breakdown? Had she fallen on her head during a big tumbling stretch?

But something in Maisie's eyes glinted, matching the shine coming from her pom-poms, held tightly in her hands. And when Cece saw it, she knew, like a punch to the gut, that she wasn't having a breakdown.

Maisie was hiding something from her.

No.

The *entire Pinewood Lions cheerleading squad* was hiding something from her.

"What did you say?" Maisie asked.

Cece's voice was small but resolute. She was a girl with nothing to lose. She fingered the bandage on her palm;

underneath, her burned skin smarted, red and raw. "I said, can I borrow your pom-poms?"

Maisie snorted. Her pom-poms responded, shuffling their strands as if in response to a strong breeze. "No. You can't."

"Yeah," Alex echoed from behind Maisie's shoulder.

Cece shrugged. "What's the big deal?"

Maisie was getting flustered. Two spots of pink lit up her cheeks. "Because I'm the captain, and they're mine."

Cece nodded, pretending to understand. Inside, though, she definitely did not. But something told her she was on the right track. There was something there. She just had to keep looking.

Suddenly, Maisie jolted. Her arms tensed at her sides; her shoulders straightened. Her face lost its color. "I have to go. Practice is over."

Cece folded her arms and stood watching while Maisie and the rest of the squad grabbed their bags and ran—literally ran—out of the gym.

Once again, she was left alone to put away the mats and wonder.

Are you safe?!?!

The text alert from her mom rang out from the depths of her backpack as Cece chugged the last of her water. She absentmindedly rubbed the sore spots on her body—shoulders, thighs, wrists—and then dug through the bag until she found her phone, the whole time conscious of the mysterious pom-pom strand still in there. She wondered what on earth her mom was talking about. She sent back a *???*

As Cece flicked off the lights in the gym, her mom responded with a link to a streaming video. When she tapped play, she froze. A hushed darkness had settled around her, and the volume of the video startled her.

Something was happening downtown, the place with all the cool cafés and gift shops, where she'd spent most of Saturday tracking the squad. An entire block was cordoned off. Helicopters circled the sky as crowds gathered on the sidewalks, and officials roped off huge areas, keeping everyone away from . . . something.

Cece peered at her phone, squinting. Citizen journalism was awesome, but whoever this citizen was, they had a shaky arm, and Cece found herself getting nauseated.

But then the camera zoomed in, offering a crystal-clear view of the situation.

And the sight made Cece fall to her knees.

Cece had seen photos and videos of villains before. Everyone had, provided they'd read a history book or a magazine or any corner of the Internet for five minutes. Even though they kept a low profile these days, villains were still part of the discourse, and everyone understood, logically, that they were likely hiding in plain sight.

But she'd never knowingly been in such close proximity to one. Ever.

On the hard, cold floor of the gym, she focused on catching her breath. The villain she'd seen on her screen was infamous—Amnesiac, they called him. He had looked straight at the camera before leaping up into the air and soaring into an open window in the building behind him, and his face—gray skin, deep crevasses etched around his eyes and mouth, dull, large eyes the color of a faraway galaxy—was seared into Cece's mind, burning her retinas. Her fingers inexplicably itched and ached. Even on a screen, looking at Amnesiac had scorched a black hole of despair in her chest. He was famous for making people forget who they were, how to live. How to love.

Cece knew then, with a clarity that surprised even her, that villains were back, and they were attacking Pinewood City.

Amnesiac had robbed a string of shops, binding and gagging everyone in his way, leaving behind a string of victims. Emergency officials had surrounded him, but Amnesiac had outsmarted them; according to the blurry videos and frantic social media posts from people near the scene, he'd disappeared somewhere in the haphazard alleyways of Pinewood City.

She gripped her phone tighter, consuming everything she could find about Amnesiac. The city streets were in chaos. Cece watched the news footage on every channel, every platform she could find, trying to piece together the updates. Her heart felt like it was inching up her throat with every breath. An emergency alert hit her phone and, presumably, everyone else's: the city was under siege. An immediate lockdown had been issued. Wherever you were, you were required to stay there until further notice.

Which meant Cece was stuck here, alone in the gym.

Maybe even in the entire school.

Dropping her phone, she glanced around, stunned. She was still crouched on the floor, sitting in the dark. Her hamstrings spasmed. Her body felt like a million bees had nested inside her, just under her skin; she was buzzing.

She could wander the halls of the school, try to find someone else to talk to, to hunker down with. Maybe kick the vending machines for some chips. No, she told herself, standing up and doing a quick back handspring, just to stretch out her body. Wandering the school didn't feel right. So what did?

The buzzing escalated. Her eyes landed on her backpack.

It was vibrating.

The squad had deserted her just as a villain had begun terrorizing Pinewood City, and the mysterious pom-pom strand Cece had found at the scene of the last unexplained incident was *vibrating*.

Inside Cece's brain, a calendar appeared. She ran through the days and months, did some quick math in her head. Last year's Nationals, when the squad hadn't shown up to compete at all? Regionals, when they'd disappeared before they could pick up their trophy? She searched those dates along with "villains" and pored over the results as fast as she could.

It didn't take long to learn the facts: On both of those days, there had been major—unexplained, unsolved—events in Pinewood City. First, a building on fire on the outskirts of town that threatened to burn down an entire development. Second, a group of employees at the big plastics factory, locked inside as a lethal chemical filled the room, slowly poisoning them.

In both instances, reports acknowledged that *someone* had saved the day. But no one knew who. The hero hadn't announced themselves, hadn't demanded any credit. A good deed done in secret.

Several times in the last few weeks, the squad had ditched practice early. Heart racing, Cece found those dates and discovered they all aligned with local news reports of other inexplicable crimes. Like what had happened on Friday evening, when she and her dad had watched the news.

Like what was happening *right now*.

Cece put down her phone, her heart a ball of fire in her chest, and stared at the banner hanging high on the far wall of the gym.

PINEWOOD LIONS ROAR! it read. And underneath: **STAY STRONG—STAY TRUE—TO THE GOLD AND BLUE!**

She set her jaw. Smoothed her yellow skirt, straightened the blue-and-gold vest with the embroidered lion's face on it, its mouth open, ready to devour the competition. To vanquish its foes.

Cece was a *cheerleader*.

It was time to freaking act like one.

The second Cece closed her hand around the sparkling pom-pom strand, she grew ten feet.

OK, not really. But it felt like it. The buzzing in her body matched the vibrations of the pom-pom, and a jolt of electricity shot through her limbs.

She had the distinct feeling that she could fly, if she wanted to.

Cece closed her eyes in anguish. All she'd ever wanted to do was fly, to be tossed into the air like Mina, to sail through the sky like a bird.

She *could* fly. Right now. Really, really fly.

And none of the Lions cheerleaders were here to witness it.

Cece's eyes popped open, and she squeezed her fingers around the pom-pom strand. Testing the burn, listening to the searing pain. She was surprised to discover that after a minute or so, the heat dissipated; in its place came a sense of control. Of power. Of knowledge.

Her eyes flicked around, from the strand to her body, her body to the bleachers, the bleachers to the locker room. Where had the rest of her squad disappeared to so quickly? So urgently? Why did Maisie's pom-poms glow so brightly? How did they contain . . . well, whatever it was they contained?

Magic? Power? Cece didn't know. But her thoughts tumbled forward like her body did on game days: fast, one after the other, until everything was a blur.

She had to get downtown.

She kept to the shadows. Pinewood City was still under lockdown, and the streets were empty, disturbed only by the slow passing of an occasional police car. She didn't know the ins and outs of this place yet, but in a way, she didn't need to; with the golden strand still gripped between her fingers, with her body still riding some kind of energetic high, carrying with it some unseen force field, she knew exactly where to go.

Almost like . . .

She didn't have time to think about how she knew where to go or why she knew with such certainty that she needed to be there. She ran. Jumped. Leapt over obstacles, ducked into alleys. Followed the sounds of the sirens.

She was close; she could feel it. She rounded a final corner, did a running front tuck—just because she could, because her body demanded that she soar—and then . . .

Cece ran smack into Maisie.

In the darkened corner of the alley, Maisie's eyes widened in horror. Cece was struck by the way she was drawn to Maisie—her hand, mostly, the one gripping the pom-pom, as if the strand needed to fuse back into the poms she held at her hips. She was in her gold practice uniform, only it looked different—shinier, Cece decided. Like it was made of something besides just cotton and Lycra.

It looked, Cece realized, like armor.

Above them, the tallest buildings in Pinewood City loomed, shadowing the alleyway. Maisie's pom-poms twinkled. The sounds of a far-off crowd seeped through the cement and brick as helicopters beat against the wind overhead and sirens continued to wail; a soundtrack Cece would never forget.

Cece couldn't help it—her fingers unfurled themselves. In her palm, the strand sparkled, glittered. Jumped.

Maisie's eyes dropped. Her jaw followed.

Something clicked inside Cece. "Give me a pom."

Crash.

Something struck the building above them, and the ground shook. Debris and chunks of brick fell from the sky. Yelping, Maisie grabbed Cece's arm and tugged her out of the way just in time as a massive piece of cement toppled from the roof above them, landing exactly where Cece had been standing.

"We have to hurry!" Cece panted. "Give me your pom!"

Something flickered in Maisie's eyes, and her mouth curled into a grin. "You're ready. Follow me!"

Maisie led her down the alleyway and around a corner, ducking behind a dumpster, avoiding the bricks and chunks of cement that now littered the alley. The sirens were louder back here, drowning out Cece's ability to think. Still, she held tight to the golden strand and to Maisie's hand. Her limbs shook—not from fatigue or effort, she knew, but from restlessness. Her body needed to move. She needed to . . . to what, exactly? She wasn't sure.

"Maisie!" someone called.

Cece peered through the dust and darkness. Ten sets of eyes gleamed back at her. Ten gold uniforms.

"You made it!" Alex cried, breaking into a grin as Maisie pulled Cece toward them.

"Wh—what?" Cece stammered as the Lions cheerleading squad encircled her, wrapping her in a group hug. There were pats on the back, kisses on the cheek, murmured greetings, all while the sky rained ash over them.

Maisie hushed the squad. She clapped once, her poms swishing against each other, sending sparks flying up. "Team! It's time!"

Flustered, Cece turned to the girl closest to her—Mina. The Lions' most famous and most frequent flyer, the girl Cece had been admiring for weeks. "Time for what?"

Mina winked. "Don't worry, Cece. You passed the test."

"You're flawless in practice," Hazel added.

Greta grinned. "Just trust us."

Cece swallowed thickly, a weak protest coming from her lips before Maisie and Mina and Alex and Greta and the rest of the squad swept her up into their tornado—an actual cheerleader tornado, Cece marveled, watching from inside as Maisie used her pom-poms to twist the squad into a unified, cohesive cone of energy, of power. They circled around and around, their feet lifting off the ground, until—together, as one—they were soaring up into the sky, past the windows, over the roofs.

Finally, Cece was flying.

What can one say about flying, really? It's just like you might imagine. If you're familiar with cheerleading, you already understand the sensations: the wind against your cheeks, the whistle through your teeth, the feeling of a thousand trampolines pushing at your feet. The ground oh so far away.

But it was more than just the act of taking to the sky.

Cece didn't need the single strand of Maisie's pom-pom anymore. Not now, when she was with the rest of the squad. *Her* squad.

Because, it turned out, as Cece would later learn—after the squad had cornered Amnesiac, after Maisie had called out their play of triple back layouts, causing twelve pairs of sneakers to knock the villain's weapons out of his hands—the Lions cheerleading squad was legendary, and not just for their winning streak, their shining trophies, their impeccable stunts and athleticism. No, they were legendary because they were superheroes.

And now, Cece was one of them.

The Pinewood High cheerleading squad had been an elite, top-secret, utterly undetectable part of the Superhero Alliance for as long as anyone could remember. "Since superheroes were invented," Greta stressed. Whoever held those golden, glowing pom-poms held the power: the ability to fight, to soar, to save anyone and anything that needed saving, provided they had a well-coordinated team behind them. The kind of team that knew without looking how everybody else moved, where their strengths and weaknesses lay; the kind of group that could catch people as they fell, that could jump over hurdles in their way.

All the things a cheerleading squad was trained to do well.

That was why it was nearly impossible for girls to make the team, Maisie explained to Cece a few days later.

Still, Cece struggled to understand some parts of the story. "Why Pinewood City? I thought the peace accords—"

Maisie shook her head, cutting her off. They were in the practice gym, collapsed in heaps on the mats, limbs tangled with limbs. The hazy, late afternoon sunlight cut stripes across the walls. "It's irresponsible to operate as though villains care about legislation."

"Villains are everywhere," Greta added. "Even Pinewood City."

Mina glowered. "Especially Pinewood City, these days. That's why we focus so much on team unity. Coordination. Without that, they win."

"So you're such good cheerleaders because . . ." Cece's voice trailed off, questioning.

Maisie's eyes flicked upward. "You saw what Amnesiac did. And he's just *one* villain. Imagine what they could do if they actually worked together?" She exhaled, her eyes round and earnest. "Superheroes learned long ago that we don't stand a chance if we don't work as a team. It's the only way we can win."

"We're in sync because we have to be," Alex pointed out.

"We trust each other," Mina said solemnly.

"So . . . this whole time?" Cece blinked. One by one, her squad nodded.

"And it's our job to stop them." Maisie crossed her arms resolutely.

Cece, thinking, stretched out her legs. They were sore. She'd spent an hour in an ice bath the night before, at Maisie's instruction—"Your first time flying is a real doozy, your muscles need time to adjust"—and now they felt loose, shaky. She glanced back at the team. *Her* team. "Why pom-poms? Why cheerleaders?"

"If it sounds cheesy, that's the point," Alex explained. "No one looks too closely at cheerleaders. We're center stage, but really, we're just the backdrop to the main action."

"People are way too busy looking at the players on the field or on the court," Hazel added.

"We hide in plain sight." Mina shrugged.

"But most of all . . ." Maisie wiggled her eyebrows.

Cece smiled, feeling the weight of the words to come, of the meaning behind it all. She remembered the feeling, the rush, the connection. The unity. The team.

"Most of all . . . we already know how to fly."

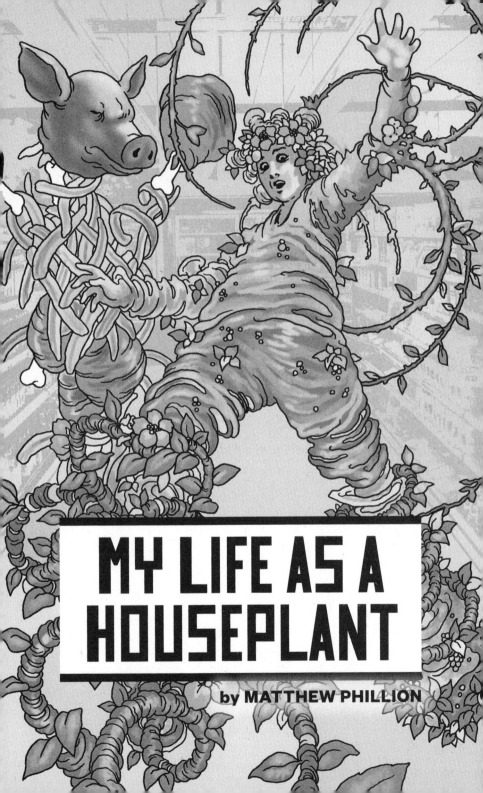

MY LIFE AS A HOUSEPLANT

by MATTHEW PHILLION

JAMIE WAS THERE WHEN THE METEORITE HIT the grocery store, and that wasn't even the weirdest thing that happened to him that day.

The incident offered him a few minutes of fame, during which he was interviewed by a young reporter from the local paper. He told the reporter, a guy named Broadstreet, everything he knew, which was exactly this: a big rock crashed through the ceiling of Trader's Market while he was mopping up the produce aisle, then bounced all the way to the deli. Yes, he told the reporter, he did touch the rock. More accurately, Jamie clarified, the rock touched him, bowling him over like a doll as it careened through leafy greens, smashing jar upon jar of pickled red peppers, and coming to a final, anticlimactic stop at the far end of the store, among the processed ham.

Jamie described the rock (rocklike) and the sound (loud) and what had gone through his head as all of this occurred (this part Jamie lied about, as most of what went through his head were curse words he wasn't shy about saying around his friends but knew better than to say for formal publication).

The reporter thanked him. Jamie punched out—after being chastised by his manager for conducting the interview on the clock—and went home.

He showered, as he not only smelled like the chemicals he'd been mopping with but also a hint of crushed onion—or rather, upscale onion, as a pile of shallots had been among the early victims of the rock. Jamie examined the angry scrapes along his arm, chest, and cheek where the rock had dinged him. He lackadaisically applied some disinfectant to the wounds and went to bed.

He had barely nodded off when a strange sensation awoke him.

The covers were moving.

Jamie leapt from his bed, knocking over his lamp as he flicked on the light, and then tripped, slamming against the floor in a slapstick belly flop. Something had tripped him, he realized, and he started to scream, a high-pitched, embarrassing sort of scream, as he saw what he at first mistook for the coils of a giant snake wrapped around his ankles.

But no, he realized—that wasn't a snake. There were vines enveloping his feet. The vines were also climbing the bed, disappearing under the covers.

He almost began screaming again but choked it back into a weird, uncomfortable gurgle.

"Are you OK in there?" his mother yelled from downstairs.

Jamie pulled on the vines and yelped as something pinched the skin on his chest, right where the scrapes were. He uttered a number of the choice swear words he had not said in front of the reporter. Vines had begun sprouting from his wounds. They curled delicately around his shoulder, thin, bright green loops of vegetation hanging all the way to his feet.

"Jamie?" his mother called again.

"I'm fine! I'm fine! I fell out of bed! I'm OK! Everything's fine!" he said.

Nothing is fine, he thought. *I'm not fine. This is not fine. This is absolutely the opposite of fine.*

He took hold of one of the thin vines and squeezed it, wincing as if expecting to feel the plant's pain. He felt nothing.

He bent the vine and still felt no pain, and then he snapped it, tossing the remnants aside.

"I'm . . . turning into Audrey II," Jamie said.

He clambered to his feet, dragging a fright wig of vines behind him, and tiptoed to his desk. Pulling out a pair of scissors, he began to cut.

By the time he got to Ash's house, Jamie's entire left arm was wrapped in a cocoon of tough, leafy vines.

The entire journey was touch and go, if he was being honest. He got dressed and quietly climbed out his window, something he had not attempted before, despite always wondering if he could. Jamie liked to think he had a rebellious streak, but breaking curfew by jumping out a window had just never come up.

Which was why he was not even remotely surprised when he slipped and plummeted from the second-story window.

This is how I'm going to die, he thought, the earth rushing up toward his face. *Struck by a falling rock in the afternoon, becoming a falling rock in the evening.*

But he never hit the ground. Instead, he felt the wild green vines swathing his side flex and stretch, and his arm jerked involuntarily upward. The next thing he knew, he was swinging, hanging from the large oak in his family's side yard, feet dangling just a few inches from the ground.

"Huh," he said, kicking his feet. The vines, as if reading

his thoughts, released the tree branch and coiled onto his body.

Jamie stole a glance back at his house. No lights on. Nobody had noticed he'd left. He had no idea how he would get back into the house, having only now realized he should have brought a key. But that was a problem for later. His right-now problem was that he seemed to be transforming into a houseplant.

Ash lived a few blocks away, easily navigable in their sleepy suburban town. Once he got there, he saw with relief that Ash's bedroom light was still on. They were probably playing video games. This was possibly the only good thing to happen to Jamie all day.

Ash was his best friend. *That's a lie*, Jamie thought. *Ash is my only friend.* But either way, they were the only person he could think of to help him with this.

He texted Ash and hoped they weren't ignoring their phone in favor of whatever first-person shooter they were playing tonight. *Hey. Big problem. Outside. Halp.*

Jamie waited a moment, watching the ellipsis dance at the bottom of his screen.

Is this because you got hit by a meteorite? Ash texted back.

I think so, Jamie responded.

What, are you developing superpowers? lollollolol

Um . . . yeah.

Instead of responding, Ash opened their window and stuck the whole top half of their body outside.

"Are you serious?" they stage-whispered. "Don't make me lose my media privileges."

Jamie lifted his vine-covered arm and waved. The vines seemed to wave with him.

"Hi," he said.

"I'll be right down," Ash said.

"You're turning into a Christmas cactus," Ash said.

They were sitting on the lawn furniture behind Ash's garage, speaking in hushed tones as Ash cast furtive glances back at their house, waiting for the lights to turn on when their escape was discovered.

"I don't want to be a Christmas cactus," Jamie said. He scratched at the vines engulfing his shoulder, alarmed that they'd begun to crisscross his chest like a bandolier. He felt an itchy sensation crawl across his right arm and looked down to find white flowers with yellow centers poking out of the skin. The skin itself had begun to turn a rather pleasant shade of green.

"Look," he said, holding his forearm out for Ash to examine. "I'm flowering. I don't even know what these are!"

"They're daisies."

"Daisies. I have daisies."

"You're growing daisies," Ash said.

"How do you know they're daisies?"

"How do you *not* know they're daisies?" Ash said. "Everyone knows what a daisy looks like."

"I don't!" Jamie said.

"Just trust me. Did you forget my father is a florist?"

"See? You have an unfair advantage!"

"One does not need a parent who is a florist to identify a daisy, Jamie. There are literary characters named after this flower."

"You're missing the point. The point is that I have daisies growing out of my elbow," Jamie said.

"But you have *superpowered* daisies," Ash said.

Jamie wagged his vine-covered arm in Ash's general direction.

"Stupidest superpower ever," he said.

"You need a superhero name."

"I don't need a superhero name, I need to stop turning into a hedge," Jamie said.

Ash hopped off their lawn chair and started ticking off suggestions on their fingers.

"Captain Planet."

"Already taken."

"The Shambling Mound!"

"Dumbest D&D monster ever?"

"Vegemite!"

"No," Jamie said.

"I mean, in all seriousness, you're so bitter about this—"

"Not funny," Jamie said.

"Poison Oak. You're irritating enough to be Poison Oak," Ash said.

"I just want this to stop," Jamie said, sliding off his chair and waving his arms around dejectedly. The vines were rapidly transforming into a kind of leafy green sweater.

"Have you thought about going to check out the rock that did this?" Ash said.

"What good would that do?"

Ash shrugged. Jamie suddenly realized why his mother hated when he shrugged at her.

"Maybe there are clues about to how to reverse it," Ash offered.

"You want to touch the rock and get superpowers, too, don't you?" Jamie said.

Ash pointed at him and smirked. "We'll be the dynamic duo of botany!"

"No," Jamie said.

"Come on, Treebeard," Ash said. "Let's break into the grocery store."

The Trader's Market was dark when they got there, of course, the employee entrance around back locked. Signs on the front doors expressed regret that the grocery store would be closed the next day for repairs, failing to mention the meteorite that had caused the unexpected closure.

"I don't suppose you have a key," Ash asked.

"They don't even trust me with a key to the bathroom," Jamie said. "You think they gave me a key to the store?"

"I have a key to my dad's shop," Ash said.

"That's because you have proven yourself to be an upstanding member of society," Jamie said. He wagged his left hand, which was now wrapped in bright green vines, at Ash for emphasis. "I, however, am an azalea."

"Do you even know what an azalea looks like?" Ash asked.

"Not a clue," Jamie said. "I just know my mom tried to get them to grow in the backyard and it didn't work."

"Meteorite gives plant powers to a kid who can't tell grass from Astroturf," Ash said. "I guess the cosmos has a sense of humor."

"Anyway, store's closed. Can we go home now?" Jamie was finally beginning to feel the raw edge of exhaustion creeping in. He might be mutating, but he'd also been awake for coming up on twenty-two hours straight, and it was catching up with him.

Ash, however, seemed to be experiencing no such crash.

"Do you think they boarded up the hole in the ceiling?" they asked.

"You'll be surprised to know that the owner did not tell me his plans for closing the hole in the ceiling," Jamie said.

"Well, we should get up there," Ash said. They started walking the perimeter of the building methodically, examining the walls. "No fire escape?"

Jamie shrugged. "I mean, it's a one-story building," he said. "Do one-story buildings usually have fire escapes?"

"I'm the child of a florist, not an architect," Ash said. "Hey, use your vines to get us up there."

"Use my what to get who where?"

"Your vines. Make them shoot up to the roof and pull us up."

"You say that like I have demonstrated any ability to control my powers," Jamie said. He scratched the top of his head with his right, non-vine-covered hand and came away with a small red flower. "What's this?"

"It's a campion."

"A champion?"

"*Campion*. It's pretty."

Resigned, Jamie tucked the flower behind his ear. Then he turned his attention to the roof.

"OK then, here goes," he said. "Use the Force, Jamie . . ."

He stretched out his left hand, aiming for the lip of the roof.

Nothing happened.

"Oh, come on," he said.

"Focus," Ash said.

"I'm tired and turning into a salad," Jamie said.

"Close your eyes and try again," Ash said.

"Fine."

Again, Jamie reached out. This time, he squeezed his eyes closed and turned away, hoping the vines would do their thing if he wasn't watching. He felt the wiry plant matter begin to shuffle and crawl across his skin. He tried very hard to not think about how much it felt like worms against his flesh.

"Nope!" Jamie said. "Nope, can't control it, it's pointless."

"Dude," Ash said, slapping him with the back of their hand.

Jamie opened his eyes. His vines had crept up the side of the building, looping in taut masses around the chimneys.

"Whoa," he said.

And then the vines began to pull.

"There you go!" Ash said, jumping onto Jamie and wrapping their arms around his neck. The vines slowly pulled them up the wall in a deliberate, stealthy manner, though Jamie noticed they seemed to grow faster and more aggressive the closer they got to the roof.

Finally, Jamie and Ash pulled themselves up the last few inches, falling onto the black, weirdly tacky roof of the Trader's Market. Two dominant sounds became immediately apparent: the low, grumpy hum of the air compressors keeping the store cool, and the raspy flutter of a huge sheet of plastic covering the gaping hole in the roof.

"That's not sanitary," Jamie said.

"Probably the best they could do on short notice," Ash said. They crouched down to pull the tarp back and look inside. Jamie frowned as the familiar smell of stale grocery store air hit him in the face.

"Work sweet work," he said.

The interior was dark but not pitch-black. Small emergency lights illuminated the sales floor, where Jamie could make out the shapes of upended cans and bottles, stray vegetables far from their home shelves, a few racks that had been knocked over completely.

"What a mess," Ash said.

"Yup. And guess who gets to clean it all up tomorrow when my shift starts," Jamie said.

"Come on," Ash said. "Lower us down."

Controlling the tendrils was getting easier, Jamie noticed. It only took a few tries to get them to loop around the compressor with enough grip for Ash and him to climb down into the store.

"Hey, I just thought of something," Jamie said as his feet hit the ground. "What if they have security cameras?"

"You work here," Ash said. "Do they have security cameras?"

"I never thought to look before," Jamie said.

"Look, we're already inside," Ash said. "What's the worst that can happen?"

"I get fired?"

"You hate this job anyway," Ash said.

"Fair enough," Jamie said. He pointed down the back aisle of the store. The deli was in the back right corner. It was Jamie's least favorite part of the store on account of a bad experience he'd never recovered from that involved cleaning up some spoiled chicken. "The meteorite bounced that way."

The duo crept with comical care down the back aisle, half expecting a security guard to jump out at them. It rapidly became clear, though, that they were utterly alone here.

"Nobody home," Ash said. Then, abruptly, they disappeared down the baking supplies aisle.

"Where are you going?" Jamie said.

"The international foods section is over here," Ash said in a whisper so loud it was nearly a shout.

"That doesn't answer my question," Jamie said, too softly for his friend to hear.

A few seconds later, Ash returned with a Flake bar.

"Are you stealing candy?"

"My aunt brought these home for us from London," Ash said. "I love them."

"You're going to steal candy from my place of employment?" Jamie said, his voice cracking just a little at the end.

"I'll leave cash," Ash said. "I need a sugar rush. I'm tired."

Jamie waved his hand in the universal gesture for *well, go ahead, then.* The motion took on a ludicrous quality as the vines flopped around for emphasis. Ash ripped open the candy bar and took an oversize bite.

"That Flake bar didn't travel across the Atlantic for you to eat it in three bites," Jamie said.

Ash finished it off in two enormous chomps, then opened their mouth to show Jamie the lumpy mess of melted chocolate there.

"Nice. That's great, Ash."

"You dragged me on this excursion," Ash said, their voice weirdly deep due to the unnatural amount of candy in their mouth. "I was happy at home playing video games till you showed up looking like a weeping willow."

"It was your idea to come to the store," Jamie said. "I was just looking for advice on what to do with my—"

Ash had stopped chewing and was staring, slack-jawed, at Jamie's face.

"What?" Jamie asked.

Ash reached out and poked his cheek with their index finger.

"Why are you poking me?"

"Does that feel weird?" Ash asked.

"You just poked me in the face."

"But how did it feel?"

"Like you poked me in the face. Why do you ask?"

"It's nothing," Ash said.

"It's clearly not nothing," Jamie said.

"You're just looking a little bark-y," Ash said.

Jamie narrowed his eyes at Ash.

"Define *bark-y*," he said.

"You are taking on a barklike texture," Ash said. "Though if I'm being fair, it's not really a downgrade."

"Can we just find the rock and go home?" Jamie said. The idea of his skin turning into tree bark cranked his anxiety to eleven. "I want to go home."

"So that you can . . . put down roots?" Ash said. They elbowed Jamie in the ribs playfully. Jamie was not amused.

"I'm an overgrown bag of arugula, and you're spitting dad jokes," Jamie said.

"Is there ever a bad time for dad jokes?" Ash said. "Hey, there's your rock."

And there, in fact, the rock was.

Jamie hadn't really gotten a good look at it earlier. At the time, the rock had been a large, jagged shape that had knocked him off his feet and then kept bouncing, and he wasn't, in his opinion, paid enough to care much about the rest of the damage it did after knocking him silly. But now that it was in front of him on a pile of processed cheese, he wished he had taken a moment to examine it sooner.

It had a rocklike structure for sure, but it was unlike any rock Jamie had ever seen. Its surface was almost reflective, so smooth in places that it had a glasslike quality, but rather than a normal reflection, Jamie thought he saw stars gleaming in the stone. In the places where it had been chipped or broken, the stone was deep black, so intense it seemed to absorb light rather than reflect it. It had a smell, too—a burnt metallic tang that stuck to Jamie's tongue. Overall, the meteorite was five or six feet long and about half that in width and depth, a giant outer space bullet of alien stone.

"It's kind of pretty, isn't it?" he said.

"Kind of pretty, but definitely weird," Ash said. They reached out to touch the meteorite, but Jamie grabbed their hand. He noticed that tiny yellow flowers had begun to sprout from the back of his forearm like a gauntlet. He sighed and wondered if he'd need to give up his bedroom and move into a greenhouse.

"What?" Ash asked, irritably pulling their hand free.

"It turned me into this," Jamie said. "You really want to turn into a walking container garden?"

"Beats living an ordinary life, right?"

"That is, at this point, somewhat up for debate," Jamie said. "I'm pretty sure my feet are turning into potatoes."

"Look, worst-case scenario, I can help the family business," Ash said.

"How do you know you'll get plant powers? I was in the produce section when this happened, remember."

"What are my other options?" Ash asked.

They both looked at their feet, currently surrounded by vacuum-sealed blocks of cheese.

"I don't want cheese powers!" Ash said.

"Nobody wants cheese powers!" Jamie said.

And then something groaned farther in the store, closer

to the deli counter. Not a human groan, either—more like weight shifting on a loose floorboard.

"Did you hear that?" Jamie asked.

"I heard something," Ash said. "Not sure what it was."

"Stay here," Jamie said. "I'll go check it out."

"I beg your pardon?" Ash said.

"I have superpowers!" Jamie said. "I think this is my job now."

Jamie promptly tripped over a coil of his own vines and landed face-first in a pile of cheese. A container of feta in water tumbled from a precarious perch and split open on the tile floor.

"Good job, Swamp Thing," Ash said. "You . . . oh."

"Oh?" Jamie said, struggling to get to his feet. He followed Ash's gaze toward the deli counter.

"Oh," Jamie concurred.

Rising from behind the counter was, without a doubt, the worst thing Jamie had ever seen. Its torso was made of uncooked pork, held aloft on limbs of bacon that had been crisscrossed like latticework made of stripes of grease and fat. At the end of each bacon-crafted arm, a hefty pink ham hung like a clenched fist.

But worst of all was what sat on the creature's tenderloin shoulders. A whole pig's head, eyes blank, mouth a rictus of rage, let loose a strangled, guttural oink, and Jamie found himself simultaneously wanting to laugh and cry.

"I think I just became a vegetarian," Jamie said.

"I want to make a cannibalism joke, but I'm too busy trying

not to lose bladder control," Ash said. "That's real, right? This is real? I'm not having some energy drink–fueled nightmare right now?"

Jamie felt a swell of adrenaline, his heart beating faster. His limbs felt loose and strong. He nodded to himself and clenched his fists, looking up at the bacon monster, which now stood so tall its porcine head scraped the ceiling.

"I think I was made for this moment," Jamie said. "Stay back. I got this."

And then a slab of ham punched him in the face so hard he flew back fifteen feet, destroying a hummus display.

The lights of the display sputtered as he scrambled to his feet, spreading smears of chickpea paste everywhere. He almost fell again as he planted his foot right on a container of grape leaves, but he held his ground.

Then Ash ran past him, holding a fire extinguisher like a battering ram.

"Back off, bacon bits!" Ash yelled, slamming the fire extinguisher into the meat monster's slippery left leg. The canister careened off, denting but not truly damaging the woven strips of breakfast food making up the creature's quad. The monster, in response, slammed its fist down sloppily, narrowly missing Ash's head. Ash laughed and reared back to strike again with the extinguisher, but the monster's other honeyed ham fist caught Ash dead center in the chest, sending them sprawling back. Jamie watched in horror as Ash bounced off the meteorite, then flipped into a display of stacked twelve-packs of seltzer, disappearing in a spray of soda water.

"Ash!" Jamie yelled, then turned his full attention on the bacon beast. "That's it, piglet. I'm not playing around anymore."

The creature answered him with a haymaker. Jamie braced for impact, but as he did, his forearm exploded with plant life, a massive sunflower appearing like a shield. The ham crashed into the flower, driving Jamie to one knee, but somehow, the yellow petals held against the attack. Growling with effort, Jamie pushed himself back to his feet and stared down the meat monster defiantly.

"Back off!" he said, and as if on command, the sunflower burst, sending seeds at the creature like shrapnel, driving it back a few steps. Jamie dropped his sunflower shield and swung his vine-encrusted hand, which tightened and twisted into a whip of thorns. He lashed out, the sharp points digging into the bacon beast's arm. The creature yanked that arm back, dragging Jamie with it, but he pulled in the other direction and immediately saw the latticework of the bacon biceps start to unravel.

"Ha! I got you, you overgrown BLT!" Jamie yelled.

The meat monster, unable to pull away from Jamie's thorny vine, changed up its tactics and charged at him. Without thinking, Jamie clamped his eyes shut, then heard jars crashing to the floor and shattering. When he opened his eyes, he found that more spiky vines had erupted from the ground in front of him, tangling the creature's feet and slowing its charge.

"I think I like being a houseplant," Jamie said, right before he took a staggeringly hard punch to the head from the creature's free arm. Alarmingly, he had to admit that the ham residue that smeared on his face wasn't that bad, all things considered, though his vision went blurry and his ears rang a bit. He felt his stomach begin to churn.

"Jamie, duck!" he heard Ash yell from behind him. Automatically, he dropped to the floor, belly flopping onto a plastic carton of black bean salad. He slid into some of his own spiked vines and was alarmed by the wooden scraping sound the tiny hooks made against his face.

Jamie looked up in time to see a burst of water strike the bacon beast full in the face, a fire hose of pressure that knocked the monster back, forcing it to shred itself on Jamie's improvised briar patch. He twisted around to look at the source and saw Ash, not holding a fire hose, but rather standing on top of the frozen fish display, arm outstretched as if casting a spell, sending a torrent of water forward.

Struggling to his feet, Jamie couldn't take his eyes off Ash, noticing that his best friend didn't seem fully there—they'd taken on an almost translucent quality, not completely see-through, but ghostly, almost blurry.

The meat monster roared again. Jamie turned his attention back to the attacker, who raised one ham fist high, ready to strike. This time, Jamie was ready. Instead of trying to stop the punch, he whipped his thorny vines upward, around the disembodied head. Even from here, he could tell it wasn't a thinking creature—there was an empty, mindless rage in its alien roar.

The vines wrapped tight. The fist hit Jamie full in the chest. He went soaring across the market, his vine weapon still twisted tightly around his hand. And, with a sickening pop, the monster's head detached from the Frankenstein's monster body, careening in Jamie's direction with horrific speed.

As Jamie smashed into a cardboard display of barbecue sauce, he saw the bacon strips unraveling, the hams falling, and heard the unpleasant sound of cutlets and tenderloins splattered on the floor.

And then he hit his head on a cooler, and the room went dark.

"Jamie," Ash said, their hands on his shoulders, shaking him. "We gotta get out of here. C'mon."

"Why does everything smell like a cookout?" Jamie said, sitting up slowly. The first thing he noticed was that Ash was soaked through, hair plastered to their face. They were surrounded by flowers and other plant matter, but, Jamie noted with some relief, most of the vines had fallen from his body and lay on the floor, inert.

The pile of previously aggressive processed meat lay nearby, heaps of uncooked bacon slowly turning to shiny grease. He winced at the sight and tried to get to his feet.

Then he saw the faint flicker of blue and red lights coming from the front of the store.

"Oh no," Jamie said.

"Is it breaking and entering if you work here?" Ash asked.

Jamie scanned the back of the store: the broken jars, the

smashed hummus containers, the pooling soda water. The hog head sat comically on top of the premade hot dog section, tilted sideways, looking almost as if it were sleeping.

"We are definitely guilty of breaking," Jamie said.

"How about the back door?" Ash asked.

Jamie nodded and led them into the stockroom, then toward the staff entrance out back, near where the trucks unloaded. He pushed the door open. And then the alarm went off.

"Did you not know there was an alarm?" Ash said.

Jamie shrugged.

"How did you not know there was an alarm?"

"Does it matter now?" Jamie said. "I think we have to run."

Together, Jamie and Ash ran exactly three steps before a dark car pulled into the lot in front of them. It turned around slowly and stopped to block their exit. The passenger door opened, and a whip-thin old man stepped out, immediately covering his bald head with a fedora.

"Great," Jamie said.

Ash put their hands up. Jamie did not.

"What are you doing?"

"Preparing to be arrested for breaking and entering," Ash said.

"Put your damn hands down, kid," the old man said. He walked over to them, calm and slow, hands in his pockets. "I'm not here to take you in."

"You're not?" Jamie said.

"Nope," the old man said, popping a white square of gum into his mouth. His face looked comically animated as his silvery mustache twisted while he chewed. "I was sent to investigate an object of cosmic origin that crashed into that there Trader's Market."

"We know nothing about that," Jamie said.

"I suspect you know nothing *factual* about it," the old man said. "Though from the look of you, and from the surveillance footage I just watched, I reckon you know a little something, at least."

Jamie and Ash shared a silent glance. Ash's hair was still dripping wet.

"Well?" Ash said.

Jamie turned back to the old man.

"The bacon monster was already here when we showed up," Jamie said. "I swear."

The old man sighed, looked up at the night sky, and shook his head.

"Of all the careers I could have had, I chose the one with bacon monsters," he said, mostly to himself. "Look, as far as I'm concerned, the rock, which has a strange effect on organic material, both living and . . . not, has been contained, and I never saw either of you. Go home. Live your lives."

"My life as a houseplant," Jamie said.

"Who knows, kid," the old man said. "You might get used to it."

"I hate everything about this," Jamie said.

The old man squinted at him.

"You've got a little something . . . growing on your . . ." He pointed at Jamie's head. Jamie reached up and found a large white puff of a flower blooming in his hair.

"Ash? Help?"

"Oh, it's a peony! I love these," Ash said.

"Can you make this go away?" Jamie asked the old man.

"Nope," the old man said. "But trust me. Most folks in my line of work, they don't regret the things they can do. Most of 'em, anyway."

"And what line of work is that?" Ash asked.

"I keep an eye on folks like you to make sure you get into the right kind of trouble," the old man said. "Power, responsibility . . . y'know, that old chestnut."

"So you're like a hall monitor for superpowers."

The old man shrugged and tilted his hat slightly to make it just a little jauntier.

"That makes my job sound about as mundane as it feels sometimes," the old man said. "I'll have my eye on both of you. Don't make me regret letting you walk away."

The mystery man waved his hand in a vaguely dismissive gesture.

"Go, do good things with your lives. Stay out of trouble. Don't get yourselves killed."

"Sure. I . . . thanks, I guess," Jamie said.

The man tipped his hat and turned to leave. "Best be getting home. It's nearly dawn," he said. "I hear houseplants need their beauty sleep."

The mysterious man climbed into the car. Jamie and Ash watched as it drove away.

"I think we're superheroes," Ash said as they began their slow walk home.

"No, we're not," Jamie said. "I'm a shrub, and you're a puddle."

"We need superhero names."

"No."

"We could be . . . Hydroponic! I'm Hydro. You're Ponic."

"I have negative feelings toward everything about this," Jamie said.

"Water Wonder and Plant Boy!"

"No."

"Come on, it'll be fun," Ash said.

The duo meandered home, unbothered by the hour, the horror of the night fading from their memory. But behind them, a new threat, cold of heart and icy of eye, began to stir. It clawed its way from the freezer aisle, leaving puddled footprints of chocolate chip cookie dough and vanilla bean.

The dairy dragon took flight into the night sky, unnoticed. But that, true believers, is a feast for another day.

AUBREY VS. THE NINTH CIRCLE OF HELL (AKA PROM)

by **ELIZABETH EULBERG**

IT'S EASY TO BE LABELED A FREAK IN HIGH SCHOOL.

Especially at Belmont Academy. Before you even open your mouth, you're judged on your attempt to make the uninspiring gray-and-red school uniform cool while still staying within the school's strict guidelines. Heaven forbid a female kneecap is exposed.

But you can't appear to be trying too hard, either.

It's the same with class. You're expected to be smart, but you can't be too eager to answer questions.

You can't be too anything, except too rich. That's not a problem, since wealth practically oozes from the gray stone building on the city's Upper West Side.

Then there are the vacations. Who traveled where. Who has the most likes on their carefully curated online profiles. If your photo didn't get at least a thousand likes, were you really on a yacht off the coast of Ibiza? Unless you're fine with being pretentious for the sake of it, which is the case for the majority of my classmates.

And don't even think of bringing coffee from a chain into school. The security guards will lock the doors if you approach with one of those white-and-green cups. No, only the most precious artisanal coffee from beans massaged by monks in the Costa Rica rainforest is allowed in these hallowed halls.

You're one slip—or sip—away from becoming the next mocking meme.

It's a fine line that I was able to delicately walk.

Until prom.

I can only imagine the damage that's been done. It's not like I wore a dress off the rack—the horror! Yet somehow, I think hovering above the entire student body after shooting actual flames from my hands and rays from my eyes did not, perhaps, go unnoticed.

Just an observation.

ONE DAY AGO

"You better not screw this up, Aubrey."

"Excuse me? You must have me confused with someone who isn't beating you in class," I fire back at Hamilton Diaz.

"Oh, are *you* the one?" He cocks an eyebrow at me. Dr. O'Malley decided to torture Hamilton and me by making us lab partners in chemistry today. "I wouldn't know from all the gloating—"

"I don't gloat." I simply state facts when anybody insults my intelligence. I might've gotten into this school because of my father's obscene wealth, but I've earned my grades and standing, thank you very much.

I've also worked on elements Hamilton—not to mention the global scientific community—doesn't even know about. I started experimenting with exousium at age ten. Never heard of it? That's because no one has. It's a compound with unlimited energy. One particle could power an entire city for a week, but my father has to keep that to himself. Just one of his many, *many* secrets.

Therefore, I think I can more than handle a simple high school chemistry experiment.

"Oh, no, *no*, you and your little group of friends are the epitome of restraint." Hamilton gestures over to the corner of the chemistry lab, where Thad Harrington the Third is dancing with two glass vials, holding them up in the air as if he's at a rave. "Is he going to break out those sweet moves at prom tomorrow night?"

I reply by connecting the Bunsen burner to the gas line.

You know that old adage that you can't pick your family, but you can choose your friends? Well, I didn't get a choice about either. I grew up alongside Thad and the other people who are labeled as my friends. Our parents have forced us together since we were in grade school. In the little free time I had as a kid—between studying, training, being trotted around to events, and my father's unconventional ways of family bonding—I didn't really have time to find my own friends.

I've always been expected to do what I've been told.

"Can we just get this over with?" I point down at our lab assignment.

"That's the spirit!" Hamilton says as he pats my back.

I look over at Bianca, who is probably my best friend, since we grew up on the same stretch of Park Avenue. She gives me one of her signature eye rolls, the kind that's made more than one maid and barista burst into tears. But this one is aimed at my partner. *Sorry*, she mouths to me.

While Hamilton can rub me the wrong way with his constant teasing and almost, *almost* beating my GPA, I have a begrudging respect for him. Not like I'd ever admit it. But unlike the majority of my classmates, Hamilton wasn't born with a platinum spoon in his mouth. I know he has to work for everything he has.

"Are you excited?" Hamilton asks as he puts on his safety goggles, the elastic strap fighting to hold down his dark curly hair.

"For what? To see the reaction of sodium chloride on—"

"Prom," he finishes.

I shrug. I'm going because it's expected of me. I know I'm supposed to be like Bianca and swoon and think it's going to be some magical, life-changing night, but it's only another obligation where we'll spend all evening hoping we don't do anything that will reflect poorly on our parents—or worse, go viral.

"Your enthusiasm today is overwhelming," Hamilton replies with a crooked smile. "But then again, given your prom date . . ."

Father decided that I'd be going with Thad, he of the basic spoiled-and-entitled-rich-white-boy variety with his perfectly coifed blond hair and blue eyes. Fortunately, Thad is pretty harmless and doesn't require much in terms of brain cells in order to have a conversation. He was deemed an acceptable date, as our pictures will no doubt end up in the tabloids and online: the son of a Wall Street tycoon and the daughter of a tech billionaire.

Some people would think this is the start of a fairy tale. I, however, consider prom to be the ninth circle of hell.

A phone pings from across the classroom.

Dr. O'Malley's head snaps up. "OK, we all know the rules, class. Phones turned off and put away, or I'm going—"

"Oh my god," Troy Lin exclaims as he stands up. "A plane nearly crashed into Brooklyn."

Dr. O'Malley opens his desk drawer to grab his phone, and everybody takes this as permission to do the same. My phone is in my locker, as I don't have the same compulsion to be attached to a piece of technology all day.

"Yeah," Troy continues as he scans his screen. "A 787 had engine failure and was attempting to make an emergency landing at LaGuardia, but it wasn't going to make it, and then . . ." He glowers.

"And then?" Trisha Callahan asks, her voice hysterical. "What happened?"

"Ah, yeah." Troy clears his throat. "It received some help."

"It received *help*?" Bianca cries out. "How could it—*oh*."

There's silence in the classroom as everybody fills in the blanks.

"It was Kastor!" Hamilton exclaims in the quiet. There's a delighted smile on his face as he scrolls through his phone. "He swooped in and flew the plane to safety just in time. And before anybody starts spouting conspiracy theories, there's footage of him, so nobody can deny his involvement." Hamilton turns his screen toward us, and we see a smoking plane with a small figure holding up the underbelly.

It's true that there's only one person who can do that.

"Oh, please. He was probably the one who caused the plane to nearly crash," Thad states in his usual bored tone. "And then, oh, look, he just happened to be nearby, how convenient. Sorry, it doesn't matter what he does. I'm never going to buy the whole superhero story."

"Yeah, I thought he was hiding out in the mountains of Utah or something," Troy replies. "What a complete coincidence he just happened to pop up right in the nick of time."

"He just saved hundreds, possibly thousands of lives, and you want to—" Hamilton begins.

"Settle down," Dr. O'Malley says as he pounds his fist on his desk. "I won't have this class disrupted by—"

But it's too late. My classmates erupt into the familiar debate. The battle lines were drawn years ago. There are some who believe those with extraordinary powers are here to help, and others—the majority—who think they're the dangerous ones, the ones who cause destruction. Kastor and those like him have gone from being called superheroes to being referred to simply as *them* in hushed tones.

"How many lives have they saved at this point?" Hamilton yells, his light brown cheeks becoming increasingly flushed.

"And how many more are *dead* because of him?" Troy shouts back.

"Guys! Guys! *Guys!*" Bianca stands on top of her stool, her loud voice cutting through the noise. "Come on. Can you all just shut up for a moment and think about what this means for Aubrey? Aubs, are you OK?"

All eyes settle on me, and I feel a pounding in my head.

I simply nod, even though I haven't felt "OK" in years.

Hamilton cringes. "Sorry, I forgot . . ."

"*They* killed her parents," Troy fills in for him.

Yes, they did.

People weren't always divided like this. Two decades ago,

Kastor and his team were celebrated. There were constant parades for them. The world owed them time and time again for coming to the rescue. Then the group started to fracture. Dr. Drevis severed ties with Kastor and his team to start his own aptly named Catastrophe Crew, because if you're gunning for world domination, might as well be alliterative.

Sixteen years ago, there was a major showdown between the two groups that destroyed an entire block in downtown Los Angeles.

More than a thousand lives were lost that day, both extraordinary and ordinary.

From the rubble that remained, a baby was recovered. She became the poster child for resilience and hope. One of the wealthiest and most powerful men on earth decided to adopt her and give her a name that means "power."

The world knows him as Richard Constantine.

But I call him dear old Dad.

After the Los Angeles attack, leaders from around the world called for the surviving superheroes—Kastor, Ajax, and Philomela—to be exiled. But occasionally, they come out of hiding to save us. Like last year, when a dictator got his hands on nuclear weapons. Most news sources claimed that "diplomatic diplomacy" stopped him, but there were other underground sites that published footage of a nuclear bomb being swept up into the sky. The explosion up above was explained as a faulty satellite.

Sometimes I don't know what to believe.

"Listen up!" Dr. O'Malley claps his hands. "If you don't

want a zero on this assignment, I suggest you all get to work now. Phones away. Yelling is over. Get to it—you only have thirty minutes left in class."

The room falls silent as everybody turns back to their assignment, but there's an unsettled charge in the room and a nervous energy in my belly that happens whenever anybody talks about *them*.

"Are you all right?" Hamilton asks, and he looks generally concerned for my well-being. It's a nice gesture and all, but I have to concentrate. I can't be distracted. For me, distractions can get messy.

"Of course," I reply coolly, even though I feel the buzzing in my body intensifying. It's something that has become harder and harder to contain. The last thing I need is to cause a scene in class. While being lauded for being a top student is fine, there are other kinds of attention I don't want. Those that will single me out. Label me as different. Make people see me as a freak.

"OK, good." Hamilton pauses. "Because I can't really afford a zero with my scholarship."

I nod. I want nothing more than to return to something I have control over, like a simple chemistry experiment.

Hamilton cautiously glances at me. "Do you really hate them?"

I don't reply. Instead I weigh out the sodium chloride.

I *should* hate them for making me an orphan, but I don't remember my parents. I don't know if I even had siblings. I know nothing about where I came from. It's hard to mourn people I never knew. My father, on the other hand, is the most anti-*them* person on the planet. He holds rallies calling on the government to banish Kastor and his ilk "back to where they came from." He uses any excuse to blast them in the media.

Father doesn't like anybody to have more power than him. While he's a billionaire and owns the world's leading tech and aerospace company, his influence remains that of the monetary variety.

My heart speeds up, and I take a few deep breathes to calm myself down.

"Let's just get this started," I finally say, but there's a waver in my voice.

Hamilton raises his eyebrow at me. "Are you nervous?"

"Please, this is easy." I tie my long wavy red hair up and put my goggles on while Hamilton turns on the gas.

It is true that this experiment is easy. It's everything else in my life that's a little complicated.

"You can do the honors," Hamilton says as he passes me the flint.

I reach out my hand when a loud *whoosh* sounds comes from the gas line. A large red flame bursts from the burner. Hamilton and I scream out in surprise as the fire nearly reaches the ceiling. Hamilton ducks under the table while I pull my hand into me. It burns like nothing I've ever felt.

How could I be so incredibly careless?

"Are you OK?" Hamilton shuts off the gas, and the flame dies out. "I didn't ignite the flint. There shouldn't have been a flame. How did— Are you burned?"

The entire class comes rushing over. Dr. O'Malley makes his way through the crowd. "What's going on? Is everybody all right?"

Hamilton shakes his head. "I was passing her the flint. It wasn't lit, but it started—"

"You OK, *hot stuff*?" Thad says with a snicker, not remotely concerned about the small explosion in the middle of class. "Dude, I told you I have the *hottest* date."

"Dude." Troy gives Thad a high five. "Nice."

Ladies and gentlemen, my eloquent friends.

"Shut up, Thad," Bianca says as she smacks him on the arm. "She could really be hurt, and right before prom!"

"Seriously?" Hamilton replies. "That's your concern right now? *Prom*?"

"Everybody be quiet," Dr. O'Malley calls out, his patience already worn threadbare. "Aubrey, let me see your hand. And someone get the nurse. Now!"

"It's fine," I assure him. "I'm fine." I keep my hand close to me, as I don't want people to see it.

Dr. O'Malley gently takes it. "Just let me . . ." he says as I slowly open my fist.

There are gasps and confused whispers.

"I don't understand," Hamilton says. "Her hand was *in* the flame."

I finally open my eyes to see the stunned reaction of my classmates.

There is not a single mark on my pale white hand.

"All right, all right, everybody calm down. Go back to your seats." Dr. O'Malley literally shoos away my gaping classmates.

Hamilton furrows his brows. "I saw your hand. It was *in* the flames."

"No, it wasn't," I lie.

"But you were—"

"Just drop it," I snap at him.

Hamilton studies me, which makes my heart race even quicker. It's like he's putting together a puzzle in his mind. Then a small smile spreads across his face. "You're always full of surprises, aren't you?"

He has no idea.

I clear my throat. "Listen, we need to get back to work if you don't want a zero."

We turn our attention back to Dr. O'Malley, who is droning on about focusing on our grades and the importance of following safety protocols. I block out his voice and Hamilton's questioning look as my mind wanders back to when I was eight. My father took me for a drive in the country. I was excited, because I was under the naive impression that I was about to get some of the quality father-daughter time I so desperately craved.

Instead, he took me to a remote forest, where we met a man dressed all in black with a hood covering his face. They proceeded to lock me in the car, flip it over, then set it on fire.

And then my father and the mystery man watched it burn with me trapped inside.

I screamed and screamed for them to let me out.

"You can do it, Aubrey! Just concentrate!" Father yelled at me.

Do *what*? What did he expect me to do?

With every second that passed, Father became angrier and angrier, while I thought he was going to stand there and watch me die.

After what seemed like an eternity, they finally extinguished the fire and got me out.

As for my father, I'll never forget what he said to me as I lay shaking on the grass.

"How disappointing you've turned out to be."

Like I said, my father has weird ideas about family bonding.

When I arrive home after school, I'm immediately greeted by Father's head of security, Mr. Hughes. He briskly guides me inside by my elbow. "It's best for you to stay upstairs for the remainder of the day," he commands in his deep voice. "Your father is extremely agitated over today's events."

Kastor saved thousands of lives, but Father has to make everything about him.

"And he is to not be disturbed under any circumstances."

As if I need to be reminded of that.

When I was little, my father was involved in every aspect of my life. He pored over my grades, got me the best tutors to focus my studies on science and math. I had a trainer who took me on runs and taught me self-defense and, at ten years old, how to use a sword. Parenting at its finest. Father received daily written reports about my progress, but no matter how many tests I aced or records I broke, it was never enough.

I was never enough.

However, on each anniversary of the Los Angeles attack, he paraded me around to the world. I attended memorials. One year, I spoke at the United Nations, a speech I wasn't allowed to write. I've always been a walking reminder not only of how "incredibly generous" Richard Constantine was to adopt a lonely orphan but of all the lives lost that day and, more importantly, who was to blame.

But here's a secret I've never been able to admit to anybody: I've always admired Kastor, Ajax, and Philomela. Their powers. Their ability to fly. They way they're special, more than enough.

I drop my book bag off in my room, change my clothes, and head to the gym down the hall.

Once my father deemed my training "a waste," he stopped bringing in self-defense experts and coaches, but I kept running and lifting weights. I've always had this pent-up energy that needed release.

But it's also something else. There are times when I feel like the energy inside me is getting out of my control. If I don't rein it in, I have no idea what could happen. I was distracted for just a moment today and nearly burned down my chemistry class. I have to do everything I can to be safe, to try to control whatever it is inside me that's desperately trying to get out. I can never make a mistake like that again.

Hamilton started asking questions. What if others begin as well? What if it gets back to my father?

With each hit of the punching bag, I let my frustrations out.

The pressure I face to fit in, to not arouse suspicion.

A surge I've never experienced runs through my body as I make contact with the bag. It splits in two, sand pouring out onto the padded floor.

I know that's not normal. *I'm* not normal.

I pick up a one hundred–pound barbell like it's nothing.

Sometimes I like to give myself tests, not that I understand what any of this means. It's not like I can google "how do you know if you have superpowers?" The FBI would definitely be knocking at the door if my father didn't get to me first.

I bring the barbell down over my raised knee, and it snaps in two like a twig.

I look in the mirror on the wall. I study my face, searching for answers, wishing there were someone I could talk to. But I can't trust anybody with this. It's too dangerous. In a way, *I'm* too dangerous.

My fist balls up in frustration. As I narrow my eyes at my reflection, the mirror shatters into a thousand tiny pieces.

Startled and unsettled, I hide in my bedroom. This feeling, this sense I've felt scratching at the edges of my muscles, has never been this powerful. It's like I can no longer control whatever this is.

Whatever *I* am.

―――――――――――――――――――――――――

Most girls at Belmont Academy dream about prom from the moment they get accepted.

If it isn't already painfully obvious, I am not most girls.

Instead, I remain numb all day as I sit in a salon, being primped and prodded with so many different torture devices: curling iron, fake eyelashes, and so much friggin' hair spray. I nod along as Bianca goes on and on about tonight. She's already envisioning a crown on her head.

All the while, I do my best to ignore the screaming questions that are looping through my head. I know it's best to bury them all deep down. At least for tonight.

An hour after returning home, there's a knock on my bedroom door, and Thomas, the head butler, pokes his head inside. "Miss Aubrey, the limo is waiting for you downstairs. And you look absolutely beautiful."

"Thanks." I force myself to smile as I look down at my floor-length blush-colored gown, personally designed by Vera Wang—my father might not care about *me*, but appearances are another matter altogether. I adjust the spaghetti straps and make sure there are no obvious lines from my biker shorts. Last year, a senior twirled around the dance floor and exposed her nether regions, which instantly went viral. All I need to do to get through this evening is smile and let everything wash over me.

As I walk down the spiral staircase of the six-story town house, I pause on the second floor, where Father's study is. There's a part of me that still craves his approval, that wants him not to regret taking me in all those years ago. Wouldn't he want to see his daughter before she goes off to prom? Though it's not as if we've ever had a normal or even functional relationship.

I hear voices as I approach his office.

"I don't care what you think; Kastor must be stopped." Father's voice rises. "We must finally purge their kind."

"It's preposterous that the mayor was considering giving Kastor a commendation for yesterday's grotesque display," a female voice says. "But I know you'll come up with a genius plan, sir."

"I don't think I need to remind you that not all of Constantine's plans are genius," a male voice replies. It's low and gravelly, slightly familiar. A memory is scratching at the surface of my brain. "Your little experiment failed. She should've been special. She was supposed to help us be rid of them long ago. Instead, we're forced to deal with these incompetent so-called leaders voted into office by people too stupid to know what's good for them."

The buzzing in my body starts intensifying as I try to work out who they're talking about. What experiment?

"And now you're stuck with an orphan."

It's like I've been hit with a ton of bricks. My hands instantly get hot, and I try to calm myself down.

They can't be talking about me.

An experiment? Maybe the exposure I had to exousium as a kid is the reason I'm now having these physical reactions I struggle to control?

"She should be powerful considering where we found her," Father responds. "Who her parents are. But she's weak and useless."

I steady myself against the wall. He's known who my parents were all this time? I was told they found me in rubble alone and had no idea who I belonged to. I've begged for DNA tests—something, *anything* to help me know more about where I come from—but he has always denied me.

"She may not be entirely useless," the gravelly voice replies. "We need to study her. Experiment. Open her up. Maybe there's a clue in her organs or body tissue that could answer some questions. Find a vulnerability we can expose. She shares their DNA, so there must be some kind of strain we can create to make them weak, just like her."

I am *not* weak.

My head starts pulsing as I try to understand what they're saying.

"She's not one of us; she's one of *them*."

I don't want to believe what they're saying, but there's a pounding in my chest that knows it's true.

It doesn't matter how careful I tried to be. The truth was going to come out eventually.

I take the compact out of my purse and angle the mirror to see who that voice belongs to. He's a tall, thin, older white man who looks slightly familiar. "She's useless."

My hand flies to my mouth to stifle a scream. I know that voice.

It's the man who was with my father in the forest. The one who watched me almost burn.

"She's not even human," he continues.

"She's not even *American*," the woman replies.

"Same thing." The guy lets out a cruel laugh.

"You can't possibly ask Mr. Constantine to give up his daughter."

"She was an experiment," Father replies tersely.

I can barely stand. I want to erase everything I'm feeling and all the thoughts swirling in my head.

That's all I've ever been to my father: an experiment. But what did he think he could mold me into? A supervillain? Someone to do his bidding? Destroy his enemies?

How could I mean so little to him?

"So . . . ?" the cruel man says.

I can almost hear the glee in Father's voice. "Have at her."

Before I even realize it, I'm racing downstairs and jumping into the limo.

"Whoa," Thad says. "Someone's excited for prom."

"Let's go."

Oddly enough, prom might be the safest place for me. The grand ballroom is flanked by security guards, protecting not only the young Manhattan elite but the millions of dollars worth of jewels that drip from our wrists and necks.

The next few hours will also give me time to figure out what to do and where to go. I can never go back to the place I called home. Who knows what will be waiting for me if I return. But most importantly, I need to figure out who I can trust.

There's also a part of me that wants to enjoy what could be my last night as a normal teenage girl. Or my last night alive.

"This is so rad," Thad says, his breath reeking of alcohol.

"I'm going to get water," I call out over the sound of the thumping bass.

I maneuver between my classmates, who are dancing like they don't have a care in the world, because most of them don't. After grabbing a bottle of artisanal water (because of course), I lean back against the wall, trying to figure out my options, which are pretty limited. I take a few breaths to steady my hands; they've been shaking since I left the penthouse.

Hamilton approaches me in a poorly fitting tux paired with beat-up Converse, which somehow suits him. "You look stunning."

"What's the punch line?"

He puts his hand over his heart as if he's been wounded. That's when I notice the tiny silver pendent on his jacket with the letter *H*.

It's what supporters of *them* wear. Though after his arguments in class yesterday, it was pretty clear which side he's on.

"Traitor!" someone shouts.

"You're disgusting," a girl practically spits at him.

"Ah, I'm going to miss our classmates so much," Hamilton says with a shake of his head. "The warmth. The wholly original and witty repartee."

A lump forms in my throat. "Why do you support them so openly?"

Hamilton raises his eyebrows. "Let me see. I'm often told to go back to where I came from, even though I was born here. I also don't exactly blend in." He gestures at the mostly white classmates in front of us. "So Kastor and I have a lot in common, even though he gets amazing superpowers while I am the opposite of invisible to security guards when I'm in stores. So really, I think I have it worse. But look, they keep doing right by us, and all we do is push them away. And yes, I know there was a cost when the group fractured, and I'm really sorry about your parents. But think of all the lives that would've been lost if they weren't still here."

I nod, knowing that he is right. And that maybe, just maybe, Hamilton could be a supporter of *me*.

"Are you going to report me to your father?" Hamilton asks.

"No, I just . . . I wanted to . . . I need to tell you—"

The lights dim as a voice booms over the speakers. "OK seniors, it's the moment you've all been waiting for; it's time to crown your Belmont Academy king and queen!" I can hear Bianca squeal in excitement all the way from the back of the room. "Can everyone please—"

The ballroom plunges into darkness. Screams erupt as the room starts shaking violently.

I instinctively grab on to Hamilton, who grasps me tightly in return.

From above us comes a loud rumbling. Part of the ornate ceiling begins to crumble. As a large crack forms, lights from neighboring skyscrapers filter into the room. My classmates rush toward the exit in a panic. Bile fills my throat when I notice that the security guards have been replaced by armed men in riot gear who aren't letting any of us leave.

A large blast throws me to the ground, and I cover my head as rubble rains down.

Screams of terror finally get me to look up. Hovering above us is a man in black spandex, an armored jet pack strapped to his back. His face is partially obscured by a mask, but we all know who he is.

"It can't be . . ." Hamilton's mouth is open wide in shock. "Dr. Drevis."

Dr. Drevis was presumed dead after the Los Angeles battle. The rift between him and Kastor began because unlike Kastor and his crew, who were born in another galaxy, Drevis had to use money and technology to give himself special powers, and he had quite a chip on his shoulder about it.

"Did you miss me?" Drevis asks with a cruel laugh.

No.

That voice.

Drevis is the man from my father's study, the one who watched me nearly burn. The one who wants to rip me open. I'm just another experiment to him.

Everyone has crowded together, hoping to find safety in one large, well-jeweled mass.

"Come out, come out, wherever you are," Drevis says in a singsong voice.

Hamilton looks around. "Who is he looking for?"

I'm frozen in fear, but I can feel my body start to pulsate. Every nerve is on edge, as if it's ready to fight.

"Oh? Do I not have your attention?" Drevis takes a laser from his pack, and the refreshment table explodes into flames, causing more screams. "There we go. Next time I'll aim for people."

Hamilton is shaking next to me. "Who does he want?"

Everyone is still except for one figure, who calmly walks into the center of the room. Father is clad in his signature three-piece bespoke suit, his graying hair covered by a large black helmet similar to the one Drevis wears. It protects them both from Philomela's powers, who can penetrate a person's brain and manipulate their cerebellum to control their movements. She can cause a running person to stop in their tracks or make someone about to pull a trigger drop their gun entirely. Kastor may have strength, Ajax the ability to manipulate the elements, but Philomela is the one Father envies the most.

There is a small part of me that hopes that perhaps Father is here because he's having second thoughts and is going to call off Drevis's attack.

"Aubrey, give up and come forward," he orders.

Then again, perhaps not.

The protective group around me jumps away as if I have mono—or worse, last season's Hermès—except for Hamilton, whose jaw is practically on the floor. Every single person in the packed ballroom is staring at me.

It's official: Prom really is the ninth circle of hell.

It turns out there's no hiding what's been stirring inside me. There's no hoping my fate away. I'm about to be a sacrificial lamb.

As much as I thought I'd be safe at prom, it actually makes sense for Father to create a public scene. He'll want the world to know that he wouldn't tolerate one of *them* living in his own house. He'll get credit for taking me down even if he never gets his own hands dirty. That's what Drevis is for.

I'm so tired of having to hide who I am. Of being scared of his reaction.

I step out into the middle of the floor. Drevis looks down at me with a sneer. "You're not worth any of this."

No kidding.

I glance over at Father to see if there's even a glimmer of remorse on his face over what's about to happen to his daughter.

His lips turn up in anticipation of my demise.

I look at the man whose attention, love, and support I've been desperate for. The man I always made excuses for when I felt hurt and rejected. He was just too busy to be a parent. He didn't really want a kid, but he did the right thing by bringing me into his home. He had done me a favor by giving me this privileged life. I didn't want him to regret "saving" me.

But now I know the truth.

My father is a gigantic selfish asshole.

Drevis bellows as he hovers from above, "Oh, that's so sweet, so touching. You thought your daddy was going to protect you." He points his laser at me.

My entire body shakes as I crouch down and put my hands over my head, like that will do anything. There's a part of me that's resisting my protective stance, that wants to fight. But I can't fight fate, even though I can't believe this is how I'm going to die.

A useless orphan killed at prom.

Bright lights blast around me, and I hear screaming. But instead of the extreme pain I'm bracing for, I feel protected. I crack open an eyelid to see that someone has cast a light blue field around me.

Wait, no. It's coming *from* me.

Well, would you look at that. Who knew? Certainly not me.

The tightness in my body loosens a little as I let the field get bigger and bigger. I stand up on unsteady legs. As I push my hands out, the field expands. I stare at my hands as if they belong to someone else.

"I knew it!" Father screams as he points at me.

"So you've been holding out on us," Drevis calls out. He looks pissed.

It's more that I was too scared of what the consequences would be if anybody knew what I was capable of. I had visions of being rounded up and exiled like the rest of *them*.

But now everybody knows. *Everybody*. I might as well see what I can do when I truly let go.

Just let my freak flag fly, so to speak.

Not that I have any clue what I'm doing.

My hands seem to be projecting the shield, so I force them up to the sky. The shield radiates out to touch Drevis. Upon contact, he falls back and hits the wall.

Holy crap. I can't believe that actually worked.

Drevis regains his composure and looks . . . pleased. "Oh, this is going to be fun."

Instead of thinking, I just let my instincts take over. I run, then take a leap, and I soar up to the balcony twenty feet in the air.

"OK, Drevis. You came for me, so what are you waiting for?"

Wait a second. What did I just say? Did I just seriously throw down to one of the evilest humans on the planet? One who has technology and indestructible armor surrounding his body, while I'm in a tulle prom dress?

Drevis lets out a laugh. "Yes, I'm so scared of a . . . *girl*." His lip curls in disgust.

"Oh, screw you." I glare at him and see red. Not like a metaphor for being angry—my entire field of vision literally looks as if a red lens has been put over my eyes.

A marble statue on the other side of the room shatters.

Oh, wait, I think I did that.

Oops.

OK, so I can shoot lasers from my eyes. That is a good fact to know. Maybe I should put that away for a bit until I can aim better.

Chaos erupts as the guards below close in on my classmates.

I jump down and put myself in front of them. I stand tall, hoping to exude confidence even though I really have no clue what I'm doing. All I do know is that I've had enough.

"Leave them alone," I shout at my father. This is all his doing. We're nothing but collateral damage to him.

"Yeah!"

It takes me a moment to realize that Hamilton is standing next to me. Maybe there's a reason he's so vocal in his support of *them*.

"You have powers, too?"

"What?" Hamilton blinks and looks surprised to be next to me. "Oh, ah . . . no, I just got caught up in the moment. Sorry."

He then smartly hides behind me.

I turn to my father. "Do what you want with me, but leave everybody else out of this."

He looks down at his manicured nails as if he's bored. "Drevis, can we just get this over with?"

"With pleasure." Drevis lowers himself several feet so I can see the glee on his face. "I'm going to enjoy watching—"

Suddenly, the guards collapse as if they've been powered off. They remain motionless. There's only one person who can control people like that.

I spin around, but I see only my confused classmates and my father.

"Hello, Drevis."

Shouts of fear and relief fill the ballroom as Kastor— *the* Kastor—flies down from the sky. The doors burst open, and Philomela and Ajax run into the ballroom. Ajax moves his hands to create a mini cyclone and throws it at Drevis, who is caught inside it and goes spinning and spinning and spinning.

"Get everybody to safety," Kastor instructs Ajax and Philomela. People start to flee the room, but I notice Father has curled up on the floor, playing possum.

Who's the weak one now, Daddy dearest?

"Aubrey!" Hamilton reaches for my hand. "Are you going to be OK?"

I have absolutely no idea, but I nod.

"I knew you were full of surprises." He gives me a wink.

"I still have one more left," I say as I pull him in for a kiss.

Hey, if I'm going down tonight, might as well kiss a cute boy first.

Hamilton's face lights up as I pull away. "Super, indeed."

"Let's go!" Ajax calls out to my remaining classmates.

Hamilton gives me a nod before rushing to safety.

While Drevis struggles within the cyclone, Kastor lands

next to me. He's even taller and more muscular in person. He towers over seven feet. His copper hair glistens in the moonlight. His biceps are barely contained by his infamous red-and-blue spandex one-piece. I'd be incredibly intimidated if he weren't looking down at me with such strange tenderness.

"Lyra, you've turned into such a lovely young woman. I never thought I'd see you again."

What? I open my mouth to reply, but I have no idea what to say to Kastor. *The* Kastor.

I can only reason that kissing Hamilton must've done a number on me, because I don't know who this Lyra girl is or why Kastor thinks he knows me. Or maybe shooting lasers from your eyes has some serious side effects, like imagining that an infamous superhero knows you exist.

"One moment," he says with a nod as he flies up to meet Drevis.

Kastor swats away the cyclone as if it were nothing. He throws Drevis down to the floor next to me. Drevis appears stunned for a moment.

He's not the only one.

That's when I see his jet pack up close. I spot a tiny opening with a purple-and-green tube running through it.

It can't be.

It's like everything falls into place. Every private science class I had as a kid starts flooding back to me. For years, scientists have tried to figure out what powers Drevis. They never could.

But I just did.

It looks like Father didn't keep exousium all to himself after all.

"I got it!" I cry out before my mind even catches up.

As one of the few people who even knows about exousium's existence, I'm aware that it's extremely unstable. Which means that a direct hit to the exposed tube would render the pack—and Drevis—useless.

"Lyra?" Kastor asks.

"I think . . ." My body begins to tingle as if it's telling me it knows what to do. My mind is getting in the way. I look down at my hands and see them vibrating.

"OK, let's see what you've got." I throw my hands out toward the pack.

And . . . nothing.

No beams. No lasers. Just me, pointing like an idiot.

Kastor and a dazed Drevis stare at me.

"Aubrey, no!" Father finally stops pretending to be unconscious when he realizes what I'm trying to do, what I know. Which means I must be onto something.

I've always done what I was told. I wanted to be good.

But I'm done trying to impress him.

"Come on!" I yell at my hands as I try again.

Nothing.

"Oh, so you worked in chemistry without me trying, but now—"

My hands heat up, and flames encircle them.

I really, *really* hope I can put this out later.

Panic fills Drevis's eyes. "No," he screams as he hits a button that causes him to shoot straight up into the air.

I jump up after him, and sweet baby Jesus, I'm actually flying.

"What's the plan?" Kastor asks as he soars next to me.

"Ah, hey, um . . ." I can't believe Kastor is asking *me* for a plan. "I can disable his power source if I get close enough. Maybe." There's a waver in my voice that does not instill confidence. Granted, most people are probably nervous the first time they *fly*.

Kastor gives me a nod before flying up to grab Drevis by his ankle to bring him closer to me.

Please work, please work, I pray as I flick my hands, hoping that a flame or something will shoot out and—

A burst of fire erupts from my hands, knocking me backward. It's a direct hit to Drevis's pack. The resulting explosion throws me to the floor, and I land with a thud. Pain radiates through my entire body, but not as much as it should, given that I dropped more than forty feet.

When I finally sit up, I see Drevis lying unconscious next to me. His armored bodysuit doesn't have a single scratch on it, while my prom dress has been singed and I'm showing more leg than one would consider decent.

Thank God for biker shorts.

"Aubrey!" Father rushes over to me and hugs me for the first time in recent memory. At least, the first time without the press around. "You did it! You have no idea what we can do with your power." He points a shaking hand at Kastor. "Let's start with him."

Kastor raises his eyebrow in amusement.

So *now* Father has decided to show me an emotion besides

disdain? He thinks I'm going to forget the small detail that he just tried to have me killed?

"Aubrey!" Father claps his hands impatiently at me. "What are you doing? Don't just stand there; you're finally able to—"

Then I do something I've wanted to do for most of my life: I punch my father square in his smug face. He crumples to the floor.

"How incredibly disappointing," I reply to his unconscious body.

I take a step back, finally taking in the destruction around me. I have no idea what any of this means.

"Lyra?" Kastor approaches me cautiously. "You were incredible. I'm so proud of you."

"Ah, thanks."

To be honest, I feel pretty proud of what I just did, too. *Me.* Not just taking down Drevis, but punching Constantine in the face.

He was never a father to me.

I did have something in me all along.

The girl who was told over and over that she was a disappointment.

Ajax and Philomela rush into the room. "Everybody's safe," Ajax reports.

Philomela takes in the destruction around us. "Guess we'll be blamed for this as well."

"Yeah, we should go," Ajax replies.

My moment of pride quickly vanishes as I realize I'll be blamed, too.

I need to flee. But to where? I don't have a family. I don't have a home to go back to.

I have nothing.

Oh, and there's also the small, teensy, super-inconvenient fact that the entire world probably already knows that I'm one of *them*.

Kastor extends his hand. "Come with us, Lyra. There's so much we have to tell you, but only if you're ready."

I look around at these three extraordinary beings. The ones the world fears.

I don't even hesitate. I take Kastor's hand.

"I'm ready."

SOMETHING BORROWED, OR THE COSTUME

by **DANIELLE PAIGE**

THE WORLD BLEW UP AFTER I SLIPPED ON THE suit. OK, "slipped on" is an understatement. It was more like shimmying and jumping up and down and then contorting myself into the suit. And maybe "blew up" is a bit of an overstatement. It wasn't the whole word that blew up, it was my world—the Lab.

I had put the suit on because it was the last night it belonged to me. After spending the better part of three months designing and tricking out the ultimate superhero suit, I had to test it . . . just once. Technically, it would've been irresponsible not to test it out. Though technically, I wasn't supposed to leave the Lab . . .

But enough with my excuses. I'll start from the beginning.

Even Harlowe wouldn't begrudge me this one night, would she? After all, wasn't this the reason she'd taken me in from The Home for the Abandoned and trained me to be her protégé? She'd had no interest in being my mother. She'd had no interest in my chubby six-year-old cheeks. It was the dimples in my brain that she'd wanted to bring home. She'd wanted to be my mentor after a story in *The Meteor* about the "orphan toymaker" brought me to her attention. I had animated one of my dolls using some wiring I'd taken from my lamp and circuits from a toy train. Harlowe had taught me the craft of suit making, and I'd become her protégé.

That was ten years ago. She'd never been much of a mother, but then, she hadn't claimed to be. "I promise you three things," she'd told me. "I'll give you a third of the profits and a skill you will have forever, and I will never make you eat your vegetables." She'd kept her promises. And since Y Corp was built on secrecy, we'd become a two-person team that served every superhero in Alcon and beyond.

We made suits for clients who demanded the utmost privacy. I had signed a nondisclosure to that effect. Not that I had needed one; I was the biggest fan of all the Super Force, from Gator Girl to Braceman. I never would've thought of betraying them.

Today had been a series of small fires I'd had to put out, which was why I had gotten so far behind on finishing Gamine Girl's suit. The Blue Raven and Voxon had both stopped by for adjustments on their suits. The Blue Raven's wing covers had shrunk, probably because he had flown too close to the sun. And Vox had wanted his suit stretched—he'd grown a couple of inches. Finally, there was Finn, aka Heartstopper, who dropped by more than anyone else for regular fittings and new gadgets.

Finn was a classic super with a tragic past and an unending drive to save the world, but there were two things that made him different from the others. He was self-taught, and he didn't have a single real power except his will and his money and his supersharp jaw.

Finn's parents had been killed by a villain named Canon who prided himself on stealing lives and fortunes from the rich. He'd left Finn an orphan with a need for vengeance. Canon had never been caught, but Finn had caught so many other villains.

"You know, you and Myron and Harlowe are the only people in all of Alcon who know who I am," he said, looking down at me after I had finished remeasuring his blue Kevlar-covered torso. Myron was his butler and his caretaker and probably the closest person in his life.

I tried to make nothing of his words, but if I was honest with myself, my heart stopped for both Finn and his hero ego. It almost felt like I was crushing on two separate boys. But I had to talk myself out of crushing at all. It was obvious that his heart was as impenetrable as the Kevlar I'd used to craft his suit. He had been seeing Gamine Girl for a few months. But it wouldn't last.

"Well, yes, it is rare company, Finn," I said.

"I didn't mean it like that. It's just nice to be around someone who knows me with and without the mask. Can I let you in on a little secret, Mags?"

I liked it when he said my name—Maggie Means. But I liked it more when he abbreviated it like this, like we had a shorthand, like we were familiar . . . like he cared. I nodded.

"Sometimes, I feel more like me with it on . . . more free. Does that make sense?" he asked sheepishly.

"Yeah, it makes sense."

We locked eyes for a long moment, and I was almost sure I felt something electric between us, but I reminded myself that the only electricity we shared was what coursed through his suit.

"I got you something—well, I got the Heartstopper something," I said, breaking the moment because I was this close to saying something that would reveal how much I liked him.

I pulled my latest creation out of my lab coat pocket and handed it to him. It looked like a case for earbuds.

He took it gingerly.

"Open it," I instructed.

When he touched the clasp, the case clicked open, revealing the earbuds. After a second, the earbuds moved to either side of the case, and a tiny propeller moved up between them. It began to spin, and the case lifted into the air.

"You can control it by voice command or with a remote on your belt. It collects audio. And you just have to wear these." I handed him another pair of earbuds with his insignia, a broken heart.

"That's brilliant. You're a genius, Mags. What would I be without you?" he asked.

"You would be just a heart*breaker* and not a Heartstopper, I guess," I quipped, remembering how when he'd first come to us, his toys and his suit had been completely rudimentary. He'd sewn a taser into either arm of his suit and fashioned a remote to control the flow of electricity. The result had been enough to stop a few Alcon villains, but he'd also gotten a few third-degree burns from the tasers. Harlowe and I had engineered a suit that still gave him the illusion of lightning but had less of a chance of frying the hero.

"I'm serious, Mags. One of these days, you're going to have to learn to take a compliment."

"And one of these days, you're going to stop bringing your suits back to me this messed up. What did you do to this one?"

"You don't want to know," he said, breaking into a smile.

"I do want to know. I can't reinforce the suit unless I know what's not working."

"Aquacast genetically engineered a whale headed for the seaport. It totally swallowed me whole. I was like Pinocchio. He spit me out after I tasered him with the lightning, but there was a little short. I'm sure it was just because of the water."

"What do you think makes Aquacast do the things he does?"

"The why never matters, Mags, only the how."

"But if we knew why, maybe we could stop more of them from being so evil . . ."

"You think if everyone got a Harlowe to rescue them, there would be no bad people?"

"I'm not that naive . . . but maybe if we knew why, we could stop more baddies from forming."

"Every second you spend searching for the reason is a second the villain spends hurting more people. It doesn't matter why it started; it only matters how you stop them."

I crossed my arms, done with the argument. It wouldn't be the first or last time we'd talk about why our town produced so many more villains than any other.

"Do you want to leave the suit? I can run a diagnostic."

"I'll drop it by tomorrow. I'm going to need it tonight and I've got the car waiting downstairs. Finn is throwing a party. You should come."

"Maybe next time. I'm way behind."

After Finn was gone, Harlowe ordered me to leave the building for the day. But I wanted to finish Gamine Girl's suit, so I clocked out and then back in to work. When I finished the suit, I tried it on.

No one would have known, only the world was torn apart.

Now there was no way Harlowe wouldn't know what I'd done. I only hoped she would understand. The suit was the most perfect thing I'd ever made. It was a pale gold with blue stitching in a delicate pattern, bat-wing sleeves, and a utility belt that curved precisely around Gamine's perfect form. It had more torque and gadgets than a fancy sports car, and it ran like a dream. It was designed for someone who had power of their own, but it also had a series of fail-safes in case the superhero got injured. And since Gamine Girl couldn't fly, the suit could do it for her.

I opened the window of the Lab and climbed out on the ledge. I took a deep breath and stepped off. For a few seconds I free-fell.

"One . . . two . . ."

I counted off the seconds, reminding myself to trust my engineering skills, to trust the suit.

"Three, four, five, six, seven . . ." Still falling.

"Eight . . . nine . . ." Still falling.

"Ten . . ."

The suit reversed course, but it felt like my stomach was still falling for another second, even as I bounced into the sky and halted, hovering above the Lab.

I extended my arms and began to fly. It was beyond anything I had ever experienced in the confines of the Lab's testing facility. Seeing the city lights blur below me, feeling the power of the suit's engines keeping me aloft. As I flew, I could feel the delicate balance between the thing I'd made and nature itself. Below, the city stretched out before me. I was in awe of how small everything was, how small my life had been before this moment. Flying through a cloud and falling into darkness for a moment, I was shaken out of my reverie, remembering the danger my town and those tiny moving dots below faced.

Suddenly, I heard a loud bang behind me, and I turned around to see that the top few floors of the Lab were gone.

The building was empty. But all our work . . . everything Harlowe and I had done . . . all the suits. We'd have to start all over again. I had lived for those suits. Every button, every stitch, every invention . . . I *was* those suits, and someone had just stolen my very being. I had to get them back.

I flew back to get a closer look. Had the Villain Core finally found us? Harlowe and I had been so very careful . . . but I couldn't think of another explanation.

I texted Harlowe.

I'm fine. But the Lab is gone. Meet me at the safe house in an hour.

I touched the camouflage button on the suit and watched it turn the color of the night sky. But I couldn't shake the feeling that whatever was out there in the dark could still see me.

I knew exactly where I had to go. Where they all would be.

"Take me to Heartstopper," I whispered.

And the suit took over, raising me back into the air and flying toward the target like a heat-seeking missile.

I touched down softly a few feet from Finn's driveway, which was filled with cars that cost more than my apartment.

As always, there was a party at Finn's manor. It was part of his cover, being the consummate rich party boy.

I knocked on the door, and Myron answered.

"Gamine Girl, we weren't expecting you back so soon."

"Um . . . I need to see Finn—it's urgent."

"But of course, I'll get him. You can wait in the study."

But we passed the grand ballroom on the way, and I saw Finn at the height of his ruse. He was wearing a tux, holding a cocktail in his hand, and he was surrounded by the prettiest girls from the local academy.

He spotted me and excused himself.

"Pardon me, ladies, it seems that a superhero has a little bit of a crush on me. I just have to let her down easy."

I stifled a laugh when he reached me, despite the circumstances. There was something about seeing him in his element but knowing his secret that got to me. Maybe I was imagining it because of what he'd said in the Lab, but it really looked like he was bored by his party and all those girls. Or maybe that was just wishful thinking on my part.

He took my arm and led me to the study.

When we got there, he closed the door behind us.

"You're not her," he said, his smile dropping as he turned to me.

"I want the same things that she does," I said, grateful for the voice modulator so he could not hear the longing in my voice.

"You definitely aren't her."

Before I could say anything more, he took a step closer. "Mags, what are you doing here? Why are you wearing Gamine Girl's suit?"

"How did you know it was me?"

"I'd know you anywhere. And Gamine Girl doesn't want to be anywhere near me right now."

"Why not?"

"We broke up. She's halfway to Henon by now."

I took a second to absorb that. I knew it didn't mean anything. He had broken up with a different girl almost every month that I had known him. Just because he was done with her didn't mean anything about him and me. He would never see me as anything but the tech he needed for his toys.

But the way he was looking at me gave me pause. Or was that hope?

"You never answered. What are you doing here?" he repeated.

"Someone attacked the Lab."

"What do you mean?" He reached reflexively for my arm. I felt the tension go out of me at his touch.

"It's gone. The only reason I made it was because I was out test-driving the suit. I just wanted to see what it felt like. It was stupid, OK?"

His eyes filled with understanding as he digested what I'd said.

"Not stupid! It saved you. And you had every right to try it on. You made it."

I knew he was trying to make me feel better. But more than that, I could see in his eyes that he was glad I was alive.

"Is Harlowe OK?"

"She wasn't in the Lab. I told her to go to our safe house."

"Good," he said, looking relieved. "The others are in the cave. We can catch them up. Together, we can fix this. Together we can do anything."

"But we don't even know who did it."

"Whoever it is won't stay silent for long. Villains are always proud of their handiwork—they have to show off, and when they do, we'll be ready."

The library's secret door swung open when he pulled out a copy of *War and Peach*. A parody of *War and Peace*, perfect for the boy pretending not to have a care in the world. I knew for a fact how much he cared and that he had read the real thing.

He put the volume back and offered up his hand in an *after you* gesture. I stepped through, like I had countless times before for fittings and adjustment to the costume. But this time I was here for a very different reason.

When we got inside, I gasped.

It took me a second to make sense of what we were looking at. Finn had raced across the room and knelt down beside one of the fallen superheroes. There were three of them. Hollow Girl was lying in the center of the floor, flickering in and out of focus like a staticky television. When she was fully visible, I focused on her face, which was frozen in what looked like pain. Next to her, holding her hand, was the Blue Raven. But something was wrong with him as well—his wings were crumpled, and he was writhing in pain. Finally, there was Voxon, who lay unmoving in front of the bank of monitors showing downtown New Ganon.

Finn looked up from Hollow Girl and said, "She's breathing; so is Blue. Check Voxon's vitals, Mags—hurry."

He called for Myron on his cell. "We need a team here stat. We have three supers in need of medical assistance. "

As I approached Voxon, I could see his muscled chest moving up and down through his suit. He looked peaceful, like he was sleeping. I shook him gently, trying to wake him, but he didn't stir.

"What happened to you?" I whispered. His lips moved, but I couldn't hear any sound. He looked like he was talking in his sleep. But then he woke for a second, and his eyes lasered in on mine.

"Someone wants to end us . . . but you're not one of us . . . you're our only hope . . . it's all up to you . . ." he whispered before closing his eyes again.

You're our only hope . . . Voxon's words echoed in my head.

It sounded like one of those things a kid would practice responding to in front of the mirror, like singing songs into a hairbrush when they thought being a pop star was possible or imagining accepting an Oscar. Only I had never even imagined being a superhero, despite my proximity to them . . . or maybe because of it. I just wanted to see what the suit looked like on me. Maybe take a selfie I couldn't post and—oh yeah—fly, if only for one night. But I'd never imagined this. I loved making suits. I knew that what I did was important; it allowed heroes to do what they did. But I had never known what it was like to have a hero ask me for help saving them, let alone the world. My pulse sped up, and my mouth went dry. I couldn't screw this up.

I looked over at Finn. "Finn, take off your suit."

"What?"

"Take it off. Someone tampered with the suits. They're hurting them."

"That's ridiculous," he said, but just then, I heard the crackle of electricity and saw a flash of light pulse through Finn's tux. He was wearing his supersuit underneath it, just as I'd thought. He fell to the ground, convulsing.

I rushed to him and began unbuttoning his tux.

Ten awkward minutes later, four superheroes were sitting before me in their underwear.

The second the suits came off, they began to wake up. But the Blue Raven's wings did not mend, and Hollow Girl was still flickering in and out of existence. Finn looked fine, though.

"What about your suit? Why isn't it affecting you?" Finn asked, looking up at me.

I looked down. I hadn't even thought of that.

"I don't know. Maybe I haven't had it on long enough? I should take it off and run diagnostics on it along with all the rest of them."

Just then, Myron arrived with the medic team to check everyone out. I excused myself to change out of the suit.

When I emerged, Finn insisted I be checked out, too. But I was too anxious about the others.

"What happened? Why aren't they healing? Why aren't we hurt?"

"You and me, Mags . . . we're not supers. Not really."

I was prepared to protest, to remind him of all his amazing feats as the Heartstopper, but then I remembered—the Heartstopper had created his own superpower. Using his incredible discipline and immense wealth, he had made himself into a superhero; he'd trained for countless hours and had tons of amazing toys created to aid him in fighting villains. He didn't have alien gifts like Voxon or genetic ones like the Blue Raven, and he hadn't fallen into a vat of radioactive goo like Gamine Girl. Finn just had his mind, his will, and his bank account.

"So the damage lasts because of their innate superpowers," I said out loud. "It has to be a villain. But which one? And what's their plan?"

"The second question is irrelevant. Only the first matters."

Finn was returning to our forever argument. After years of battling supervillains, he thought it didn't really matter why, only how. They all had their reasons, and even if there was no reason at all, the effect was the same. The world was in the crosshairs, and the superheroes had to save it. In the past, I'd thought he was wrong—that maybe if we knew the villains' reasons, we could figure out how to stop anyone else from turning evil. Now I wasn't so sure.

Every second you spend searching for the reason is a second the villain spends hurting more people. It doesn't matter why it started; it only matters how you stop them, he was forever saying.

Now, on the other side of the suit, I was coming around to his way of thinking.

The doctor who treated me in the mini lab ordered me to take it easy.

"The Doctor and Myron are going to settle the others upstairs," Finn volunteered.

Finn's house didn't just have a secret super lair—it also had a hospital room upstairs.

"Why was the whole team here?"

"Voxon had detected some unusual activity around town. Some of the supervillains have been developing new tricks.

We were all going to scout together after I made an appearance at the party."

"What kinds of new tricks?"

"I don't know. We never got to have the conversation."

"What else did they tell you? Any clues as to who did this?"

Before Finn could answer, our attention was drawn to the lair's giant television screen. On the screen, there was a shot of the destroyed lab. Harlowe was there, speaking to a reporter, instead of in the safe house like I'd told her. "No . . ." I whispered.

"I can't believe anyone would do this. We're just a simple design house. Who hates dresses this much?" Harlowe said.

Villains have a way of showing themselves, Finn had said.

And Harlowe and I were the only ones with access to all the suits.

I started putting the pieces together. It was like putting together a suit, anticipating the hero's every need . . . only this time, the hero was me. When I was done using Finn's mini lab, I showed him my results, my heart sinking.

"I tested the suits. Each one contained a foreign compound. For Voxon, some powdered meteor that counteracts his powers. A paralytic lined the Blue Raven's wing covers. And for you . . ."

I held up the suit to show him the places where the liquid had burned right through the wires that conducted his electrical current.

"What is that?" he asked.

"Some kind of acid. "

"You were right—someone sabotaged our suits," he concluded.

"The only people who had access to them were Harlowe and me," I said slowly, each word feeling like a dagger inside my heart.

"You don't think . . ." he said, trailing off and shaking his head.

"I don't want to think . . . but I need to go find out."

"Then I'm coming with you."

"You're hurt—you can't go anywhere," I protested.

"I'm coming with you," he repeated. But there was a look in his eyes that told me he wasn't as sure as I was about Harlowe's innocence.

"She would never do this . . ."

"I'm coming with you," he repeated.

I made a decision. He would see that he was wrong, and he would be there to assist me if Harlowe needed help.

"Then you're going to need to wear that," I said, pointing to his old suit, which was in a case on the wall.

Just then, Myron retuned to check on us. I looked at his cardigan, then back at the screen showing Harlowe's interview with the press.

"Myron, I need your cardigan and ten minutes in your lab."

When we got to the square, I made a beeline for Harlowe. I wore the suit under my street clothes, feeling bulky and conspicuous, but Harlowe didn't notice. She began to cry when she saw me.

"You're here. You're alive."

I draped the cardigan over her and gave her a hug.

"All our work is lost. Who would do this?" she asked, her eyes filled with tears. I wanted to believe she was innocent.

"Someone who hates the supers . . ."

"Well, tomorrow, we start again. Tonight, we rest."

I nodded.

She moved to give me the cardigan back. I shook my head. "Keep it. Let's get to the safe house."

"I have a few more questions to answer for the officers."

I watched her walk away. Then I met Finn a couple of blocks from the square.

"Did it work?" he whispered.

I lifted up my wrist to take a peek at the suit's wrist panel.

The tracking dot was blinking.

"Now we wait."

A few minutes later, the tracking dot I'd placed on Myron's cardigan began to move, and we followed. Like I'd suspected, she wasn't going home. She was heading to the warehouse district.

She entered an old, unmarked warehouse building. We could see through the walls with the infrared from our goggles. There were two figures in the center of what looked like a duplicate lab, and all around her were hundreds and hundreds of suits.

"Do you see what I'm seeing?" I asked.

"Maybe it isn't what it looks like . . ." he offered. "Let's listen."

Finn produced a boomerang with tiny sound-collecting

speakers on it. He threw it with expert efficiency; it whizzed through the air, suctioning itself to the wall by the window.

He put in his earbuds. "I'm not getting anything—I think the window might be soundproof."

"Then allow me—I made one for Gamine, too," I explained, producing one of the new audio drones I had shown him that morning.

I raised my arm and released it. We watched as the drone slipped inside one of the air vents.

I pulled out my own headphones from my utility belt.

"Before we listen, I just want to say . . ."

He trailed off, and his eyes met mine. And then he kissed me. The kiss was sweet and soft, and I could feel his heart breaking for me.

"I'm sorry, that came out wrong. I just—"

"It felt right to me," I whispered.

"I know how much she means to you. If she . . ."

I gave him one of the earbuds. We were so close together, I could feel his breath on my cheek.

"Then we'll have to stop her," he said quietly. "But first, let's be sure."

Within, Harlowe stood next to a man who remained in the shadows.

We heard her voice through the buds first.

"Your funds have been received."

"One million dollars. Steep . . . but a small price to pay for taking down the heroes."

"Our business is completed. Maintenance is included in the fee, but I require discretion for obvious reasons."

"Speaking of reasons . . . you never told me yours . . ."

"I believe in balance. I am just tipping the scales."

I ripped the bud out of my ear as if it were on fire. Harlowe had betrayed us all. Finn looked at me, eyes full of empathy. He touched my shoulder.

"I'm so sorry . . ." he whispered.

"I'll take her. You take the customer," I said just as quietly.

Using our suits' flight capabilities, we flew through the window. I felt a rush as the glass broke and I saw the expression of surprise on Harlowe's face.

"Stop where you are," I demanded.

My voice didn't sound like my own through the voice modulator. I turned it off. I wanted her to hear me. I wanted her to know it was me, and I wanted to know the answer to my question, too—why?

"Doesn't this ever get old?" Finn quipped. "This is why you can't have nice things, Raptor."

I recognized the name. Raptor was a longtime foe of his, and he was wearing Heartstopper's suit.

But this time, Raptor was ready, and his suit was much newer than Finn's. The punch that should have sent Raptor flying through the warehouse and possibly through the wall instead landed with a thud.

Raptor threw a punch in return, sending Finn sliding across the floor. I knew it had to have hurt his new wound.

"Finn!"

"I got this." Finn was already flying through the air, pushing the guy back.

Meanwhile, Harlowe revealed that she, too, was wearing

one of our creations. She unbuttoned her dress and revealed a tiger-printed suit that was one of the test models we'd been working on for Hollow Girl.

"You were selling suits to our enemies? Why would you do that?" I asked, using my own voice.

"What matters is that I've put enough suits out in the world to change things. We're all equal now. And we can decide which people are more equal than others."

"What does that mean?"

"That we choose. That *we* have the power now. We've had it all along. It's our brilliance that keeps them safe, that makes them great, and we get none of the glory. I know you're tired of the shadows; that's why you put on the suit."

I shook my head.

"In your heart of hearts, you know it's true. We make quite the team. We could put them in their place forever."

How had I not seen how deep her jealousy ran? How had I not seen that she didn't value what we did at all, that she was playing the long game, that she had been using me all along as an unwitting accomplice?

We came to blows in the air. I pinned her to me in what must have seemed like a hug to her. She had forgotten that I had helped her design her suit.

I reached around her back and released a new feature I'd added to all of Hollow Girl's suits—a parachute. I pulled the cord, and Harlowe was pulled backward with great velocity, hitting the back wall of the warehouse and slipping down the wall like a cartoon.

Suddenly, air was whooshing behind me. I whipped around to see that Finn and Raptor were picking up speed as they circled each other and traded punches, blurring into a red-costumed tornado. I considered flying in, but as I approached, I was pushed backward. Then the air stopped as suddenly as it had started. They were spinning slower now, but Raptor was wearing electric cuffs.

"Nice job," I told Finn.

He went over to Harlowe and cuffed her as well.

"Goodbye, Harlowe," I said through my tears.

On our way out, Finn called the police and told them where to find the factory.

"Wait, we can't just leave the suits. If they fall into the wrong hands . . ."

"I'm on it."

I went over to the console that monitored the suits' progress and entered a series of numbers.

Within seconds, the suits began to disintegrate.

"When did you add that feature?"

"I did it because of you. Remember when you said that we should make the suits more environmentally friendly? I changed the polymer . . ."

When we got back to his lair, the enormity of the day hit me.

"You OK?" Finn asked.

"No, but I will be."

"About what I did back there . . ."

"What?"

"The kiss. I wanted to explain why I did it—"

"I thought there was never time for whys."

"There is with you. Mags . . . there is no one like you. You're the only one who—"

Before he could finish, I kissed him again.

"Come and get me, sucker." A voice from the television interrupted our sweet, perfect kiss.

On-screen was Canon, the villain who had killed Heartstopper's parents, and behind him was a line of others wearing identical suits, suits that looked like the ones from our lab.

"For too long, we've been under the rule of the superheroes—they decide who to save and who not to save. We will no longer live according to their whims. Anyone can be a superhero now . . . for a price." A number flashed on the screen like a commercial. Then the screen went black again.

"Can you use the disintegration button on those suits?" Finn asked quietly.

Once I got a drone into place near the square, I tried pushing the button on the remote console, but nothing happened.

"It's not working . . ." I said, pushing the button again.

"Canon is smarter than that. He must have reconfigured it. What are we going to do?" Finn asked, sounding anxious.

He was always cool under pressure, but Canon was the one exception.

"We're going to need new suits—tons of them. He's building an army. And we're going to need a bigger one."

I reached out and took his hand. He squeezed it. I was a hero now.

THE KNIGHT'S GAMBIT

by VARIAN JOHNSON

BEFORE I'VE EVEN STEPPED OUT OF THE SEDAN, I know that there's a horde of freshmen loitering in the commons area, just waiting for me to appear. And no, it's not because I have super hearing. Or because I can see through brick walls. Nor is it because I have one of those weird superpowers, like the ability to feel people's heartbeats through vibrations in the earth or smell the sweat dripping from their armpits—no crazy shit like that.

It's because that's the way it's always been at Millicent Academy, ever since I was a freshman.

They're not jocking me because of anything I've done.

They like me because of my dad.

I wait for my bodyguards, Orville and Grady, to give me the all clear, and then I step out of the vehicle. My dad, Knight Justice, might be bulletproof, but I'm not. And the last thing the government wants is for some dumb villain to try to take me out. They probably think Dad would destroy half the city trying to get revenge. Don't get me wrong—he'd rip apart the city, but only because he'd finally have an excuse.

Sure enough, as soon as we step inside, I hear all the usual gasps and shrieks. A few people even take pictures.

But then, one kid mumbles, "That's him? He's so . . ."

Small. Skinny. Normal.

Black.

Here's the thing. My dad is Black, too. Biracial, technically. But unlike me, Dad is light enough to look exotic—you know, like The Rock. He's that "safe" kind of Black. The acceptable type of minority.

But me? I'm about as dark as they come, thanks to Mom. Wherever she is.

Orville and Grady fall away as I near two of my friends, Thom and Drew. Well, I guess they're neighbors more than friends. Their parents are important, like mine, but in different ways. Thom's father owns three dental offices. Drew's mom is an architect.

It's kind of messed up that my dad has to be a freaking superhero in order to live in a neighborhood with dentists and architects. But it's a lot better than the two-bedroom apartment where we used to live, back before he revealed his secret identity to the world.

"Yo, Raymond! What's up?" Thom and I do that stupid bro hug thing he does to prove he's "down with the cause." He pulls away, then says, "That must have been some wild party you guys were having on Saturday night. My pops wanted to call the cops, but I was like, you don't call Five-O on Knight Justice. He *is* the cops."

"Thanks," I mumble. To be fair, the cops wouldn't have done anything. Plus, it wasn't like Dad was having some mega party. I was the one who'd turned up the music. That way, the neighbors wouldn't hear him yelling at me, daring me to "man up" and sleep with one of the groupies he'd brought over.

Heroic, right?

"But yo—which one of those freshmen are you gonna pass off to me?" Thom starts to survey the crowd, then smiles as he spots a Black girl looking at us. "What about the sista over there?" He nudges me. "I can say that now, right? Since we're cool?"

By "cool," he means that he's been over to my house for dinner once. Not that I've ever been to his house.

"You sound disgusting," Drew says, before adding, "I'm not picky. I'll take any of them."

Out of the corner of my eye, I see Zora sitting at a table by herself. She spots me, smiles, and waves me over.

"I'll catch y'all in class."

"Aww, come on," Drew says as I begin to walk away. "Not Zora again. You know you don't have a shot with her."

"I have a better shot with her than y'all do with any of those freshmen," I say over my shoulder.

OK, fine—I really don't have a shot with Zora. Even though she's only been going to this school for a year, I've known her for a lot longer. We grew up together in Lincoln Heights. She was my neighbor. No—my *friend*. We had playdates and everything. Even back then, I had a crush on her, though I was too young to understand what a crush really was.

Once Dad revealed his secret identity and we moved away, she and I lost contact. But last year, while Dad and I were touring the old neighborhood for some stupid cable documentary, our old building caught on fire. While I called the fire department, Dad rushed in and saved everyone.

Afterward, Dad pulled a few strings and got her father a new job and her enrolled here, and voilà—now she's the closest thing I have to a best friend. She's certainly the person I trust the most.

And that's why trying to have a relationship with her would be super weird. At least, that's what I keep telling myself. But I won't lie—sometimes I can't help but wonder what it would be like to date her. Would I be happy? Or would I end up like Mom and Dad?

"Guess what's happening in the Linc this morning?" she says as I sit down beside her. She angles her phone so I can see the screen. It's a live feed of a convenience store robbery.

"Hey, that's Mr. Santiago's store!"

She nods. "I heard about it on the way to school this morning. Looked it up as soon as I could get on the Wi-Fi."

The feed we're watching seems to be coming from a drone. Two robbers slowly exit the store, one of them holding a hostage, who is screaming his head off. "Do you know him?" I ask.

"Seriously? Does he *look* like he's from the neighborhood?"

OK, she had me on that one. The hostage was white—clean-cut, with spiky blond hair and a fancy blue suit. Even on Zora's small screen, I could tell he was sporting some expensive shoes.

"The robbers probably didn't pick a Black hostage on purpose," she says. "For all they know, the police would have shot all of them."

"Unfortunately for them, there was only one Black guy walking around town with bulletproof skin, and he doesn't shop at convenience stores."

She sneaks a look at me, then turns back to the screen. "One . . . for now."

I swallow the spit in my throat.

Eventually, the robbers and the hostage make it to the middle of the street. Then, all of a sudden, the police turn around and face the spectators. "Back up!" they yell. "Back up for your own safety."

Well, that's what it *sounds* like they're saying. But I've seen this rodeo enough times to know that the live feed is dubbing over their words. What it looks like they're actually saying is, "Back the fuck up, or he might kill you, too."

I sneak a look at Orville and Grady. They're chatting it up with Mrs. Polansky, the very fit gym teacher.

I pull my phone from my pocket and quickly open up a browser. No one knows it, but the last time Dad was drunk and passed out, I logged in to his computer and found the link to the real drone with the real audio—along with a stash of other videos too hard-core for the general public to see. I'd been hoping to find information about Mom, but this was a decent consolation prize.

"Here, let's watch this one," I say, sliding my phone toward her.

She frowns. "It's kinda grainy."

"Trust me. There are some things you don't want to see in high definition."

While we're waiting for Dad to show up on the scene, she asks, "So, how are you?" She knows a little about the meltdown on Saturday, but not the entire story. There are some things I absolutely do not want Zora to know—like how Dad makes fun of me because I'm a virgin.

"Things were better on Sunday. Almost normal."

Her eyes cut into me. "Things haven't been normal for a while." She quickly tucks a strand of hair behind her ear. "He's getting worse, isn't he?"

That strand of hair is about to fall out of place again, and I so badly want to tuck it back behind her ear, but I keep my hands to myself. "Define *worse.*"

"You have to take care of him, Raymond. The city needs him."

I laugh. "The last thing Dad wants is compassion from me."

"Raymond, don't be so hard on him . . ." She stops, however, as the bystanders begin to cheer. A few second later, Dad shows up, passing through the crowd like he's freaking Moses and they're the Red Sea. I swear, one lady even tries to flash him.

"Look, I'm gonna be real with you," Dad says. "I've got a fucking hangover, and I've got a tee time at—" He stops as he looks at the hostage, who is whimpering like a lost puppy. "Man, will you shut up? You sound like my son."

I sense Zora looking at me again, but I don't return her gaze.

"So how about this," Dad continues. "Y'all put down your weapons now, and I don't rearrange your spleens."

"Fuck you, Knight Justice," one of them yells. "We ain't scared of you."

"We should do a drinking game the next time this happens," I say. "One shot of tequila for every time someone does something corny like that."

The robber with the hostage turns his gun on Dad.

"Duh, he's bulletproof." Zora nudges me. "That would be a double shot of tequila, right?"

OK, so maybe it's time to raid Dad's liquor cabinet.

The only time I came close to making out with Zora was this past summer, when she'd had too much to drink at one of those stupid pool parties. But of course the Boy Scout in me wouldn't let me take advantage of her. She thanked me for it afterward, which helped. Plus, superpowered father or not, her long-time boyfriend, Antonio, would have kicked my ass if something had happened between us.

I lean closer to her, toward that strand of hair threatening to untether itself from her ear. "So if that's two shots, what would it take for—"

BANG!

I jerk my head back toward the screen. One of the robbers—the one with the hostage—has fired at Dad.

And Dad . . . is holding his shoulder. "Son of a bitch!" he yells. He bends down and picks up something from the ground. It looks like maybe it's the bullet.

I realize I'm holding my breath and exhale.

"Since when does your dad feel pain when he's shot?" Zora asks.

Good question.

The robber must be as shocked as we are, because he slowly lowers his gun. And that's when Dad strikes. In the time it would take you to snap your fingers, he's hurled the bullet at the robber's head.

It goes clean through, splattering blood all over the hostage.

And then, as Mr. Fancy Suit begins to scream again, the other robber drops his weapon and takes off. But it's too late. Dad's already on him. And once Dad takes him down, he keeps pounding his head into the pavement, over and over and over.

Finally, the screen goes black.

I look at Zora. "Anything on your phone?"

"It went dead a while ago. They said something about technical difficulties." She puts her hand on my arm. "Is he OK?"

Zora's touch makes my voice go high. "He's Knight Justice. Of course he's OK."

Zora frowns as she pats my arm once more. Then she moves her hand, and my arm suddenly feels very cold. "Well, I bet those robbers won't try to cross him again."

"Zora, those two robbers won't ever *breathe* again. Don't you think he went overboard?"

She shrugs. "For all we know, those were the same guys who assaulted Misty, the lady who lives on the floor above me. Remember her?"

"No. Sorry. I don't." I shake my head. "But those guys . . . they at least deserved a trial, right?"

She shrugs. "Tell that to Misty."

I try calling Dad and leave him three messages, but it's clear that he doesn't want to talk to me. Throughout the day, I get more and more worried. But I try to remain calm. I do my breathing exercises and even sneak in some yoga poses during lunch.

Dad wears his emotions on his sleeve. Me, my goal is to always keep mine buried. Hidden. At bay.

Dad's not home when I get there after school, so I try to focus on other things. I finish my homework. Our cook makes me a delicious dinner of steak and potatoes.

I eat my food in the dining room. By myself.

Dad eventually makes it home a couple of hours later. He's changed out of his Knight Justice uniform (he almost took my head off once when I called it a costume by mistake). Now he's wearing a silk robe. Even though I don't have the power of super smell, I can still pick up the scent of a woman's perfume.

"Heard you were looking for me," he says as he pops open a beer can and sits down at my desk.

"I saw the robbery this morning. Are you hurt?"

He pauses, the beer almost at his mouth. "I thought they cut the feed. How did *you* see what happened?"

"Um . . . a kid showed me a video from one of those conspiracy theory sites."

"Fucking technology." Dad takes a long swig of his beer, then belches. "I told those cops to make sure they confiscated all the cameras. I do all the freaking work for them—the least they can do is keep stuff off the Internet." He finishes the rest of the beer. "I'm starting to lose my invulnerability."

"What?" I bolt upright. The way he says it so nonchalantly makes me think I must have misheard him.

"Don't start crying. I'm fifty, for fuck's sake. You know it eventually happens. But I still have my other powers. For now." He sighs. "You ready to man up and get your own powers?"

"I'm trying, Dad—"

"Bullshit!" He slams his hand down on my desk, cracking it. "You know how our powers are triggered. By aggression. Anger. Passion. You'd think your powers would have kicked in when Miranda abandoned you."

"Dad . . ." There's an edge to my voice. I can tell he's glad to hear it.

"Look, we need to *do* something. You're running out of time."

"The last time you *did* something, I almost died." I pull back my shirt collar to show him the scar on my shoulder. "Or do you not remember stabbing me?"

"Better to die like a man than live like a bitch." He stands. "What about that girlfriend of yours? You tried to—"

"Me and Zora aren't like that. We're just friends."

Dad snorts as he reaches into one of his robe pockets. Of course he has another beer on him. "If you're not careful, you're going to be normal for the rest of your life."

"What's wrong with normal?" I ask. "I don't want to be a hero anyway."

"This ain't about being a hero. It's about having power." He opens the can. "When you're in charge, you get to decide what's right and what's wrong. And trust me—it's better to be the one deciding than the one having to live with the judgment." He walks toward the door, then pauses. "I might be an asshole, but I guarantee that hostage today would rather I be an asshole who saves his life than some nice guy who buys flowers for his funeral. And I bet your *girlfriend* feels that way, too."

My great-grandfather was the first one in the family to gain superpowers. And no, he wasn't an alien, and he didn't get them from a radioactive insect. He got his powers the good old-fashioned way: through government experimentation. Most of the other test subjects died, but him—well, he was so mad, so angry, so *furious*, all that emotion triggered something, and all of a sudden, he had these kick-ass powers. The problem was, the anger didn't go away. If anything, it became stronger. Like adding grease to a fire. Ever since then, our family's powers have been passed on from son to son, all triggered by traumatic events.

At seventeen, I'm the oldest of the Burke men not to have developed my powers yet. Supposedly, if I don't manifest them by the time I "come of age"—whatever that means—I may never get them. Which, honestly, is fine by me.

Dad has always been an asshole when it came to my powers, but he started going overboard about a year ago. First, there were the taunts and belittlements. Then the training sessions that would become a little too physical, with me ending up with a black eye or sprained arm.

And then he stabbed me with a kitchen knife.

Mom flipped when she found out. She actually charged at him. Dad responded by slamming her against the wall enough times to break the drywall.

Mom left the next day, but Dad and the government wouldn't let me go with her.

I'm sure she's still in the city, hiding. At first, I was mad at her for abandoning me, but she was only doing what she needed to do to survive. I know I'll find her eventually.

That is, if Dad doesn't kill me first.

Everything is normal for the next couple of weeks. No evil geniuses trying to take over the world, no superpowered fathers trying to kill their children. One night, I'm supposed to go over to Zora's place to help her with some homework, but at the last minute, she texts and asks if she can come over to my place instead.

I want to say no, but Dad is out for the day—a meeting with the governor. And while I don't like having Orville and Grady around all the time, they aren't snitches. They won't tell Dad that Zora was over.

Though maybe that would finally get him off my back.

She texts me when she's getting dropped off, and I do my best to remain cool as I rush down the stairs. I open the door before she can even knock.

"Wow," she says. "I didn't know your house was so big."

"You've been here before."

She shrugs. "You're right. I guess it just seems bigger when it's empty."

We sit down and get to work, but she can hardly concentrate. She's fidgety and makes silly mistakes on almost every calculus problem. Finally, I put my pencil down. "Zora, what's going on? Is something wrong?"

"There's just a lot on my mind." She closes her book. "Can we watch a movie instead?"

"Uh, sure. We can either watch something on the big screen in the den or down in the basement—"

"The basement sounds great." She stands. Her hand falls on my shoulder, close to my scar. "Do you have anything to drink?"

My heart starts thumping. "You mean . . . like juice? Or soda?"

"Raymond . . ." She run her hand over my head, then tugs my ear. "Something stronger."

The movie isn't on for five minutes before she's downed her first drink. I try to keep up, but she is on a mission. She drinks another—and I resort to taking shots.

After her third drink, she turns to me. "So do I have to ask you to kiss me or what?"

That's all it takes—I'm on top of her, my tongue pressing against hers. And then she's taking my hand and guiding it all over her body. And then . . . she's reaching for my belt buckle.

I pull back. "Wait. Are you—"

"Don't you want to?" Her voice is rushed. "I thought—"

"Yeah. Of course. It's just . . . I don't have any protection."

"Don't worry, Boy Scout," she says, reaching for her purse. "I came prepared."

My head is still spinning an hour later. She lies against me, her skin warm and soft. I keep my eyes closed as I hold on to her.

Maybe to try to capture this moment in my mind . . . or maybe because I'm afraid I'm going to throw up.

She taps my chin. "Hey? You alive there?" she asks, finally sounding like her normal self. "How do you feel?"

I peek at her. "Um . . . great?"

"That's all I get? *Great?*" She begins to pull away, but I wrap my arms tighter around her.

"Sorry! I mean . . . I feel spectacular! Outstanding! Or any other SAT word you want to use." I pause, then add, "I also feel confused. What just happened?"

She doesn't speak for a long time. Finally, she says, "Just something that's been in the works for the past year." She sits up and grabs her phone. "I have to go."

I sit up as well, and the room starts to spin. "Wait. We should talk. We should—"

"No, it's OK. I'm ordering a car now." She quickly collects her clothes while I lie back down.

After she's dressed, she leans over me. I can't focus on her face, but I know it's beautiful.

Then she grabs a hunk of my skin and squeezes it.

"Ouch!"

She looks genuinely disappointed. "I guess this wasn't passionate enough to kick-start your powers, huh."

I stick my tongue out at her. "Don't worry. I'm happy to give you a chance to try again."

Her face falls. "Raymond . . ." Instead of saying whatever is on her mind, she leans over and kisses me. But not passionately, like before. There's no heat. No spice.

But hey, beggars can't be choosers.

"So, I'll call you later?" I say.

"Yeah," she says. "Later."

I watch her exit the basement, then fall asleep.

"Raymond, get your ass up here!"

I jolt up. It takes a second for me to realize that I'm still in the basement.

"Raymond! Don't make me come down there!"

I quickly throw on my clothes and scurry up the basement stairway to the kitchen.

Dad is sitting there, a beer on the table in front of him. He's sporting the biggest shit-eating grin I've ever seen. "So, now do you feel like a man?"

"You don't have to be so crass," I mumble. "I'm going to grab a drink of—"

"Think fast!" he yells as he throws something at me.

"AAUGH!" Something strikes me squarely in the side, causing me to stumble backward. I'm not sure, but I think at least two of my ribs are cracked.

I look down and see a baseball rolling between my feet.

"Felt that, huh. Well, fuck." Dad stands up from the table. "And I hoped Zora was wrong."

"Are you fucking insane?! You could have killed me!" Then I process what he just said. "Wait, you talked to Zora?"

"Of course I did," he says. "What? Does that hurt your little feelings?"

"Dad . . ."

"Trust me, what's coming next is gonna hurt a lot more."

I hold up my hands. "Dad, please. Hitting me isn't going to trigger my powers."

"I'm way past physical pain, son." He turns to the back door. "Come on in, Miranda!"

My breath catches.

Miranda?

Mom?

Sure enough, Mom steps through the doorway and into the kitchen. Her eyes are wet and shiny. "Hey, baby."

Ignoring the pain in my side, I rush to her and throw my arms around her. I'm crying, and I know it'll just make Dad mad, but I don't care.

"Where were you?" I ask. "I was looking everywhere for you. Are you OK?"

She leans back. "Sweetie, there's something you should know." She looks at Dad, then back at me. "Me running away . . . it wasn't real."

"Let me tell him," Dad says. "It's better that way." He pulls Mom away so that it's just him and me. "About a year and a half ago, I realized I was going to have to take drastic measures in order to kick-start those powers of yours. You were too much of a baby to do it on your own."

"I know," I said. "I still have the scar."

He laughs. "Please, I knew that knife wasn't going to do anything by itself. But I thought . . . maybe if you saw me beating up on your mom, you might grow a pair. Fight back. *Feel* something."

I narrow my eyes at him. "You hit her . . . just to get a rise out of me?"

"Why the fuck else would I do it? I love her."

I turn to her. "Mom, don't listen to him. He doesn't love you. He's insane."

Mom walks forward . . . and puts her hand on Dad's shoulder. "Raymond, I know you're upset, but this is for your own good. For the good of the world."

I take a step backward. "You were in on it?"

"In on it?" Dad laughs again. "It was her idea!"

"But . . . but . . ."

Now I do throw up. But not from the alcohol.

"Is this part of the process?" I hear Mom ask. "Did you vomit when you gained your powers?"

"You guys are sick!" I yell at them. "I'm getting out of here."

"And where are you going to go? Zora's place?"

"Yeah. I am."

"Remember how I said I've been planning this for a year and a half?" Dad asks. "Think back. Wasn't it amazing how I just happened to be in the right place when her apartment building caught on fire? And how you happened to be with me?" Dad picks up his beer from the table. "Do you know how long that took to organize? How many people I had to pay off?"

I point a shaky finger at him. "You're lying. I don't believe you. Zora would never be in on—"

"You're right. She wasn't in on it—not at first. Just her parents. She didn't know about any of it until this summer, when I prepaid her college tuition and told her to make you a man."

I stumble backward again, but now my back is against the sink. I don't have anywhere else to go.

"She chickened out this summer, but she finally came through today." He winks. "To be fair, she *does* like you. Like a puppy, I mean, but what do you except? How could she be attracted to someone who refuses to be a man?"

My body begins to shake.

My eyes lose focus.

My insides feel like they're on fire.

"Come on, son," Dad says. "You must be pissed off at me. At all of us!" He takes a step toward me. "Hit me!"

Yelling, I lunge at him, my right hand balled into a fist, swinging it like a sledgehammer.

I strike him square on the jaw.

And break every bone in my hand.

═══════════════════════════════

Nothing is the same after that.

Once I'm out of the hospital, I run away from home . . . but not before leaking all the private videos of Dad's "heroics." Once people see how demented he is—how much he enjoys tormenting people—they turn on him.

As far as I know, he and Mom have run off to South America.

The government eventually tracks me down. But once I tell them I've downloaded more info—like proof about the secret experiments they did on my family and how they covered up everything my dad did—they agree to help me so I won't leak it.

A few weeks later, I change my name. Enroll in a different school. Fabricate brand-new grades.

And then I sit down with the guidance counselor to discuss my options.

"Well, Richard," he begins, looking at a printout, then back at me, "your grades are exemplary. And you have some nice community service projects listed here. But I'm afraid this isn't good enough for most top-tier schools. I just can't recommend you."

Of course, having hacked his computer while he's been talking to me, I already know that he recommended three rich white students with lower GPAs to these "top-tier" schools last week.

He slips off his glasses. "My suggestion is to take a year off. Maybe volunteer at a homeless center. Or tutor urban kids—that always looks good on an application."

"Ah, yes, of course," I say. I close my eyes and connect with his laptop again. Two seconds later, I've not only updated my application but have sent off glowing recommendations on his behalf to five different schools.

And, of course, I eviscerate those other students' grades.

I stand up, and we shake hands. "It's nothing personal," he says. "I don't want you to think this is a race thing. It's just, you can't be normal in times like these. You have to stand out. Do something spectacular. Heroic, even."

"I'll keep that in mind." Then I close my eyes and transfer all of his savings to the homeless center in Lincoln Heights.

See? I'm a hero after all.

THE NIGHT I CAUGHT A BULLET

by STERLING GATES

THE LAWYER ARRIVED THREE WEEKS AFTER the funeral.

Our house was still in disarray, every shelf and countertop full of the food our friends and neighbors had left to express their sympathies. I was clearing breakfast remains from the kitchen table when there was a curt knock at the front door.

"Nessa!" I yelled toward the front of the house.

"On it," my little sister said, darting from upstairs. *She's getting faster*, I thought, scraping egg residue off my plate. As I retrieved Nessa's plate from the table, I glanced at Dad's seat, untouched the last few weeks. Mom wouldn't let anyone sit in it, even after the reception.

You'll never get to see how fast Nessa becomes, I thought.

"Casey?" called Nessa. "It's a man."

"Actually, dear heart, we prefer to be called lawyers," said a deep, melodious voice. "Is your mother home?"

I walked to the living room to find a short, stocky man in a dark suit standing next to my sister. His white hair was trimmed neatly, and he was wearing a crimson vest under his suit coat. A gold chain dangled from one of the vest's pockets. A briefcase hung from his hand.

"Mom's asleep," I said. Since Dad had passed, Mom was sleeping more and more. "Can we help you?"

"Yes, Miss Dodson," said the lawyer. "You can. My business here pertains to the both of you."

"He has a card," Nessa said, handing it to me. It read **JOSEPH FRACTION, ESQ.** A phone number was printed across the bottom.

"OK, so you're a lawyer. What do you want with us?"

The lawyer pulled at the gold chain, producing a heavy pocket watch that opened with a *KLIK*. He frowned. "It might be better to tell you with your mother present, but I'm afraid I don't have much time here," he said, slipping his watch home. "May we sit?"

He sat on the couch, then gently set the briefcase down on the coffee table. Its latch snapped open. Nessa and I sat in the chairs opposite him.

"I was very sorry to hear of your father's passing. Very, very sorry."

"It was fast," Nessa said quietly.

"I know, dear," said the lawyer. "You may not have heard of me, but I have heard a lot about the two of you. I've known your father, Henry, since we were boys. I've been watching over his affairs since he turned the tender age of twenty-one, long before he met your mother and well before you two came along. He asked me to execute his wishes in the event of his . . . well, at a time like this." Tears suddenly welled in the lawyer's eyes. He pulled a handkerchief from his pocket and wiped a tear away. "I'm sorry, children. It's just that . . . I'm going to miss your father. He was my friend." The lawyer's voice got quiet. "I wish we'd had more time."

My brow furrowed in confusion. Dad had friends, sure. They'd all sat behind us in the funeral parlor three weeks ago, dozens of crying eyes staring at the casket as Mr. Philips gave his eulogy. Mr. Gresham. Mr. Landrum. Even Steve Jones had come out, and I hadn't seen him since Nessa was born. All of Dad's friends approached Nessa and me at the reception, looking at us with dewy eyes as they told story after story about how great our father had been. Dad had a lot of friends, and they'd mourned his passing, just like we had.

. . . like we are.

But never once had any of Dad's friends made mention of Joseph Fraction, Esq.

The lawyer opened his briefcase and removed a small black box. He set it on the table in front of us.

"What is that?" I asked.

The lawyer cleared his throat. "Your inheritance."

"I thought inheritances were money," said Nessa.

The lawyer tapped the box with one long finger. "Not always. Your father got these during a . . . well, during a trip somewhere far away. Upon his return, he entrusted them to me. And now I am delivering them to you."

"When did Dad travel? He was a bank manager," I said. The lawyer just smiled.

I picked up the box. It was made of dark wood stained a deep ebony. There was a small symbol carved into the lid. It reminded me of an elaborate hourglass.

"What's the symbol mean?" I asked.

"The symbol is called a *gibhann*, which means 'make your own time.' It's a lucky phrase in certain cultures."

"Open it," Nessa said.

A gold latch held the box closed. I undid it and opened the box. Inside were two silver bracelets, the *gibhann* symbol engraved on each.

"Holy smokes," said Nessa. It had been one of Dad's favorite phrases, and Nessa had adopted it since he'd passed. "They're beautiful."

"Very capital, are they not? One for each of you."

I picked one up. The metal was light and cool to the touch.

"What are they made of?" I asked.

"I believe they're a type of silver."

"Are they valuable?"

"In their own fashion." The lawyer smiled again, two rows of perfect white teeth glinting in the light. The hair on the back of my neck stood straight up. *Why would Dad send this man to give these to us?*

"I wouldn't try selling them, however. Your father wanted you to wear them. They'll bring you good luck if you wear them in times of need. Now," he said, closing his briefcase, "having delivered these to you, my work here is done."

"Wait, Mr. Fraction," I said as he started toward the door. "My mom is probably gonna wonder where these came from—"

"And she can call me at any time. You may as well, if you have more questions. I'm sorry to leave so quickly, children, but as I said, I don't have much time here."

Nessa darted around him and opened the door, the *gibhann* bracelet already on her wrist. "Thank you so much, Mr. Fraction," she said.

The lawyer paused at the door. "You're welcome, Vanessa Dodson. Your father wanted you to have these when the time was right, and that time is now. Please give my regards to your mother." The lawyer nodded once at me, and then he was gone.

"What do you think?" asked Nessa. She held her arm out to admire the silver bracelet on her wrist.

I checked the time on my phone. "I think that was ultra-weird. And kind of creepy. I also think that if we don't hurry, we're gonna be late. Go wake up Mom and tell her we're leaving."

"On it," Nessa said, running upstairs.

I ran my thumb over the *gibhann* engraved on my bracelet.

"'Make your own time.' Sure, Dad," I said to the empty living room. I slid the bracelet into my pocket, then went back to the kitchen to finish the dishes.

"Where do you think Dad got these?" asked Nessa, examining her bracelet in the morning sunlight. The front suspension of my ancient Honda groaned as I turned in to the Fanto Falls Middle School driveway.

"I don't know. Europe?" I said. The car shuddered once as my engine misfired, then continued to creep slowly across the pavement.

"Dad never went to Europe. He used to joke about never even leaving the state, remember? 'I saw a big city once, girls. It's how I know the small ones are good enough for me,'" Nessa said in her best impression of our father.

"I don't know, Ness. I'll ask Mom," I said, chewing on a fingernail. "And . . . don't you think it's weird that the lawyer just gave us these, then left?" All I'd thought about since leaving the house was the stranger's visit.

The whole thing just didn't sit right. Dad is—*was*—such a practical man, straightforward as they come. Why send us our inheritance in such an unusual way? And why had I gotten such a weird vibe off that guy? His clothes, the loud pocket watch, his odd mannerisms . . . I felt like I was staring at the pieces of a jigsaw puzzle strewn across the kitchen table and didn't know where to start.

Dad was so great with puzzles, too. Mom would sort the pieces by color while Dad looked for the edges.

"First you have to build the borders, Casey. Set the parameters, and then you'll know exactly how everything fits inside."

. . . I miss him.

Nessa brought me back to reality.

"Why's that weird? Mr. Fraction's a lawyer. Lawyers do that kinda thing."

"Yeah, I dunno. There was just something off about him. Like, who even says things are 'capital' besides that old man on *The Simpsons—OH MY GOD!*"

I slammed on the brakes as two girls darted in front of the car without looking. I laid on the horn, but they didn't break their stride. One girl turned around and stuck her tongue out at us.

"Step on out there and meet Jesus, why don't you?" I muttered.

"That's Abigail Lowther," Nessa said. "I'm racing her in track after school."

"She's not gonna race anybody if she gets herself hit by a car," I grumbled as I pulled into the drop-off lane. "What time's your race?"

"Three thirty. You gonna be there?" Nessa asked. Hope gleamed in her eyes.

"If I can get over here in time." I didn't really want to go; Nessa's track meets were complete snoozers.

"I know you'll make it."

The blast of a car horn behind us startled me. In my rear-view, a Drop-Off Mom wearing expensive sunglasses motioned for us to move faster. I told Nessa to hurry up.

"I'm going at my own speed."

The Drop-Off Mom honked again.

"Well, make that speed faster. I don't want to be late, too."

Instead of hurrying up, Nessa held out her bracelet. "Do you think Dad might've gotten these for him and Mom—"

A third honk.

"Nessa! *Go!*" I hissed.

Her eyes filled with hurt, and I was immediately sorry I'd snapped.

"Fine," Nessa said. She pushed open the car door and climbed out, slamming it behind her before I could speak. I'd definitely have to make that up to her.

Adela Anklesaria had been my best friend since the first day of sixth grade. We'd met in marching band when we'd both volunteered to play the tuba. Mr. Smith had given the tuba to Matt Morrow instead—"Sorry, girls, neither of you is big enough to carry a tuba on the field"—so Adela and I had decided to become the Trumpet Queens.

This morning, she was waiting for me in my parking space, and she was frantic.

"*Where have you been?*" she demanded before I'd even gotten my door open. "I've been texting you for, like, an hour. The cops are looking for Rodney Cady! He told Andi Loomis he was gonna shoot up the school!"

"Oh God. Why?" Rodney was our school misfit, a class clown who was always trying to make people laugh instead of studying. His grades had taken a deep dive last year once he'd discovered he could get more attention for making dumb Internet videos than for making straight Bs. One of his videos had gone semi-viral and hit half a million views.

But threatening the school with violence? That was a new level of attention-seeking.

"He got suspended after Mrs. Cunningham caught him cheating last week and flipped the eff out!" Adela shook as she spoke, and my own adrenaline started surging. She hated guns. We both did.

Up until the citywide ordinance two years ago, Fanto Falls had been an open-carry city. You'd see rifles in the back windows of pickup trucks, pistols on hips in coffee shops—just another piece of small-town living.

Mayor King's ordinance had caused some grumbling—well, a *lot* of grumbling, actually—but it made me feel better out in public. My dad, too. Whether he was waiting for a slice of pie at Erma's or standing in line for the movies at the Poole Theater, Dad was always scanning the room. I asked him why once, and he'd told me, "Better to see the threat coming than come under the threat."

I took a deep breath and looked up at the clear morning sky. *Rodney, what the hell are you doing?*

Surrounded by dozens of other students all buzzing about

the same thing, we made our way toward the building. Adela flicked through her phone obsessively.

"I've gotten, like, seventeen texts about Rodney in the last fifteen minutes. This is insane." She held the door open for me.

I looked through the doorway and saw dozens of teenagers pushing and pulling, everyone trying to get their books and get to their classrooms and get settled and *there were just so many kids and they were all gonna look at me and I could already feel the panic forming inside me—*

Adela looked up from her phone. "Hey. You OK?"

I bit down on my lip. It helped pull apart the panic.

I can do this. I have to do this.

"Yup. Just need a sec."

"Still weird to be back?"

It was. After Dad died, I hadn't gone to school for two weeks. Adela brought me my assignments, but I'd struggled to focus on homework. I was falling behind in trig and chemistry.

What was worse, though, was feeling the stares every day. People staring at me in class. Staring at me like I was the first person in the world to lose a parent.

. . . staring at me like I was the first person in the world to cry in my car at lunch.

"How much you wanna bet we get a 'random' active shooter drill today?" Adela asked as I flipped open my locker.

"Not taking that bet." I pawed through the pile of books at the bottom. "You know Dr. Rector likes doing drills. And if everyone knows about Rodney, we'll likely have one just to remind us what to do."

"Probably not a bad thing," Adela said.

"Knowing what to do in an emergency is never a bad thing . . . Crap, where *is* it?"

"Where's what?" she said, scrolling through her phone. "Bulletproof vest?"

"Not funny, Del. I can't find my trig book."

"This it?" asked a deep voice behind us.

I turned. And beheld the glory of Fanto Falls High star running back Jamal Giles (*swoon*), my trig textbook in his hand.

I somehow managed to keep my voice even and stutter-free as he handed it to me. "Yes. Thanks. Where was it?"

"And how'd you know it was hers?" Adela asked.

Jamal opened the front cover of the book. Below a list of student names going back to the 2000s was **CASEY DODSON**.

"I found it out in the parking lot—you musta dropped it," Jamal said. "You hitting the fall festival tonight, Dodson?"

My heart dropped through my stomach and dissolved on the spot.

"Uh, I—"

Adela saw my struggle and heroically looked up from her phone to wingman. "Yes. Yes, she is. We both are. Are you gonna be there?"

Jamal nodded. "Me and my boy Jason are gonna be there at seven, if you wanna hang with us."

"Um, sure. But why . . . uh . . ." I stumbled.

"Why not meet us at six forty-five?" Adela said.

"Dope. See ya," Jamal said. He smiled at me before disappearing into the crowded hallway.

Adela spun back to me, excitement bubbling through her. "Can you believe what just happened?!"

"I can't believe you just did that." My hands shook as I spoke. Turns out I could only handle two big adrenaline rushes in one morning . . . even if this one was a good one.

"Prompting Jamal Giles to ask you to hang out at the fall festival? I know, I'm basically a saint. Hold on, I'm telling everyone you've ever met." Adela began typing furiously on her phone.

I stopped her. "Please don't. It's no big deal."

"It's the biggest deal on the planet, Casey."

"Bigger than someone threatening to shoot us at school?"

"C'mon, Casey. Odds of Rodney getting up the courage to actually come in here with a gun seem slim. He's just talking Big Talk. He'll probably sulk for a couple days, then make a sad video and get over it. Let's focus on the good, mm-kay? You've had a crush on Jamal since, like, you were born, and he just asked you out!"

"He didn't ask me out, he asked to hang out at a public event," I shot back.

"Which is, by definition, a date!" Adela squealed as we rounded the corner into Mr. Brand's classroom.

"It's not a date."

"Jamal Giles asked you out on a date? *You?*" Kristi Crosby scowled at me from her desk. Kristi was Fanto Falls High's resident queen bee . . . and the "bee" stands for exactly what you think.

I feigned innocence as I slid into my seat. "Um, no. Where'd you hear that?"

Kristi held up her phone. "Del texted everyone in the school. She says you were practically suck-face with him in the hall."

I turned to Adela, who shrank behind her textbook.

"We weren't suck-face," I told Kristi. "He just asked me to go to the fall festival—"

"Jamal and I used to go out, you know," Kristi interrupted. "And me and the girls will be at the festival tonight. So keep that in mind." Kristi's three hench-friends, Kerry, Melissa, and Amber, glared at me from their own desks.

I felt hot blood hurricane through me. I was suddenly both angry and embarrassed all at once. "Great. See y'all there."

"Bless your heart," replied Kristi—Oklahoman for *go to hell*. I was gonna try to get one last word in, but Mr. Brand entered the classroom with a hefty stack of papers.

"All right, everyone. Good morning." Beaming, Mr. Brand walked the aisles, placing papers facedown on everyone's desks. "Do not turn these over till I tell you to."

"Mr. Brand, is this a test?" asked Amber.

"Yep. Surprise! Not to worry, if you've been keeping up with the homework, this should be a cinch."

The class groaned.

Mr. Brand stopped at my desk. "Casey, I know you're a little behind because of . . . well . . . I'm not sure if you'll want to take this."

Every eye in the room turned toward me to see what I'd do. I could feel Kristi's eyes boring into the back of my head.

"No, I'll take it, Mr. Brand. Thanks."

"OK," he said, setting a test on my desk. "And everyone, as a reminder . . ." He pointed toward a metal sign hanging at the front of the room: **YOU CHEAT, YOUR PAPER GOES IN THE TRASH. NO EXCEPTIONS. (THIS MEANS <u>YOU</u>!)**

He leaned against his desk and watched the clock on the wall, waiting as the second hand noisily ticked to the top of the minute. *Tick . . . tick . . . tick . . .*

We all watched him watch the clock, tense with anticipation.

"OK, class, you have fifteen minutes to complete as many problems as you can. On your marks . . . get set . . . annnnnd . . ." *Tick . . . tick . . . tick . . .* "Go."

Twenty-five tests flipped over at once. I was the twenty-sixth, turning the test over slowly.

I recognized almost nothing on the first page.

Page two was even worse.

Anxiety welled up in my chest. I glanced at Adela as she flicked to the second page, the first page already completed. She'd always been a monster at math, and she prided herself on usually being both the first person finished *and* the one with the highest grade in the class.

"Eyes on your own papers, please," Mr. Brand admonished from the front of the room. "I catch anyone cheating, you know where your test goes. Fourteen minutes to go."

I closed my eyes, bit down on my lip, and tried to calm myself. Every tick of the clock reminded me that I had absolutely no idea what I was doing. My palms were sweaty.

I was gonna need the best luck in the world to get through this.

Which made me think of the *gibhann* bracelet.

I reached into the pocket of my jeans and pulled it out. *Hope this is actually lucky, Dad*, I thought. I slid the bracelet onto my wrist, steeled my nerves, then reread the first problem.

A triangular parcel of land has sides that are 725 ft, 650 ft, and 575 ft long. Find the measure of the largest angle. Then, estimate the acreage . . .

My nerves shattered. My body vibrated with dread. The bracelet made my wrist itch.

Tick . . . tick . . . All I could hear was the clock. For every click, my heart thumped in my ears three times. *Tick . . . thumpthumpthump . . . tick . . . thumpthumpthump . . .*

Is this what a panic attack feels like?

I moved to problem two. It was even more complicated. I turned to the next page, then the next. The test got harder as it went.

Now I was really sweating. I scratched at my wrist.

Tick . . . thumpthumpthump . . .

I was so screwed.

"Eyes on your own paper, Mr. Briggs!"

Eyes came up as Mr. Brand made a beeline for Ben Briggs. I stared at my test instead. It would take me ten minutes to solve even the most basic of these problems.

A hole formed in my chest as all my fear and anxiety took over. The bracelet itched even more. *Why had I put it on in the first place?*

Mr. Brand took Ben Briggs's test from him.

"Hey, I didn't do anything! I was just looking around!" said Ben.

Tick . . . thumpthumthump . . .

I decided. I'd just turn the test over and wait out the rest of the time. I'd tell Mr. Brand that I couldn't do it. He would understand, right?

Or would he tell me I should have said that from the beginning?

"Mr. Brand! Mr. Brand!" pleaded Ben.

Our teacher made his way back to the front of the room, Ben's test in hand.

The skin around my bracelet screamed at me. I pulled back my sleeve to scratch some more.

Tick . . . thumpthumpthump . . .

There just isn't enough time for me to figure out how to solve my problems. These problems.

Mr. Brand crumpled up Ben's test.

"C'mon, Mr. Brand!"

"The sign's clear, Benjamin. Cheating will not be tolerated in my class."

Adela swished over to another page of the test.

"Mr. Brand!" cried Ben.

Mr. Brand took aim at his trash can.

That's it. I can't do this. Whatever happens happens.

I closed my eyes. Sweat rolled down my back.

There's just not enough time.

The bracelet grew cold against my wrist.

Tiiiiiiiiiiiiiii—

The sound of the clock changed.

It didn't stop; it just turned into a . . . a *constant*.

An elongated tick.

I looked at the clock. The second hand had stopped.

It wasn't the only thing in the room that had stopped, either.

Mr. Brand was frozen in place. Ben's crumpled test floated in the air between his fingers and the trash can.

Adela was stopped in mid page flip.

I glanced at the other students. They were frozen, too. Shonda Offord chewed thoughtfully on her pencil's eraser. Kristi was counting on her fingers. Ben Briggs's arms were still in the air as he made his case to Mr. Brand.

They. Just. Weren't. *Moving.*

Is this a joke? Are they all in on it?

KRAK! I stifled a scream as the tick finished and the second hand slammed into place. Then the room went silent again.

What is this?

"Adela?" I whispered. She didn't move, didn't respond in any way.

What if I'm stuck like this?

The bracelet was still cold on my wrist. I pulled my sleeve back. The *gibhann* symbol, so delicately carved into the silver, shimmered.

Was it . . . *glowing?*

No, it had to be just a glint from the overhead lights.

Unless . . . unless I'm frozen between seconds?

Well, that's just madness, Dodson.

Tiiiiiiii . . .

The clock's second hand started to move.

That's when it dawned on me . . . I wasn't *between* seconds. *I had just slowed the seconds down.*

"Make your own time," I whispered. The *gibhann* seemed to glow in response.

I knew then exactly what had happened. I'd needed more time . . . and Dad had given it to me.

I flipped back to the first trig question.

I can do this.

I have the time.

I got to work.

I pushed open the stall door just as the vomit hit the back of my mouth. I even managed to get most of it in the bowl. Once my stomach was empty, I sat on the floor of the stall, pulling in deep, heaving breaths.

What the $%^& just happened to me?

As soon as I'd finished my test, time had snapped back to normal. Like nothing had happened. Ben Briggs's pleas didn't sway Mr. Brand from throwing away his test. Adela finished hers in record time. Kristi Crosby and her hench-friends side-eyed me the rest of the hour.

The second the bell rang, I'd run out of there and into this stall.

I cleaned up the vomit that missed the toilet, then moved to the sink to wash my hands. I splashed water on my face, then looked at my dripping self in the mirror over the sink.

"What did you do?" I asked myself. The *gibhann* bracelet shimmered in my reflection. I pulled it off my wrist and inspected it.

"What are you?" I asked the bracelet.

It didn't answer.

"Case? You OK?" Adela asked. She was standing at the bathroom door, concern on her face. Students shuffled past in the hallway behind her.

"Peachy," I lied.

"You left your backpack." She held my bag out to me.

"Sorry. I was gonna be sick, so . . ."

"Happens to me sometimes, too. I think I have something for it . . ." Adela started rummaging in her purse.

"No, thanks. I'll be OK, Del." I slung on my backpack and headed for the door. "I need to go check on my mom."

"You're ditching?"

"I'm taking a sick day. I'll have my mom call in. OK?"

Adela nodded. "I'll see you tonight? Around five?"

"Sounds great."

"And pick out a cute outfit!" I heard Adela call as I pushed past several students in the hall. I headed for the parking lot.

I wasn't lying to her; I *did* need to go home.

The business card was where I'd left it: the corner of the living room coffee table. **JOSEPH FRACTION, ESQ**. I pulled my phone from my pocket and dialed the number. The lawyer's melodious voice greeted me after the third ring.

"Good day, my fellow strider. You've reached the voice-mail of Joseph Fraction, Esquire. If this is an emergency, please hang up and dial the local authorities in your time zone. If you need to speak to me, please leave a message, and I'll contact you as soon as the clock allows. Thank you, and have a capital day."

There was a long, shrill beep. I debated hanging up, then cleared my throat.

"H-hi, Mr. Fraction. This is Casey Dodson. We met this morning. I'm having some . . . trouble, I guess, with the bracelet Dad left me. The *gibhann* bracelet. I'd like to ask you a couple questions about it. Please call me back."

I left my number and hung up. The bracelet was cold on my wrist.

The Fanto Falls Fall Festival was the biggest event of the year for us. It couldn't compete with the state fairs in Tulsa or Oklahoma City, but we did pretty good. And everyone went: all the kids from school, their parents, their teachers. Sometimes even kids from nearby towns came, like the time Dante Malveaux stole his dad's truck and drove it up from Pauls Valley to tell a girl he liked her. (Still together, last I heard.)

The fall festival was where you went to be *seen*.

Adjusting the small mirror on my vanity, I wanted nothing more than to be invisible.

Nothing looked right. I tried putting my hair up—hated it. Tried wearing it down—hated that, too. I laid every top I had out on my bed—hated every single one of them. Nothing seemed cute enough for the night ahead of us.

Adela was no help. Instead of helping me pick something fun to wear, she was rifling through my closet.

"Can I wear this?" she said, holding up my favorite blue crewneck.

I knew saying no wouldn't do much, so I gave in. "Go for it. The color'll look good on you."

"Sweet," she said, stepping into my closet to change.

I turned back to my mirror and examined my stupid, stupid face. Why did I look so . . . *like this?* How was I going to hang out with Jamal Giles looking like, well, *me?*

"Is Nessa coming with us?" Adela asked from the closet.

"She's going with her friend Josie. They both won their races today, so they're getting celebratory pizza at Captain Cheesy's."

"Carbs are *always* the best reward. You talk to your mom much today?" Adela said, stepping out of my closet. I gave her a thumbs-up; the blue really did look good on her.

"Long enough for her to call me in sick, but then she crashed out again." I sighed.

Adela sat down on my bed. "It's really hard for her, huh?" she asked.

"For all of us. There's just . . . just . . ." I looked for the words but couldn't find any. There was a Dad-shaped hole in our lives now, and nothing was gonna fill it. Nothing would bring him back. Mom wasn't handling it well. Neither was Nessa.

I was just trying to keep my head above water in the well

of grief. Kicking hard to stay afloat. And every time I tried to talk about it—to actually tell another human being how I *felt* about all of this, how much I was struggling, how I wanted nothing more than to wake up from the nightmare and just have everything be all right and everything be normal—my brain just shut down. On permanent overload.

I looked at Adela as tears welled in my eyes.

"It was so fast, Del. So damn fast. We just blinked, and . . . and he was gone. And all I want is . . . is . . ."

All I want is to have him back.

"I know, Case. I know." Adela pulled me into a long hug.

It was exactly what I needed.

Then Adela tried her best to pivot. "Wellll, what are you excited to ride tonight with Jamal Giles? The Himalaya? The Bell Ringer? Oh, I know—the Zingo! 'Oh, Jamal! Hold me as this roller coaster takes my breath away!'" Adela feigned a swoon, falling backward onto the bed and into Jamal's imaginary arms.

I wiped away a tear and tried to muster some enthusiasm. "Trying to cheer me back up?"

"And keep you from smearing too much of your makeup."

"Heh. It's mostly waterproof. And honestly? The thing I'm most excited for tonight is the food. Mrs. Cunningham's fruit whips. Mr. Fry's electric pies. And, of course—"

"Mr. Song's pot sticker madness!" Adela and I laughed at the same time. We'd made ourselves sick eating pot stickers from Mr. Song's booth the last two years in a row. We were hoping for the hat trick this year.

As I tried on yet another shirt (green with yellow stripes), Adela's phone chimed. She opened her messages and gasped.

"What is it?" I asked.

"Rodney Cady's in a car chase with the cops!"

I frowned as I checked myself in the mirror. "That idiot should give up at this point. If you tell everyone you're going to shoot up the school, you can't be surprised when cops come after you."

"It's definitely not gonna end well for him." Adela typed a reply, then pocketed her phone. "You ready?"

"Ready as I'll get, I guess," I said. I threw on a jean jacket and presented myself for inspection. "What do you think?"

Adela's brow furrowed as she gave me the once-over. "Not quite there. Hold on." She went to my vanity and pulled opened my jewelry box.

"Del, wait a sec—" I started.

"Aha!" Adela plucked something out of the box. "Perfect!" It was the gold necklace Aunt Gayle had given me the summer I turned thirteen. "This'll look great with the jean jacket. *Tsk.* What would you do without me, Case Face?"

"Be a happier person?" I said, fastening the necklace around my neck.

"But you wouldn't look as nice. Let's *go!*" she said, already clomping down the stairs.

"I'm two steps behind." I waited a moment before turning back to the open jewelry box. The *gibhann* bracelet sat on top, its silver gleaming in the light of my room.

"And *you* are staying here," I said.

I closed the box and headed downstairs.

"Wow, Dodson," Jamal said. "You look . . . uh . . ."

"Doesn't she clean up nice?" Adela wingmanned.

"Definitely." Jamal smiled at me.

"Th-thank you," I mumbled, hoping he didn't notice the blood rushing to my face. The four of us stood awkwardly in the cold and crowded parking lot: Adela, Jamal, his friend Jason, and me. Dozens of kids and parents moved around us, all heading into Hathaway Park, where we could see the lights of the rides poking up over the tree line.

"So, uh, what are we doing first?" I asked.

Jamal gestured toward the lights. "Start with the Bell Ringer? Get the long lines out of the way first, then hit the smaller stuff later?"

"Iph whut we did wast year, worfed OK," Jason said, talking through a mouthful of hot dog.

Adela linked her arm with his. "First thing's first, chum. Show me where you got that delicious-looking dog."

"Iph a turkey dog." Jason smiled at her. We all headed into the park.

At the festival entrance, the four of us waited patiently while security guards waved their metal detectors over us and checked our purses.

"This is weird," I heard Jamal whisper to Jason as we got clear of the checkpoint.

"They're just worried about Rodney, man. You know the drill."

"Cotton candy, dead ahead, kids!" Adela grabbed us by the hands and pulled us into the thoroughfare.

The festival was here, and we were gonna enjoy it to the fullest.

We waited half an hour for the Bell Ringer, a spinning ride that used centrifugal force to pin you to the wall before dropping the floor out from under you. Jason threw up right after . . . then asked if we could ride it again.

Adela and I went through the Phantasmagoria Scare House together because the boys didn't want to. They claimed it was because they wanted funnel cakes instead, but Del and I decided they were too scared. (. . . it was actually pretty scary.)

After we got off the Himalaya, the four of us split up, Adela with Jason and me with Jamal.

"You hungry?" he asked.

"Starving."

"Wanna hit the food trucks?" Jamal held out his hand. I looked at it, stunned. *Jamal Giles wants to hold my hand.* He cleared his throat, and I snapped out of it.

"The 'Corridor of Cuisine'? Yes, please."

I took his hand. His skin was so smooth, not at all what I was expecting from an athlete who played as hard as he did.

Adrenaline crashed through me. My whole body tingled with excitement.

Even my ears.

If I wanted to be invisible tonight, though, holding hands with our star running back while walking the main festival thoroughfare was definitely not the way to do it.

Everyone saw us together. Like, *everyone*. Nessa and her

friend Josie spotted us as they waited in line to ride the Zingo. Mr. Brand smiled as we passed him and his wife. Mrs. Cunningham winked at me as she sold us two strawberry whips. Ben Briggs gave Jamal a high five, then squinted at me as he chewed on a massive turkey leg.

"We have trig together. Sorry about your test," I said to him.

"Grades are whatever." He shrugged, then disappeared into the crowd.

Jamal and I smiled at each other, then walked on. I tried not to notice Kristi Crosby and her hench-friends glaring at me from a nearby table, but it was hard to miss them. I took the high road and smiled at them as I entwined my fingers with Jamal's.

"You good?" he asked.

"Great."

And I was.

For the first time in a long time—in weeks—I felt happiness deep in my chest. I'd forgotten how good, how intoxicating joy could feel. After spending the last three weeks trying to rush through everything so I didn't have to feel anything, I wanted this feeling, this moment, his hand in mine, to last forever.

Naturally, that was when my little sister appeared.

"I need to talk to you," Nessa urged, pulling me away from Jamal. "Right now." She and Josie were panting, panic putting color in their cheeks.

"Sorry, this is my sister, be right back!" I called out to Jamal over my shoulder.

Nessa dragged me behind a ticket stand. She was sweating hard.

"Have you been running?" I asked. "Wait, are those my earrings?"

"Yes to both. I've been looking everywhere for you. You're not answering texts. Mom is freaking out."

I pulled out my phone. Seven texts from Nessa, sixteen from my mother. I opened Mom's first.

ARE YOU AT THE FESTIVAL?? SOMEONE SAW THAT CADY BOY THERE, COME HOME RIGHT NOW!!!

"They spotted Rodney Cady here?"

"Casey, we saw him two minutes ago! By the food trucks!" Nessa said. "We tried to tell a security guard, but there was a fight outside the livestock show, so they're all dealing with that."

"We should get out of here—wait. He was by the food trucks?"

Nessa nodded. Realization hit me first, then dread.

"That's close to Mrs. Cunningham's fruit whip stand. What if . . . what if he's here for her because she got him suspended?"

"Casey, he was carrying something," Nessa said, hushed seriousness in her voice. "I think it was . . . it could've been a gun."

The hair all over my body stood on end as that sank in.

I took off running, heading for Mrs. Cunningham's stand. Nessa was the runner in the family, but I had to do something. I didn't know why, really. I was no hero. I just felt the need to find a guard, get an adult, stop Rodney, *something*. Because . . . because . . .

. . . because my dad would've done something.

I was two hundred feet from the Corridor of Cuisine when I heard the first scream. It wasn't the scream of someone having fun on a ride, or even someone freaked out by the paper ghosts in the Phantasmagoria.

It was a true scream, one backed with real fear.

I ran faster.

I rounded into the Corridor of Cuisine at top speed, only to find a wall of people in front of me. I pushed to the front to see Rodney Cady and Mrs. Cunningham.

Rodney had a pistol pointed directly at Mrs. Cunningham's chest, and they were surrounded by a circle of onlookers. Many of them were familiar: Kristi and her friends, Mr. Brand, Ben Briggs. Even Shonda Offord looked on.

Rodney was distraught, his clothes and hair disheveled, angry tears in his eyes.

"This is all your fault!" he yelled at Mrs. Cunningham, wiping tears away with his free hand. The gun shook in the other. "It's your fault they want to take me away! Your fault my parents don't want me in the house anymore!"

"No, Rodney, you're confused. This is *your* fault," Mrs. Cunningham said, her voice full of a teacher's calm. "*You* chose to cheat on my test, *you* chose to tell people you were going to hurt others, and *you* were punished by your parents for your actions."

"You got me suspended! The cops are after me! I'm probably gonna go to jail for this!" Rodney's hand shook harder. "And nobody go anywhere! You're all gonna watch this!" He waved the gun at the crowd. Everyone stood very still; many of the teens in the crowd were recording the scene on their phones.

"Rodney, give me the gun." Mrs. Cunningham held out her

hand, a small woman in a fruit-patterned apron standing up to a crying teenager with a gun.

"You're out of your mind if you think I'm giving this up. This is the only thing keeping me safe." Rodney took a step toward her. "You don't get to take this from me. In fact, the only thing you're gonna take is a bullet." He pulled back the gun's hammer.

"Freeze!" shouted a voice.

All of us turned to see two security guards, a woman and a man, pushing their way into the circle of onlookers. They both trained their guns on Rodney.

Rodney grabbed Mrs. Cunningham, putting her between himself and the security guards. Just like that, it was a hostage situation.

"Let her go!" said the male security guard. "This doesn't need to get worse for you, kid."

"Look at me. How do I come back from this?!" Rodney screamed. The security guards split apart, making it hard for Rodney to keep his gun on them and Mrs. Cunningham.

"None of these people deserve to get hurt tonight," the woman security guard said gently. "Everyone came out for a good time, not for this."

"I know what people wanna see. That's why they watch my videos. I always show them something fun," Rodney said. His motions were growing more erratic. He whipped the gun back and forth, trying to keep it trained on one of the guards. The crowd grew thicker as more people came over to see the commotion. I spotted Adela and Jason across the circle from me. Adela's phone was out, recording it all.

"Let's just put our guns down and talk this out. Like adults," said the male guard.

"Yes, Rodney. Listen to the nice man," said Mrs. Cunningham.

"You shut your mouth!" Rodney screamed at her.

Rodney didn't notice the third guard coming toward him until it was too late.

It all happened at once.

The guard grabbed Rodney's arm—they started to struggle—the crowd panicked, some of them ducking, some of the teenagers still recording on their phones—Rodney pulled the trigger—BLAM!—a roar filled my ears as he fired into the air—I gasped—the guard kept fighting him—Rodney's gun waved in all directions, pointing this way and that—he fired again— BLAMMM!—the crowd scattered, trying to anticipate where he'd aim next—everyone was reacting now except for Adela—she kept recording on her phone—then the gun was pointing right at her—I saw her register she was in danger—I rushed forward to do something, anything, just trying to get between Rodney's gun and Adela—but I wasn't fast enough—how does a teenage girl outrun a bullet?—he was pointing the gun right at my friend, my best friend, my Adela—Rodney pulled the trigger—the gun thundered as the slug broke the sound barrier—I closed my eyes—

BLAAAAAAAAAAAAAAAA—

And then the roar of the bullet slowed.

And then it held in the air, one long note.

Just like . . . *just like* . . .

Just like the clock in the classroom.

There was a cold tingling on my wrist.

I opened my eyes.

Everyone and everything around me was perfectly still. Dozens of scared faces, all frozen in fear. Kids trying to run, adults pushing each other over, Ben Briggs tripping over Kristi Crosby as they tried to get away, everyone scared of the panicking teenager and the gun in his hand.

But no one was moving.

Time had stopped.

Not slowed down, like before.

Nothing was moving.

Time had completely *stopped*.

I looked at my wrist. The *gibhann* bracelet glowed brightly. Nessa stood next to me, her hand just above it.

"Holy smokes. I can't believe that worked," Nessa panted, pulling her hand back.

She'd put the bracelet on me.

"What did you do?" I asked. "How did you—"

Nessa pulled her sleeve back, revealing her own *gibhann* bracelet. "Uh, don't be mad? I wanted to wear your earrings, so I went by the house before we came to the festival. I opened your jewelry box, and there it was."

"So why did you bring it here?"

"Um, again, don't be mad? I wanted to show Josie what it could do . . ."

"How did you know what it could do?"

Guilt crossed over Nessa's face. "I am not a faster sprinter than Abigail Lowther."

My eyes went wide. "*That's* how you won your race today? You used Dad's bracelet?"

"Casey, focus. And *look*." Nessa pointed.

The bullet hung in the air between the barrel of Rodney's gun and Adela.

One more millisecond of real time, and it would strike my best friend.

I walked through the sea of frozen people and stepped up to the bullet. There was no way Adela could dodge this, like some superhero on TV.

In another millisecond—the blink of an eye—I would lose my best friend.

If I didn't do anything, Adela would die.

I reached for it.

"Casey, be careful," said Nessa.

"I will be." I gingerly touched the round with my fingertip. It was hot to the touch. I held my hand out, hovering my palm directly over the bullet.

Deep breath, Casey. You can do this.

I closed my fingers around the lead round.

The bullet fizzled as the laws of physics broke and it lost all momentum. I opened my fingers. The bullet sat loose in my palm, now completely harmless.

"Holy smokes," Nessa said. "You just caught a bullet. Like, out of the air!"

I smiled at my sister. "And saved Del."

Nessa ran her hand over the *gibhann* bracelet. "Casey, what *are* these? How are they so powerful you can catch a bullet? And, like, do you think *I* could catch a bullet?"

"I hope you never have to. And we're not gonna figure any of that out right now"—I turned back to Rodney and Mrs.

Cunningham—"because first, we've got to do something about *him*."

"What do you think we should do?" Nessa asked.

The answer struck me like a flash of lightning.

"I'm on it," I said.

"I just don't get it. He brought a gun to the fall festival to hurt your teacher, but, what, he loaded it with blanks . . . ?" Mom asked.

Nessa and I exchanged a quick smile, and then I shrugged.

"Rodney has never been too bright. Just likes getting a lot of attention," I said. The three of us were eating breakfast at the kitchen table, a copy of the *Fanto Falls Times* spread out in front of our mother. The story was all anyone could talk about. Splashed across the front page was a picture of Rodney Cady being loaded into a police car. Mrs. Cunningham stood by, watching the whole thing. **HERO TEACHER STOPS SHOOTER**, screamed the headline in a font twice the normal size. If you squinted hard enough, you could read the photo's byline: Adela Anklesaria.

She'd gotten the whole thing.

No one could figure out why there wasn't any damage from Rodney's shots. The popular public theory—and the theory Mayor King was happy to go with to keep us out of national news—was that Rodney loaded the gun with blanks. A prank gone wrong.

"I'm just glad the woman he took hostage managed to get the gun away from him. And it's a miracle you girls weren't hurt." Mom stood and kissed us both on the tops of our heads, just like she had when we were little. "I also hope it didn't mess up your date with, ah, what was his name?"

"Jamal *Giiiiiiles*," teased Nessa.

"It wasn't a date. More like a . . . get-together," I said, red rising in my face.

"Well, I hope you and Jamal have another get-together planned," Mom said. "One not interrupted by a gunman."

"We do. This weekend," I muttered.

Mom smiled at me. "Go get 'em, kiddo." She drained her coffee and put the mug in the sink.

As she passed Dad's empty seat, she slowly ran her hand across the top rail.

"I need you girls to do me a favor," Mom said, her back to us.

"Sure," I said.

Mom turned toward us, tears in her eyes. "Can you both hug your mother for a second?"

Nessa and I got up and pulled our mother into a long, lovely hug. I could feel Mom's heart beating fast against my arm. Nessa's breath was hot on my shoulder.

For the first time in a long time, it felt like we were a family again.

I looked at where my father used to sit at the head of our kitchen table.

Our family had spent hundreds of nights at this table, talking about the mundane parts of our days, from doing jigsaw puzzles to debating history and books and TV shows and movies. Dad offered us advice when we needed it, consolation when we wanted it, and education when we least expected it.

He was our father. We would always miss him.

I would always miss him.

Always.

But we had each other.

Mom, Nessa, me.

Our family.

We had each other.

We would keep going.

We could do this.

For him.

That night, Nessa and I sat at the kitchen table, both of us wearing our *gibhann* bracelets.

"Ready?" I asked.

"Do it," she said.

I dialed my phone and turned on the speaker. The line rang twice before someone picked up.

"Hello, dear hearts," said the lawyer. "I am so thrilled you stopped Mr. Cady from shooting Miss Anklesaria."

Nessa and I looked at each other, astonishment on our faces.

"Mr. Fraction, how did you know that?" I asked.

"Oh, we Time Striders tend to know things," he said. You

could almost hear the twinkle in his eye. "I trust you have questions about your bracelets."

"We do," said Nessa. She leaned closer to the phone. "Are they really from our dad?"

"Yes, Vanessa Dodson, they are. Your father was a Time Strider, like me. He asked me to give you those whenever he thought you'd need them."

"What's a Time Strider?" I asked.

"Time travelers, of course. We make wrongs right. Your father was one of us, a very well-respected Time Strider, before he met your mother and retired to Fanto Falls."

"Are we . . . are we Striders, too?" I asked.

"Not yet. But you might be someday. The *gibhann* bracelets are the first trial for any potential Time Strider. We have to see how you'll use them. Will you use them selfishly? Or selflessly? For good or for bad?"

Nessa and I looked at each other.

"Um, Mr. Fraction, I cheated on my track race," admitted Nessa.

"And I used mine for my math test."

"Minor infractions both. Your *real* test was when Mr. Cady attacked the festival," the lawyer said. "And you passed it with flying colors. You could have quite the future with us."

"Was . . ." I swallowed, working up the courage to ask the next question. "Was Adela going to die yesterday?"

"Yes. But *you* stopped that from happening. And I'm sure your father would be very proud of you for doing so."

"Does our mom know about all this?" Nessa asked.

There was a pause on the line. "She does not, dear heart. And I don't think Henry would want her to, do you?"

Nessa shook her head. "Probably not."

"I agree," said the lawyer. "But now that you've saved Miss Anklesaria and seen what the *gibhann* bracelets can do, would you like to know more? Would you like to start the second trial of the Time Striders?"

I looked at the bracelet, its silver metal bright against my skin.

I had spent so many hours alone in my room, thinking about Dad being gone. Thinking about the Dad-shaped hole he'd left behind. Wondering why he had to go before we did, wondering why it happened, wondering who had cursed us so, that we'd lost the man we loved most.

Mourning.

Mourning what our future could have been.

Mourning that future snapping shut in front of us.

But Dad planned ahead. He knew we'd want to know more about him once he was gone. He left this legacy for us.

There was comfort in learning there was still more to know about him. About his life before *we* were his life.

It was a way to fill the Dad-shaped hole.

Then a question occurred to me, and I knew I had to ask it.

"Mr. Fraction?" I asked. "Can Time Striders . . . *meet* former Time Striders?"

"What do you mean, Miss Dodson?"

I can do this.

"You're telling us time travel is not only real, but that our dad used to do it, right? So what I'm wondering is . . . if we get involved with you, if *we* time travel with you . . . is there a way we can see our dad again?"

Nessa gasped.

The phone was silent. The clock in the living room ticked off several seconds as we waited to hear the lawyer's answer. *Tick . . . tick . . . tick . . .*

Finally, his answer came.

"If you pass the trials, yes. That is a possibility. But it will be very, very dangerous, both for you and for him. And you would have to pass all six trials with perfect scores, dearest, which isn't easily done."

I held my hand out to my sister. "It'll be dangerous, he says."

"Very, *very* dangerous," she said. "But worth it." Nessa took my hand, the *gibhann* bracelet shining against her wrist.

"Mr. Fraction, we'd like to start the second trial," I said.

"Capital," said the lawyer.

There was a curt knock at the front door.

I stood up from the table.

"On it," I said.

I opened the door and started our future.

MECHA GIRL

by AXIE OH

I HAD THOUGHT TIME AWAY FROM PEACECROFT
would clear my mind and put a stop to the rumors that began
right before school let out at the end of last year. I was wrong
on both counts. Shame on me for thinking problems disappear
if you just ignore them. Of course, the irony was that this all
began *with* a disappearance—of my sister, Ji-eun Shin. Even
now, the authorities haven't discovered her whereabouts, nor
that of the ten billion in school property she'd taken with her.

"You're not really going to accept his challenge, are you,
Auri?" My best friend, Gabby Tarigan, huffed and puffed as
she followed me across campus, clutching my helmet to her
chest. It was the final piece of the armor I'd donned back in our
dorm room. "We just got back. We haven't even unpacked yet."

I slowed my pace. "This won't take longer than a minute.
After I beat his ass, we can go grab breakfast."

Sighing, she conceded, "I think I saw dim sum on the menu."

We continued our steady march, the manicured grass
soft beneath our feet. Peacecroft was beautiful at all times of
the year, but there was something about late August that reminded me of the first time I stepped onto school grounds, the
humidity clinging to my skin like a balm. The great trees that
surrounded the campus swayed in the breeze off the Pacific.

We were an island school, not affiliated with any country
but close enough to a few that we often caught pleasure yachts
in our waters, and sometimes the occasional military vessel.

A banner that read **PEACECROFT, SCHOOL FOR THE FU-
TURE LEADERS OF THE WORLDS ALLIANCE** hung from the
Founder's Building, which seemed like a bold claim, but the
students here would literally inherit the Earth. Among them

was Olufemi Fall, heiress to the militant Fall Foundation; Gabrielle Tarigan, second daughter of the Spice Queen of Singapore; and Phineas Delaune of the infamous Delaune family, which had already established a dozen space colonies between the Earth and the moon.

As for me, I was a scholarship student, a nobody, given a spot at the prestigious school because of my brilliant sister, the youngest professor in the illustrious history of Peacecroft. When the school approached her about a position five years ago, she had only one condition: If they wanted her, they had to take me as well.

Gabby and I approached the massive Mori Athletics and Training Hall, a donation from the powerful Mori clan, and stepped through the automatic doors that hummed as we entered.

The building was impressive inside, boasting several gymnasiums and workout rooms, three swimming pools, and a sauna. The martial arts facilities were located in the back and included a traditional Japanese dojo, complete with tatami mats and papered windows letting in natural light.

The room was already packed wall to wall with members of the kendo club, but also students in years ten, eleven, and twelve. It wasn't every day that the top students at Peacecroft sparred. Not that I was the top girl in my class any longer; my grades had dropped soon after my sister's disappearance.

Noticing my arrival, the students parted to make way, the whispers ratcheting up a notch.

Waiting in the center of the room, his back to me, stood Takashi Mori.

A summer vacationing on a hover yacht in Singapore had left me tan and soft.

A summer spent in the forests of Japan had also left him tan, but definitely *not* soft. His shoulders seemed wider, and it wasn't just the padding on his protective gear. What had he done all summer? Sat shirtless beneath a waterfall?

Beside me, Gabby whistled low, then handed over her water bottle. "Drink up."

"Ladies!" Phin Delaune approached, holding a tricolored flag. "I'm refereeing this match. No foul play," he said with a wink, then added as he took his position outside the mats, "Unless it's entertaining, of course."

"Auri," Gabby said, glancing around the room at the crowd of students, at Takashi, who stood beside Olufemi Fall, saying whatever tall, perfect people say to one another. "I'm not sure about this. You haven't practiced in months. Maybe you should forfeit."

"Aurelia." Takashi's voice traveled from across the room, sounding *bored*. "Are we doing this?"

It drove me up a wall that he called me by my full name. No one ever called me Aurelia except for my sister, and only when she was angry. Auri was for most of the time, and Eun-kyung, my Korean name, was for when she was feeling nostalgic and thinking of our parents.

Eun-kyung-ah, life isn't always easy, but we'll get through it together.

"Give me my helmet," I said, and Gabby relinquished it with a sigh, plopping it into my hand. I lifted the headgear over my head, the metal bars obscuring my line of sight.

I turned to face Takashi, who'd already taken his position on the mats, his legs apart, his weapon—a curved, single-edged wooden sword—at his side.

Walking over, Phin handed me an identical sword, then raised his voice for the crowd. "In the interest of fairness, both competitors will be using practice swords. First to draw blood wins." The crowd gasped, and Phin laughed, clearly amused by himself. "I jest. Three strikes to the body will end the duel. Victory goes to whoever makes the third strike."

I raised my sword, and Takashi mirrored my movement.

We began slow, circling, testing each other's grips on the weapons.

I might not have trained all summer, but my muscle memory kicked in. Sliding my foot forward, I dodged his block, raising my sword to connect with his shoulder.

Phin's flag went up. "First strike goes to Auri Shin!"

Gabby's victory yell drowned out all the other cheers, as well as a few boos, which, wow, *rude*.

Maybe this wouldn't be so hard.

Then Takashi rushed me. I barely raised my sword in time, bracing my legs. The impact pushed me back a few inches, my feet skidding against the mat.

His sword slid against mine to the hilt. I felt a dull pressure as the edge of his blade dug into my shoulder.

Phin yelled, "Second strike to Mori!"

Takashi didn't immediately step back. Through the slits of his helmet, I could see his arrogant, upturned chin. "You're not even trying to win, are you, Aurelia? It's the same as last year. It's like you've given up."

"You should be happy," I seethed. For years, Takashi and I had tried to one-up each other, vying for that number one spot, ever since I'd arrived in year six and ended his ubiquitous reign over the school. We'd competed in athletics, in academics, even in the arts. "There's no one to challenge you. Your place as top of the class is secure. Congratulations, you've won."

Takashi put pressure on my sword, then stepped back. "I take no pleasure in an empty victory."

We'd each taken a strike, but it didn't matter. Only the last would determine the victory. Just one more hit, and I could go back to my dorm, wallow in the unfairness of it all. Who cared what Takashi thought? It was my life, my future. I could throw it all away if I wanted to.

"Maybe the rumors are true," Takashi said, "that your sister was working for an illegal tech dealer. That she stole school property for the money. That she resented the privileged students she taught, the families that destroyed her own."

He was saying aloud everything that had been churning in my head for months. Why had Ji-eun left without a word? Where had she gone? What was she hiding?

"That she abandoned you."

My breath caught, and then anger filled me up, powerful, uncontrollable. I rushed at him, raising my sword and putting all my force behind the strike. Even knowing that this was wrong, that this was just a duel, that with this much force, I could truly hurt him.

For once, I was glad for Takashi's fast reflexes.

My sword splintered against his. I felt a sharp, fleeting pain as a shard of wood shot through the bars of my helmet and sliced my cheek. The momentum drove me forward, and I fell to the floor. Behind me, I heard him curse thickly. There was a stunned silence, and then the students who'd been watching rushed onto the mats. Most went to Takashi, though a few, like Gabby and Phin, came to me.

"Auri, oh my god, are you all right?" Gabby helped me to my feet. I yanked the helmet from my head, whipping around to face Takashi, who'd already taken off his own.

Before I could say anything, he said, "That went too far. Forgive me."

Something in his expression made my heart clench. He searched my face, his eyes dropping to my cheek and widening slightly in alarm.

"You're bleeding," he said. "Aurelia." He took a step forward, his hand reaching out, an almost unconscious movement.

"I don't need your pity." Turning, I fled from the room.

In the infirmary, I laid my head back against the exam chair, closing my eyes as Hana, the school nurse, applied a Band-Aid to my cheek.

"First day back, and you're already in my office." She clicked her tongue. "Ji-eun would not be pleased."

"Well, she's not here, is she?" I said, then immediately felt like a brat. After me, the person most affected by my sister's disappearance was Hana, who had been her closest friend at Peacecroft. They'd bonded over their shared identities as Korean women and similar backgrounds. Hana wasn't a war orphan like Ji-eun and me, but her family had been torn apart when a huge conglomerate had ousted them from their ancestral home to build a military base. It was ironic that both she and Ji-eun had ended up on the Peacecroft campus, catering to the children of the rich and privileged.

A shadow fell across the room as an aircraft flew over campus.

Hana followed the movement with a frown. "She didn't tell me either, you know."

I looked up to see an odd expression pass over her features. It almost looked like . . . resentment, but then it was gone, the sun appearing through the window.

"You look exhausted," Hana said with a closed-lipped smile. "Classes don't start until tomorrow. Why don't you get some rest? You can use one of the beds in the back room."

"I'm fine," I said, getting up from the chair. "I'll go back to the dorm."

"Here." She handed me a small paper cup with a single blue pill in it. "This'll help you go to sleep."

I took the cup. "Thanks, Hana." But her face was already turned to the window.

I didn't head back to the dorms; instead, I ended up in the basement of the science building. It was mostly laboratories down here, plus a room my sister and I had dubbed the Hideout.

Like my sister's classroom and office, the Hideout had been thoroughly searched.

I righted a chair and picked up a glass soda bottle from the floor, dumping it into a recycling bin that was already packed full of them.

I flopped down on the couch, coughing as a cloud of dust rose in protest. Waving my hand in the air, I looked around the room. I'd left the lights off, and only the blue glow of a vending machine against the back wall illuminated the space.

My eyes landed on the jukebox that Ji-eun had installed in the corner, which only played songs from our favorite video games. A large bookshelf was stuffed with manhwa, graphic novels, and books; beside it was another case filled with plushies, board games, and robot kits. The walls were decorated with posters.

Not posters of famous scientists or singers, but magical girls.

Girls with brightly colored hair. Girls with weapons as accessories. Girls who fight for love and justice.

You're always so practical, and then there's this side of you. A memory rose up of Ji-eun the last time I saw her. We were on this couch, a starry pink blanket strewn across our legs as I played a video game on a handheld console while she watched the latest episode of a TV show starring magical girls.

"This *is* practical," she responded.

I put down my game, and she made room for me beneath the blanket, and we watched an episode where the heroine transformed from an ordinary high school student to a magical girl with superpowered attack moves that had names like "infinity heart ignite" and "love aperture springtime blossom," saving the world in time to perform at a school talent show in front of her crush.

"So, tell me about this fight," she said as an ad began to play before the start of the next episode.

I grimaced, not wanting to recall the event. Earlier, an upper-classman had said disparaging things about me, like that I was only allowed into the school because of Ji-eun. It didn't matter that I was *almost* at the top of my class; I didn't deserve my spot. In a burst of anger, I had flattened the twelfth-year with a kick to the stomach. Afterward, I'd been taken to Headmistress Peacecroft's office. When Ji-eun had arrived a few minutes later, the disappointment on her face had been all the punishment I'd needed.

"No matter how upset you are, you can't lash out like that. Consider the consequences. You might have been expelled!" She sighed. "Sometimes you just don't *think*, Aurelia."

When I surfaced from the memory, I was still holding the cup with the pill in it. Was that why she'd left me behind? Had she finally realized I was a burden after all?

Sighing, I looked around for something to take the pill with, and my eyes landed on the vending machine, glowing blue in the darkness.

Ji-eun had stocked it with her favorite drinks from all over the world—bubble fizzes from Japan, milk sodas from Korea. It didn't take standard currency, only coins that Ji-eun had fashioned herself. I fished in my pocket, surprised to find one caught in the seam. For a moment, I stared down at the simple design—a round coin with a square hole cut in the middle—a sudden heat at the corners of my eyes.

I inserted the coin and pressed the buttons with my initials, A and *S*. Inside the vending machine, the metal claw began to spiral. As it released a peach soda into the chute, I noticed there was something *behind* the can. A small box. Quickly, I inserted my last coin, once again pressing my initials.

The claw began to move, and I willed it to go faster. When the box finally fell, I crouched down and took out both the can and the box, putting the can aside.

What could it be? Had Ji-eun left me a message, a clue as to where she'd gone?

Slowly, I opened the box to reveal a pendant necklace. The chain was long enough that I could fit it over my head, the pendant falling to rest beneath my collarbones.

It was a beautiful necklace. The chain was silver, the heart-shaped pendant a single bright red jewel. A ruby? I brushed my thumb over the faceted surface, only to notice that there was a catch on the back of it.

I pressed down and jerked back when the vending machine made a loud hissing sound. Then it *opened*.

Cool mist swirled out, enveloping me. When it cleared, I stood, staring slack-jawed at what was inside.

It was a suit of armor.

It looked nothing like any armor I'd ever seen. First of all, it was *pink*. Well, not pink, exactly, but a vibrant fuchsia color with aquamarine accents.

It also appeared to be a single continuous piece, from the long, sleek legs to the chest, complete with contours that would fit snugly against a body, flexible gauntlets, and even a stylish helmet. Here the accents were the most striking—the shield of the helmet was an opaque blue.

A . . . mecha suit. What was it for? And why had Ji-eun left it for *me*?

Because of the cramped space of the vending machine, the armor was folded in on itself. I knew without a doubt that it would look magnificent when it was standing tall, its legs extended. I reached out a hand.

A loud boom rocked the building; plaster fell from the ceiling and hit the ground.

An explosion?

Then the intercom blared. "Attention all students, faculty, and personnel. An unknown military force has breached campus defenses. Peacecroft is under attack. I repeat, Peacecroft is under attack."

Crouching behind the front doors of the science building, I watched as a group of soldiers in fatigues cornered two underclassmen on the lawn. One of the boys made a break for it, and the soldiers raised their guns.

I pushed open the door, stumbling outside. "Stop!"

An electric shock hit the boy in the back, and he crumpled unconscious to the ground. They began to tie him up.

My relief that they were using stun guns, meant to debilitate only, was replaced with anger. They were taking students, likely to ransom them to their wealthy families.

When they finished securing the boy, all three soldiers turned their heads in my direction.

Oh shit. I scrambled back into the science building.

I raced through the halls, slipping inside the first open door and shutting it behind me. It was a classroom, the long tables cleaned and pushed to the side.

Shouts echoed in the distance. The soldiers would be here any minute.

I felt a heat against my chest, above my heart, and my hand moved to grip the pendant. Palming the necklace, I looked down.

Before, the jewel at the center had been red, but now it was a vibrant, glowing blue. It almost seemed to pulsate. I pressed down on the jewel, and there was an audible *click*. At first, nothing happened, but then I heard a crashing sound, coming closer. An object burst through the wall.

The armor.

It must have flown from the vending machine, *through concrete*, directly to me.

A calm, vaguely feminine voice issued from the armor. "Permission to begin transformation sequence?"

I stripped down to my underwear—because that just seemed logical—and said, "Permission granted."

In a whir of motion, the armor broke apart, and then reformed around me. It truly was like a transformation, pieces adhering to my arms and legs. The jewel pendant unclasped from my neck and attached to the front of the armor at the center of my chest.

The whole "transformation" took less than a minute.

The helmet slipped over my head, and data immediately begin to flit across the inside, like a screen.

Heat signatures appeared as soldiers streamed into the classroom, surrounding me. My armor scanned them, identifying weapons and other potential threats, even their spiked heart rates.

One of the soldiers released an electric shot. It hit me in the shoulder and . . . fizzled.

Well, then.

I attacked them in a fury, all those martial arts classes paying off.

I'd thought the armor would limit my speed, but it was the opposite, feeding into my reflexes, powering my strikes. The suit warned me of incoming threats, guiding my body when necessary, sort of like an auto-lock mechanism.

In a matter of minutes, all the soldiers were either unconscious or groaning on the floor.

I didn't linger, sprinting back to the quad.

Sarani Peacecroft might have been a pacifist, but she was also a pragmatist, and the school had a defensive system in place for instances like this. I looked up at the great dome that now encased the campus, which I knew stretched to the edge of the island, ending at the shore. Only those with school IDs could cross the barrier. As long as the students made it to the beach past the dome, they'd be safe.

I caught sight of movement at the edge of the forest.

Olufemi stood with a few of the younger students, shepherding them beneath the trees. Turning back, her eyes widened. "Takashi!"

I followed her gaze to where Takashi was sprinting across the lawn, carrying two first-years in his arms. He still wore the armor from our bout this morning, though his helmet was missing, his hair plastered to his brow.

Immediately, I noticed what had caught Olufemi's attention. A large piece of concrete had broken off the nearest building, and Takashi and the first-years were directly in its trajectory.

I raced across the quad, but I knew I wouldn't make it in time. I wasn't fast enough. On the screen of my helmet, an icon appeared, and the voice from earlier said, "Activate flight mobility?"

"Yes!" I shouted without stopping.

"Affirmative. Flight mobility activated."

My body jerked into the air, toes barely skimming the ground, as thrusters ignited from the back of the suit. I arrived in time to catch the piece of concrete.

I tossed it aside, turning to find Takashi crouched on the ground, his body covering the first-years. He spoke to them briefly, then released them before turning to face me.

"Who are you?" he demanded. "Why are you helping us?"

I scowled, though he couldn't see my expression beneath the helmet. It was just like Takashi to ask questions instead of responding normally to this situation. Would it hurt him to say *thanks for saving my life*?

"Thank you," he said haltingly.

"N-no problem," I responded, my voice altered by the helmet.

"Their leader passed through earlier," Takashi said,

"heading toward the headmistress's office. If you stop them, you might be able to end this whole operation."

I was annoyed at him for taking control of the situation after I'd just saved his life, but . . .

That *was* a good plan.

"Aurelia," Takashi said. My heart almost short-circuited. How did he know it was me? But then I realized he was speaking to Olufemi, who'd jogged over to us. "She was on her way to the dorms. She could still be there now."

"She's fine," I said, exasperated with him. Why did he always have to look out for everyone, as if he were personally responsible for each student at Peacecroft? "She can take care of herself."

His head, which had been canted in the direction of the dorms, now swung back toward me.

I tensed as he studied me—the armor covered my body head to toe, but it was also rather . . . formfitting. His eyes lingered on the pendant.

"Let's go, Takashi," Olufemi said. "Mecha girl is right. Auri Shin isn't top girl for nothing."

Takashi let himself be led away, though I could feel his eyes on me as I sprinted toward the main building, flying the last few leagues and bursting through the wall of the headmistress's office.

The red sighting lights of a dozen guns pinned me. I took in the scene. Headmistress Peacecroft was facing off against the leader of the soldiers, who whipped her head around to look at me.

I blinked, then blinked again.

The leader wore a suit almost identical to mine, but for one difference. While mine was fuchsia and aquamarine, hers was purple and black.

Only one person had this technology.

I gasped. "Ji-eun?"

Why was she attacking the school? Why was she kidnapping students? I wanted to ask so many questions. *Where did you disappear to? Why didn't you tell me you were leaving? Why didn't you take me with you?*

A loud beeping sound drew my attention to a huge digital map on the wall behind the headmistress's desk. Several green blips were approaching the school from the east side. My suit notified me of the same thing, green text scrolling across the bottom of my screen. Reinforcements from the militaries of the surrounding countries would arrive in fifteen minutes.

"Return my students, and I'll allow you to escape," Headmistress Peacecroft said.

"This isn't a negotiation." Ji-eun's voice came out hard and unrecognizable. "And you're coming with us."

"I will not let you take me without a fight." Mistress Peacecroft spoke with certainty though she held no weapon.

Ji-eun sneered. "I thought you were a pacifist."

"I am. Violence is unconscionable, but I will defend the liberty of myself and my students until my very last breath."

"Then let this be your last!"

I noticed then that Ji-eun held a sword, black like her armor with a purple blade.

One swipe, and she'd cut Headmistress Peacecroft down. I needed to act, but half the soldiers still had their stun guns pointed at me, and the others had theirs pointed at Headmistress Peacecroft. That many electric shocks hitting her body at once might kill her.

The door to the office flew open, and the entire kendo club burst into the room, led by Takashi and Olufemi.

In the chaos, I sprinted toward Ji-eun.

"Threat identified, weapon activated, releasing sword."

A sword ejected from my gauntlet. In a single motion, I grabbed it, sliding between Ji-eun and the headmistress in time to block Ji-eun's downward swing. The force of our connecting swords reverberated throughout the room.

Ji-eun glided backward with her thrusters, releasing me. And then she flew out of the room through the hole in the wall.

I spared a glance for my classmates—Takashi was holding back soldiers with his katana, while Olufemi twirled a long pole and the rest of the club pummeled the soldiers with their wooden swords—before following my sister.

Ji-eun waited for me on the lawn.

"Little sister," she sneered, "let's see what you've learned while I've been away."

She attacked, her thrusters igniting.

Immediately, I was put on the defensive, desperately parrying blows. She was faster, stronger.

She backhanded me, and I went flying across the grass, somehow managing to hold on to my sword.

I couldn't defeat her. She was more familiar with the suits' capabilities; she'd *designed* them.

But that wasn't the reason I was going to lose. I was going to lose because I didn't *want* to fight her. How could I? She was my *sister*, the one person I looked up to most in the world.

She was my hero.

Ji-eun flew at me, and this time when I raised my sword, she knocked it out of my hand.

"You're pathetic," she said, and my heart felt like it was breaking. "I've always been disappointed in you."

The memory rose up from earlier, the same memory of Ji-eun and me on the couch as we watched her magical girl show.

"Sometimes you just don't *think*, Aurelia." My stomach dropped at her words. Why did I always have to act out and disappoint her? Why couldn't I just keep quiet?

"But that's what I admire about you," she continued, and I looked up, tears pricking the corners of my eyes. She was smiling. "You're all heart.

"He deserved it, didn't he?" she said, and when I started to nod vigorously, she poked me in the forehead. "Well, even if he did deserve it, you shouldn't use your powers for harm."

"Powers?" I laughed, rubbing my brow.

"Yes, a magical girl only uses her powers in defense of love and justice."

I laughed again, then said haltingly, "I—I'm sorry. I never wanted to disappoint you. I want to make you proud of me."

She looked at me, her eyes bright with warmth and accep-tance. "A day doesn't go by when you don't make me proud."

On the lawn, I got to my feet.

I might have lost my sword, but I had one more weapon in my arsenal. I lifted my hand to the pendant, pressing down on the jewel. Immediately, the voice flooded my helmet, and I recognized it now, though I hadn't before, hidden beneath the robotic overlay: Ji-eun's voice.

"Activating Aurelia's secret heart power."

I rolled my eyes. Of course Ji-eun would name the weapon something ridiculous.

A bright light exploded from my palms.

In the aftermath, I reached down and tore off the helmet of my opponent's smoking, stolen suit. Looking at me, defeated but furious, was Hana.

"How did you know?" she fumed. I knew what she was ask-ing. How did I know she wasn't Ji-eun? How did I know it was an imposter beneath the helmet?

"Because," I said, "there's no one in the world who believes in me more than my sister."

The suit was a prototype. Hana had stolen it from Ji-eun's lab shortly after my sister's disappearance, though she hadn't had an opportunity to use it until the first day back from summer break, when the dome was deactivated to let in returning students. Her plan was to pin the kidnappings on my sister, who she truly believed had stolen billions of dollars worth of tech. The soldiers were mercenaries who had been promised a cut of the ransom money. Surprisingly, she hadn't meant for me to get involved. The blue pill she'd given me in the infirmary was supposed to knock me out.

I learned all this later from Headmistress Peacecroft. That morning, after leaving Hana incapacitated, I'd managed to stash my own suit in the vending machine before pulling my clothes on in the classroom and stumbling outside.

Gabby, who'd been holed up with Phin and a few others in the dojo, rushed over. "Where were you?" she cried. "I was so worried."

"I was taking a nap." I rubbed the back of my head, grinning sheepishly. "I slept through the whole thing." I felt bad for lying, but I didn't want to tell anyone about the suit—not yet. Once I did, I knew it would be confiscated, and I needed it if I was going to find Ji-eun.

"Sleeping, huh?" Takashi and Olufemi made their way over from the Founder's Building. Already, the reinforcements were rushing across campus, securing students and faculty.

It was Takashi who'd spoken. His eyes lingered on the necklace that was back around my neck. Grabbing the pendant, I tucked it beneath the collar of my shirt.

"You missed out on all the fun," he continued.

"Only you would think an attack on the school was fun," I scoffed.

"We had some help," he said offhandedly.

I thought he would mention Mecha Girl, as Olufemi had dubbed me, but he refrained.

"We never finished our duel, Aurelia," Takashi said, moving closer to me as our friends started discussing Hana's arrest. "Are you interested in a rematch?"

I frowned. "Why do you always call me by my full name? You're the only one who does. It's incredibly annoying."

I didn't think he'd answer, but then he said, "Auri is only two syllables; Aurelia is four."

"And?" I asked, exasperated.

"When I call you Aurelia," he said, drawing out the syllables of my name, "I have your attention for that much longer."

I gaped at him.

He walked away.

I shook my head with a sigh. Would I ever understand Takashi?

Looking around the Peacecroft campus, a feeling of peace settled over me. A lot had been damaged in the attack—smoke billowed from some of the buildings—but as my eyes lingered on the blue sky, I felt something I hadn't in a long time: hope.

Ji-eun was still out there somewhere, waiting for me. No matter what it took, I would find her, and I would bring her home.

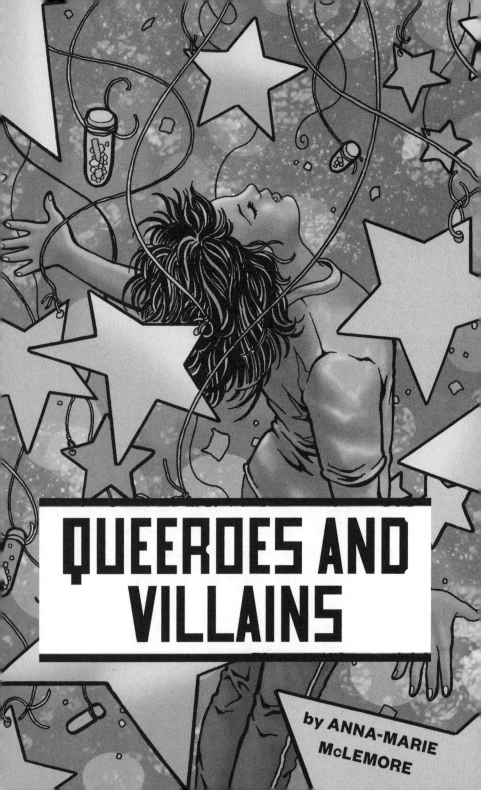

QUEEROES AND VILLAINS

by ANNA-MARIE
McLEMORE

WHEN I GET OUT OF THE SHOWER, IT'S WAITING for me.

Sitting next to a glass of water is the same kind of orange plastic bottle that might hold naproxen or antibiotics. Except I know this one didn't come from the CVS, because what's in this bottle doesn't officially exist. So the standard prescription container seems like a sad attempt at pretending this is all normal.

I lift the bottle off my dresser. The pills are somewhere between lavender and purple, which seems in poor taste.

And the pills are huge, worse than the ones I had to take for my sinus infection.

But what did I expect? That medication designed to make me not be una lesbiana was gonna come in tiny easy-to-swallow tablets?

On the way to my bed, I dodge the dozens of mobile strings hanging from my ceiling. One end of each string is masking-taped above me. The other holds a paper heart, or a sparkly D20 (the theater tech director at school helped me drill little holes), or the kind of plastic star-shaped weight they put at the ends of balloons.

Your room is one big modern art exhibit, Papá always says with a roll of his eyes, though I can see the pride in his smile. He likes that I'm weird.

He just doesn't like that I'm the kind of weird that makes me look more at Prudencia Reyes than her brother.

I sit on my bed, wet hair dampening the shoulders of my shirt, pills rattling as I pass the bottle back and forth between my hands. My stuffed animals bob in response to the shifting mattress (yeah, I'm sixteen and keep stuffed animals on my bed, so what?).

I'm lucky. I know that. When my parents found my love letters to Pru Reyes, they didn't yell at me or tell me I was going to hell. They didn't even ask me why I hadn't told them or demand answers about me, about Pru, about any of it.

They just looked at me with overwhelming pity. Which was almost as humiliating as the sweet, sympathetic smile Pru gave me right before telling me she thinks I'm great, just not like that.

Mamá knocks on my door. I can tell her particular knock from Papá's.

"Come in," I say, almost hiding the pill bottle before remembering it's my parents who got it for me.

Mamá holds a ceramic mug in her hands. The smell of cinnamon and masa drifts from the cup.

"I thought it might be nice to take your first dose with something besides water," she says.

My mother almost never makes champurrado on weekdays. She likes to let the pot simmer for hours. Our family's secret recipe is always better with an afternoon on the stove.

I can still see the sadness in Mamá's face from when she and Papá found out about me, the worry that drove them to ask their friends and friends of friends until they found someone who knew someone who knew someone who could get me into a clinical trial. They think I'm gonna end up like Tía Adelida, whose abuela won't even speak to her and who lives thousands of miles away with the woman our family won't acknowledge as her wife.

Tía Adelida always seems happy when we visit her. But I know my great-grandmother's refusal to return her calls has left a little of her heart broken.

Ending up with a heart that's only a little bit broken, my parents say, is the luckiest it gets in this world for someone like Tía Adelida.

For someone like me.

My parents have pretty definite ideas about what kind of life a queer brown girl can have, and what kind of life she can never have.

My mother leaves the champurrado on the table next to my bed. But then she pauses, hand on the doorknob.

"What you are," she says, a wince creasing her perfect eyeliner, "it's not wrong. There's nothing wrong with it. You know that, right?"

I nod. Reflex.

"It's the world that's wrong," she says. "And maybe it's going to be better for your children or your nietos. I hope it is, but it's not better yet."

I keep nodding, a way to hide the prickling along my eyelashes.

"We just want you to live a happy life in the world now," she says.

I have good parents.

I just wish they'd asked me, even once, if I want this. But so fast, we were all swept up in phone calls, and appointments in unmarked buildings, and interviews about how long I'd had *homosexual inclinations* (not even kidding, I wish I were making this up), and pages and pages of paperwork. Oh, the sheer volume of paperwork. Forms and questionnaires and surveys and waivers and medical record summaries and confidentiality agreements. If it turns out that I failed my finals, it's going to be because nothing else could fit in my brain after all that paperwork.

But because they didn't ask me what I want, I don't ask myself.

I take the first pill, the purple dye and the coating bitter on my tongue as it goes down.

Nausea. Chills. Fever. All reasons my parents wanted me to take the course of pills over winter break.

The men in expensive-looking suits and ties that matched the colors of their company's logo went over the possible side effects with us. But they glossed over the fine-print list and said I might, maybe, have some loss of appetite. Vomiting. Possible sensitivity to sunlight, but that was in a truly insignificant percentage of subjects, barely worth mentioning.

Papá read the whole list, though. So thanks to him, I know that anything from a high fever to temporarily blurred vision is possible. He made sure the warnings printed in nine-point font did not include cardiac arrest or kidney failure or anything else that the men in nice suits wanted to go over too fast for us to catch. He actually made them wait while he and my mother read every word. And even though their throat-clearing impatience made me shift in my chair, I loved my father for that.

A few days in and half my doses later, I wake up in the middle of the night with my back soaked in sweat. I catalog everything I'm feeling. Fever: normal. Chills: normal. Trouble sleeping: normal. All listed in the common side effects.

It happens again the next night. I blink into the dark, my pulse hard in my neck and my damp hair sticking to my forehead.

As my vision clears, the air in front of me wobbles.

The silhouettes of everything dangling from the ceiling— the paper hearts, the tiny vials I filled with dyed sand, the tissue paper flowers—sway. They look like a draft from an open window is pushing them, even though the December weather means my window's been shut and locked for weeks.

Fever dreams, not just fevers. They should add that to the list of symptoms. And it's worse the next night, when, in addition to swinging back and forth, each piece of my room-sized mobile glows, haloed in light the same purple as the pills in the bottle.

I stumble out of my room, stomach feeling fragile and unsteady.

"You OK, mija?" my dad asks. I realize it's already afternoon by the way the sun's coming in the kitchen window and how Papá is taking off his work shoes instead of putting them on. "You're looking a little green."

I nod, hand to the back of my neck to check if it's still damp.

My mom's purse isn't on the hook in the front hall. Her shifts start and end later than my dad's. I check the clock on the oven. In a little while, she'll come through the door with her makeup touched up and her hair neatened, something the men at her job think is for them but is always for Papá. She likes batting freshly mascaraed eyelashes at him when she comes home.

"Want water?" I ask.

Papá gives me a look. "Only if you're having some. You look like you need it."

I round the corner into the kitchen. "Thanks a lot."

I don't reach for glasses yet. I'm just thinking about them. But then purple light flashes along the handle of the cupboard, and it eases open.

My head snaps back toward the living room. My dad's distracted, turning on the TV.

I look back to the cupboard, and two glasses float toward me. The clear and red pebbled plastic glows bright and cool with lavender light.

I catch another violet glow out of the corner of my eye.

A constellation of ice cubes drifts across the kitchen, each one lit up purple from inside, like the northern lights through icicles.

When did the freezer even open, and why didn't I hear the cracking of the ice tray?

I rush to shut the cabinet door and the freezer. I grab the floating cups and use them to scoop the ice out of the air just before Papá turns back toward me.

As soon as I touch everything, the purple glow fades.

I stand in the middle of the kitchen, still on the linoleum, holding two plastic cups of ice.

My dad studies me. "Estás bien?"

I nod and fill the cups from the tap.

Side effects may include:

Not knowing qué demonios is going on.

This side effect continues when I find a tumbled purple gemstone—an amethyst, maybe?—on my windowsill. It catches the last of the light in its swirling purple center.

I open the window and grab it. I put it in a tiny glass jar and hang it from my ceiling, both because it's pretty and because it seems like the safe thing to do. Keep an eye on it. Especially if, somehow, I made it appear.

Fever dreams. Nightmares. Add them to the list of side effects, right alongside floating objects and purple light.

I try to surface from the twisting, whirling dreams that make my brain feel like it's folding in on itself. And I don't know whether I wake up screaming or if I start screaming when I see the storm of glowing violet brightening the darkness.

The pieces of my room-sized mobile are breaking free of their strings. The star- and sun- and rainbow-shaped balloon weights are flying around in streaks of lavender light. The paper hearts spin like leaves, throwing lilac rays across my bed. The D20s tumble across the dark, each facet of the dice winking brilliant purple. The glass bottle with the amethyst spins through the air, bright as if it were full of liquid light. Even my stuffed animals join the party, dancing toward the ceiling.

The door of my room opens. I sit up in bed.

My parents' eyes follow the shapes whirlpooling through the room. Their faces show horror and incomprehension, like they're a little confused this wasn't listed in the paperwork.

Mamá blinks a few times before snapping back into herself.

"We won't tell anyone," she says, eyes tracking an orange tissue paper flower that's lighting up purple at the edges. "We'll make sure no one finds out."

The words inside me open my mouth. "Like you want to make sure no one finds out about me? Who I really am?"

Papá stares at me.

The orange flower crashes into the window, and now Mamá stares.

I grip my comforter. "What else would you change about me?"

"What are you talking about?" Papá asks.

I bunch the comforter against my stomach and chest, backing toward the side of my bed that's against the wall. "What else would you change about me to make my life easier?"

I don't know if their eyes are widening because of what I'm saying or because everything is spinning through the air even faster, the purple glowing brighter.

"Would you make me not even look like you?" I ask, the words bitter on my tongue. "Make sure I never sound like you?"

Everything spins fast as winter wind. Both the air and the light feel like they're rushing inside my head now.

"What about me is worth keeping?" I ask.

Half the apartment building probably thinks I'm the worst kind of daughter, yelling at her parents—I have never yelled at any of my relatives before, because I value my life—but right now, I don't care.

"If you could change everything about me," I say, "would you keep anything?"

Mamá and Papá say my name at the same time. That chorus has the weight of truth behind it—they love that I am brown like them, that I can never strip my handed-down accent out of certain words.

And that they also know the world may never love the things about me that they love.

I will never forgive them for doing this to me.

I will never stop being grateful for why they wanted to.

The spinning gets stronger, and violet brighter, until my brain can't hold it all. It's too fast. The frequency is too high, too strong.

Everything falls in the same moment that the world turns the deepest purple, and the depth of it pulls me under.

When I wake up, it's quiet and still dark. The dice and paper cutouts are on the floor.

When I see a wink of purple, I flinch. But I scramble toward it, blinking.

Another amethyst, resting on the outside of my windowsill.

I lift the pane just enough for my hand to get through, and cold air sweeps in. When I move forward to reach for the stone, I see another fleck of purple, and another.

A trail of these little stones crosses the apartment building courtyard.

My parents are asleep deeply enough that I can hear their breathing as I creep down the hall. Even though guilt pricks at me—I know I'm the reason they're so exhausted—it doesn't stop me from sneaking out the front door and down into the courtyard.

I follow the trail of little violet stones out of the apartment complex. Then there's one every few squares of sidewalk.

I follow them down the street, past our church and my mother's work. I nod at Mr. Contreras, opening the taquería for early-morning prep. I pretend I'm bending down to tie the Converse I threw on so he won't see what I'm picking up.

The purple stones lead me onto a street that's mostly old houses but also has a couple of boarded-up businesses. The houses all look occupied, a few windows lit, but the storefronts don't look open. Which is part of why I hesitate where the last stone is, in front of a door that could have been painted orange or could just be that color from rust. I can see the outline of where a sign used to be, but there's no clue left about what is, or was, inside.

I also hesitate because the seams of the door are glowing purple.

Before I know I'm thinking about reaching for the door, the handle is lighting up violet, and it's opening.

I stay on the threshold, staring into the belly of what must have once been a bar. The floor is swept clean, and it only smells a little of dust and cobwebs and old cardboard boxes. The remaining stools are worn at the edges, the wooden bar scratched pale.

The first two people I see are two blonds who look like twins. The reason I see them first is because they're flashing, in unison, between being about six inches tall and ten feet tall. Not everyone here is a gringo, though. A lot of them have brown skin like me, like Mamá and Papá, like Tía Adelida.

And purple light follows all of them.

One guy sticks his head and arms into an aquarium that's filled with water but has no fish, and his mouth and nose light up purple like he's breathing underwater. He grins through the glass, and two friends cheer him on.

A girl flies through the air, dodging the old light fixtures, a comet blur of purple behind her. Underneath her, another girl blurs into a translucent lavender version of herself, barely visible.

Someone else turns into a giant lavender dragonfly. Another person appears at one corner of the bar, disappears in a puff of purple smoke, and then reappears clear on the other side.

And then does it again, reappearing in front of me.

"Welcome," they say. I can't tell if there are still threads of purple smoke around them or if pieces of their hair are dyed purple.

They hand me a sweatshirt the same violet as the pills I've been taking, something between a zip-up hoodie and the kind of jacket all the X-Men wear in one of the movies. Everyone in this room is wearing one. Some have jabbed safety pins through the sleeves or enamel pins into the collars. Two people who seem like a couple have identical glitter-painted unicorns on the backs of theirs. Others have even artistically slashed at the fabric or bleached clusters of pink spots.

Even with the alterations, the sweatshirts look like what I'm slowly realizing they are:

A uniform.

"Suit up," the flying girl calls down to me.

I look at the sweatshirt, my stomach wavy with the memory of swallowing those pills.

"Who are all of you?" I ask.

The guy breathing underwater pulls his head out of the aquarium. "We're superqueeroes," he says with the grandeur of an announcer from an old-timey TV show.

"That's not gonna catch on, dude." One of his friends shakes his head, purple sparks coming off the tips of his hair. "Give it up."

"I still have faith." The aquarium guy shakes his own head, sending out a spray of water.

"Suffice it to say"—the flying girl lands and sits on the edge of the bar—"the clinical trial is not working as they hoped. We're all as queer, trans, and nonbinary as we started out."

The purple dragonfly lands and turns back to human form. "Plus a few unanticipated side effects."

"What does she do?" asks one twin, currently almost as tall as the ceiling and looking down at me.

The teleporter, the one who handed me the sweatshirt, leans their head back. "Didn't we *just* talk about not assuming pronouns?"

"Sorry."

"I'm she/her," I say.

The teleporter nods. "They/them."

As soon as I even think about showing them what I can do, before I can decide not to, an old empty bottle that used to hold some fancy liqueur flies off a shelf. It kicks off dust, every mote lighting up bright violet along with the bottle glass.

It comes toward me fast. I catch it before it can slam into the opposite wall.

"Yessss," the aquarium guy and his friends say, stretching out the word with approval. Their eyes glow purple in a way that matches their delighted smiles.

The teleporter nods. "Nice."

I look around at the peeling wallpaper, the neon sign that would probably short-circuit if you tried to plug it in, the disintegrating advertising posters behind the bar.

My brain tries to catch up. The shades of lavender and purple. The possibility that all this—the breathing underwater, the teleporting, the flying—came from each of us being given pills to make us something other than what we are.

"How did you all find each other?" I ask. "How did you find me?"

"Don't worry." The translucent violet girl turns into herself again, solid, visible. "We'll catch you up."

Remembering my mother's words stops me.

It's the world that's wrong. And maybe it's going to be better for your children or your nietos. I hope it is, but it's not better yet.

I understand that place my parents live in, wanting something better for all of us but not wanting to dream it too hard, not letting themselves want it too much so they don't break their own hearts.

If I hope for that world where it's better for all of us, I could break my own heart.

But I also know that we'll never get it unless we go after it. That world they want for me, where I can be who I am, will never exist unless we make it.

"So, what do you say?" the second twin, currently about a foot tall and standing on top of a barstool, asks.

The teleporter nods at my hands, one holding the bottle that just flew through the air, the other holding the sweatshirt I am considering putting on. "You in?"

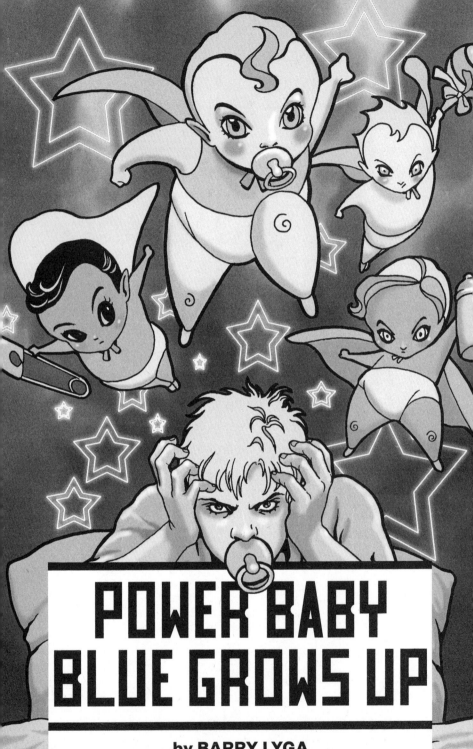

POWER BABY BLUE GROWS UP

by **BARRY LYGA**

DON'T TELL ANYONE I SAID THIS, BUT SOMETIMES
I miss the cape and diaper. Life was a lot simpler back then.
Good conquered evil every single time; might always made
right. But more than that, there was no boredom. No self-
doubt. No paparazzi or gossip columns, and none of the crip-
pling fear that came with the certain knowledge that you'd
peaked right around the time you were toilet trained.

If you've been paying attention to the world at all, you already know my story. They took my life and turned it into a
cartoon series on Netflix, for god's sake. You can probably recite the opening lines of every episode by heart:

*Four toddlers have been chosen by the Nanny to possess the
powers of the ancients! Each one holds an item of great power!
Tyler is . . . Power Baby Blue! Cordelia is . . . Power Baby Pink!
Jonny is . . . Power Baby Green! And Brian is . . . Power Baby Red!
Now it's time for evil's lullaby!*

And, of course, the theme song:

Power Babies! Power Babies! Get up and go!
Power Babies! Power Babies! This is your show!
Power Babies! Power Babies! Fighting the good fight!
Power Babies! Power Babies! Evil goes night-night!

If there weren't actual video footage of me—*at the age of
three*, mind you—flying around with my three best friends,
literally getting cats out of trees and rescuing lost puppies
and—oh, yeah—saving the world once or twice, I would've
just chalked it up to a fever dream. Most kids have imaginary
friends, and mine just happened to be a thirtysomething in a
cable-knit sweater who claimed to be from an another planet

and who gave me and three other kids at our daycare "objects of mighty power!" to use as fucking *baby superheroes*.

Brian got the Rattle. Pretty cool. He could throw it around, and it always returned to him. It also shot fire. Nice, right?

Cordy had the Diaper Pin. Which . . . who the *fuck* uses a diaper pin in the twenty-first century, but whatever. That Pin, man . . . it could turn into a sword, a javelin, all sorts of things. I remembered Cordy tossing it at The Stink once—that motherfucker *ran* like someone had lit his shoes on fire.

Jonny got the Bottle. It could magically squirt out enough liquid to put out a fire, refill a reservoir (like the time Dream Lady nightmared away all the water in the city), knock down a barricade.

And me? Tyler? Power Baby Blue?

I got the fucking Binky.

The Fucking Binky

Funny thing is this: According to my parents (and don't get me started on *them*), I never, ever used a pacifier or anything like that. Didn't even suck my thumb.

But the Nanny handed off the Binky to me that day, told me to "fight evil and bad dreams." I was the leader of the Power Babies—the Binky let me fly, gave me enhanced strength, resistance to harm, all that nonsense. And for a couple of years, it seemed as though the world had decided to play along.

We did good deeds and helped people out, and then things got really weird, as if toddlers with superpowers wasn't weird enough. That's when The Stink showed up. And then Bad Teddy with his stuffy army. And Dream Lady. And KnightLight.

And.

And.

And others.

Others, yeah.

Anyway . . .

Anyway.

We did the superhero gig for a couple of years, and then most of the bad guys seemed to go away, and we started to feel a little ridiculous, so we stopped.

But then we all got back together in third grade for our big reunion that the animation people arranged. None of us really wanted to go—by third grade, we were all more than a little bit embarrassed by our past—but the money was good, and our parents made us do it. Pictures from the reunion went viral in a heartbeat. Cordy with her Pin wrapped in ribbons and clipped in her hair. Bri with a bad-ass handle grafted onto the Rattle. And Jonny had a fucking *holster* for the Bottle.

And me?

Look, there's no way in the world to make a goddamn binky look badass, OK? By then I was wearing it on a necklace, but at the end of the day, in order for my powers to kick in, I had to jam the fucker in my mouth. Do you know what it looks like to suck on a binky at age eight?

At age ten?

At age sixteen?

And you wonder why I gave up superheroing.

Marty

I woke up to discover that the heat was out again. Which was probably half the reason for my shivering. The other half being the dreams.

Fucking Dream Lady. We'd banished her to the Other Side of the Pillow back when we were toddlers. It had taken her more than a decade, but she made her way back, haunting my dreams, trying to get into the Real World. Fucking bitch.

"Fucking bitch!" I said out loud, even though I knew she couldn't hear me when I was awake.

I hopped off the bed, landing a few feet away. Which was ridiculous, because the Monster wasn't there during the day, but it was force of habit.

Sure enough, a quick check of my phone showed that I'd neglected to pay the heating bill this month. And last month. And the month before. Only a matter of time before they cut it off.

Being emancipated at age fifteen wasn't easy, but it was necessary. My parents were bleeding away all the money from the cartoon, shoveling it into some very sketchy investments that never paid off. Flash forward two years, and I'm seventeen, dead-ass broke, living on my own in an exceptionally shitty apartment in a mostly shitty part of the same city I'd once saved from Bad Teddy.

And it wasn't like I could go public and ask for help or set up a GoFundMe or something. I was Power Baby Blue! Leader of the Power Babies! Do you know how embarrassing it would have been to go begging?

Instead, I scrolled through my list of deals to see when I could expect some cash to come in. There was a royalty check for the new toy line, but that wasn't due for another six months or so. Other than that, there was nothing on the horizon, and fall was almost over. I'd freeze if I didn't pay those back bills and get the heat turned on. In September, it had seemed like a good bet to skip the heating bills. Not so great at the end of November.

So I had to call Marty.

I hated Marty.

I really fucking hated Marty.

And I knew it was, like, projection, or something like that. Marty was my agent, my manager, the guy who kept the money coming in. The only adult I could trust, and I loathed him for that.

Fucked up, right? Right. Glad we agree.

So I called Marty.

"I need some money, man," I said without preamble. "You gotta get me something."

I could practically hear his shrug over the phone. "Ty, if you can hold out to the first of the year, I can probably squeeze out an advance on—"

And I just lost it. Like I always lost it with Marty. Because Marty always had bad news, or good news that was never good enough.

"The first of the year? My place is ball-shriveling cold *now*, Marty! Get me a guest shot on a talk show or something. Something that pays today."

"But—"

"I was the fucking leader of the Power Babies, and I've got dick to my name! Look, Cordy's got a sweet endorsement deal. Jonny's got that TV thing, and Brian has—"

"Look," Marty said with his trademark infinite patience, "I'm doing my best. I'm out there every day, but it's been tough getting you gigs ever since that last TV thing."

That Last TV Thing

It was supposed to be my big return to the spotlight. The *Reed Wilson Show*, a daytime talk show hosted by the guy everyone called the male Oprah. Reed's show started as a scrappy little fifteen-minute webcast on some Black-centric site, then got picked up and went national *fast*. He was a kingmaker. Presidential candidates did his show. Musicians. Actors. Celebrities who had fucked up big-time and needed to make the appropriate apology noises.

And superhero toddlers, now past puberty and trying to make a comeback.

There was the obligatory chitchat after a *very* nice standing ovation. I felt pretty good. Pretty settled in.

It started out easy. Reed said, "I know you get asked this all the time, but I just have to—what was it like?"

I have a long-practiced chuckle I haul out for just this question. "Honestly, Reed, that's tough to say, because for me it was just normal, you know? I mean, I was three years old! What did I know about normal? A woman shows up and gives me a magic pacifier, well, sure, OK!"

Here I mugged a tiny bit, and the audience went nuts for it.

Reed and I laughed and watched some old footage of me in action as well as some clips from the cartoon. Everything was going well.

Until it wasn't.

"But wasn't it frightening?" Reed asked. "You were practically a baby, and you were out there fighting KnightLight and The Stink, Bad Teddy and the Stuffies, Dream Lady—"

"Well, we only did that stuff a few times, really. Most of what we did was helping people out. Getting Frisbees off roofs, stuff like that. The more, uh, intense stuff was pretty infrequent. The only time I remember actually being scared was when we fought the Monster Under the Bed."

Why did I even say it? Why was I so fucking honest? Why did I even bring it up?

You could see me shiver on the video. The audience laughed, but it wasn't a put-on. Every time I think about the Monster . . .

Brr.

Why? Why did I say it? As soon as I mentioned the Monster, it was all I could think about. My brain jumped backward, and I was three years old again, and the Monster . . . the damn Monster . . .

I tried to focus. Tried to stay in the present as Reed showed a still from the cartoon on the big screen mounted between us. The Monster Under the Bed. It looked like what you'd expect—some fangs and fur, big bulbous eyes. Maybe a little unsettling for young kids, but nothing that would get the PTA up in arms.

And it was all bullshit. Because when the Netflix people asked us to describe our villains for their animators, the one *none* of us would talk about was the Monster Under the Bed. No way, nohow.

Some nightmares you share and they get better.

Some you never, ever talk about.

So they just made up the Monster, but still, every time I see even the cartoon version . . .

I get a little sweaty. I have a little trouble swallowing. Because it takes me back. Takes me right back to the first time the Monster crawled out from under my bed.

The Binky made me impervious to physical harm, but not psychological harm. And the Monster Under the Bed was a mindfuck brought to life. That was when we all learned what true fear was.

I tried to cover. I tried my best not to let the studio audience or the people watching see that I was rattled. Unless you knew what to look for—my fingers clutching the armrests of my chair, my feet pressed too hard against the floor—you never would've known.

I probably could have recovered and rallied if Reed hadn't chosen that moment to Get Real.

(That's an actual segment on the show, with a logo and fanfare and everything.)

Reed leaned in, and the lighting in the studio shifted subtly. The studio audience went still. When Reed Got Real, everything changed, and my laughing buddy suddenly looked incredibly serious. I barely registered it. Sweat had started to gather at the nape of my neck. I wished they would wipe the ersatz Monster from the big screen. I wanted to speak, but I was afraid to.

Reed didn't seem to notice. He just went on like everything was fine.

"I can't help pointing out," he said, "that all four of the Power Babies were white. And only one was a girl."

"Um . . ." I wasn't sure what he wanted from me, and I was only barely present, anyway.

"Now, in the cartoon," he went on, "they introduced Leo, an African American Power Baby. But that was in the third season, and there was never a Black Power Baby in real life, right?"

You could see me squirm a little in the video. I flicked my eyes from the Monster to Reed, then back, and back again.

"Look, I was literally a toddler." I've heard myself saying this on the video, but I have no memory of it. "I didn't *choose* to have powers, and I didn't choose who else had powers."

The sweat was gathering at my hairline now. My palms, pressed tight against the armrests, went slick. I barely heard Reed as he went on.

"I'm not saying you did." He offered up a smile that I'm certain was meant to be comforting, reassuring. The cameras cut first to a very serious-looking white woman, then to a Black lady who nodded just slightly, her lips set in a grim line.

"I'm not saying you have any culpability at all," Reed continued. "But you're older now, so what I'm asking is this: In retrospect, does it seem odd to you that the Nanny chose four straight, white, cisgender toddlers on whom to bestow her power?"

On the video, my mouth puckered and gaped for a moment, like a gasping fish on a dock. All I wanted in that moment was to run. Run like hell from the studio, away from that stupid image on the screen and the man badgering me with questions I had no answers for.

Reed, no doubt thinking I was stalling, pressed me: "Tyler, doesn't it seem odd to you?"

I needed a second. Just a second of silence. To gather myself. To regroup.

"Tyler? It's odd, right? In retrospect?"

And I just couldn't stop myself. It just exploded out of me.

I jumped out of the chair, fists clenched, glaring at Reed, finally able to tear my gaze away from the goddamn Monster. I was sweating freely now, my breath coming hard, fast, and hot. My brain was a cotton candy swirl.

"Are you [BLEEP]ing kidding me with this [BLEEP]? We were [BLEEP]ing *toddlers* flying around in capes and [BLEEP]ing diapers, fighting nightmares and [BLEEP]ing aliens! Are you [BLEEP]ing me with this [BLEEP]ing [BLEEP]? What kind of [BLEEP]ing moronic [BLEEP] are you?"

And finally, at last, I was allowed to leave.

Adam

So, yes, I could see how it might be tough to get me on TV. And it wasn't Marty's fault, and I apologized to him, like I did every time, and he promised to keep trying, like he did every time, and I stood there, realizing it was already noon because I'd slept forever because who the fuck cares, right?

I slipped my earbuds in. I'd stopped using the wireless kind, because they kept falling out during flight and getting lost.

I put the fucking Binky in my mouth, and I hopped out the window, soaring up into the sky.

Flying isn't nearly as cool as it used to be. Everyone is like, *Wow, what's it like to fly?* And I want to tell them the truth—that you have to dodge birds, and you occasionally get splatted by a bug, and it's *cold* up there, so you have to wear a leather jacket, and sometimes smart-asses with BB guns take potshots at you, and also there are drones to worry about, so that's nice.

But I have to admit, it helps clear my head.

I flew up to the highest point in the city, the skyscraper that Mega-Ape climbed. Not in real life, of course. That was on the cartoon, where they made Mega-Ape a ginormous purple thing with a bandolier of bananas and a faux Italian accent. (Why Italian? I have no fucking clue.) In real life, Mega-Ape was just this poor, confused ape who escaped from the city zoo and couldn't cope with the world around him. We used our powers to rescue him from a busy intersection and brought him back to the zoo.

But now, up at the peak of the skyscraper, drifting around the radio antenna mounted there, I couldn't help but think that maybe the cartoon had gotten it right. Mega-Ape *should* have been terrifying and majestic. He *should* have stopped the city in its tracks.

Instead, he'd just freaked out and run into traffic. Barely made a blip on the news.

I banked left into some clouds, let the needle-sharp pricks of cold water assail me, spattering my jacket. Then I dipped low, plunging out of the cloud cover, the Binky clenched in my teeth. The usual traffic along Central Avenue was missing, replaced—from my altitude—with bustling Chiclets of color.

I dropped down a little more, and the colors solidified and resolved. Central Avenue was jam-packed with protesters marching from Hilton Street down to City Hall at the intersection of Central and Amerigo Boulevard. From my altitude, I could hear the chanting but couldn't make out the words.

There were cops lining Central and a phalanx of them at the intersection, protecting City Hall from . . . what? Pissed-off citizens exercising their rights? Man, I hate that shit. If you just let people have their say, no one gets hurt.

Not my problem, of course. Once upon a time, there was talk of officially deputizing the Power Babies, but it got all mixed up with politics and who got credit for what, and it just never happened. So I had no compunction about just flying by, which is what I planned to do.

Except . . .

Except I noticed a scuffle off to the side, along the sidewalk. A couple of cops had gotten involved with the protesters. One protester in particular—a Black guy, I could see as I flew down farther—was being singled out, dragged from the scrum of protesters. A circle of protesters had formed around them, and the cop looked panicky.

Shit.

I dropped down farther. By now, the cop had his gun drawn. I landed between him and the Black guy. As long as the Binky was in my mouth, I was impervious to harm.

I held out my arms, trying to project calm.

"Hey, what's going on here?"

(I've been talking around the Binky my whole life. Second nature.)

The cop tried to wave me off with one hand while the other aimed right through me. "I have this under control. Step aside."

"Dude, why do you have your gun out? He's unarmed. Be cool."

"Power Baby Blue!" the cop snapped. "Step aside! I've got this!"

(Ugh. I hate being called Power Baby Blue. I so wanted to drop-kick him over the horizon for that.)

"Stop being a dick," I told the cop. Belatedly, I realized I was surrounded by cell phones and this was going to be up on YouTube, like, five minutes ago.

Shit. Marty's gonna kill me.

I held out one hand, palm up. "Come on. Put the gun away. Let's make this a boring-ass news day."

The cop glanced around. Maybe he realized he was being recorded, too. Maybe he actually cared about that.

He slipped his gun back into his holster. It made me think of Jonny and the Bottle, and I almost giggled, which probably would not have been the best move.

Instead, I gave him the sternest look I could manage with the Binky in my mouth. Then, arms akimbo, I waited and glared until the crowd parted and the cop rejoined his comrades on the sidewalk.

I figured I should probably stick around for a little while longer. Just to make sure things didn't get out of control.

The guy who had drawn the cop's ire fell back into the march. I sidled up next to him.

"Tyler," I said.

He snorted. "I know."

"You got a name?"

For a second, I thought he wasn't going to give it to me. "Adam."

We said nothing for a little while. He didn't even look at me, just focused on the march.

"Uh, you're welcome," I told him.

He blinked a few times. "Oh, you want me to thank you?"

"For saving your life? Sure."

A laugh. Not the merry kind—the short, annoyed kind. "How about those ads you did a while back? 'Listen to the police—they're your friends!' All that money you raised for the police unions just by standing there next to 'Officer Friendly'? Yeah, thanks a lot. I don't need your white savior narrative, OK?"

The crowd was almost at City Hall. *Fuck this*, I decided, and took off.

Everyone looked up to watch me go. Everyone except for Adam.

What Dream Lady Wants

I killed the day flying around. Did a couple of good deeds—the usual shit, nothing to write home about. Happened to overhear a guy yelling at his wife, which always got me nervous. But when I hovered outside their apartment window, I saw that it was just a TV show.

Some days, it sucks to have superpowers.

(That was actually the tagline for the ill-fated Power Baby Blue spin-off cartoon that was canceled halfway through the first season. Because I suck on a pacifier, get it?)

By nighttime, I wanted nothing less than to go home. I would have to kick around my cold, empty apartment, trying to remember what other bills I'd forsaken and what else might be cut off at any moment.

Plus, as it got darker, I started thinking about sleep.

I didn't like thinking about sleep.

Because of her.

Because of . . .

This is stupid. You're seventeen years old. You have magic powers. Go into your apartment and go to bed.

I flew in through the open window. Stupid to leave the window open—it just made it colder inside.

It was too early to sleep. It was almost *always* too early for me to sleep. I stayed up as late as I could so that as soon as I hit the sheets, I was out cold. It was safer that way, even though it meant *her*.

I watched TV. I considered calling Brian or Jonny, but I pussied out, like I always did. I deleted a bunch of texts and voicemails from my mother. I had nothing to say to her, and there was nothing I wanted to hear from her, either.

Midnight cranked around, then one a.m. What I should do, I realized belatedly, was just stay up all night and sleep during the day. That would be safe, right? *It* wasn't around during the day.

I didn't think.

Except that one time.

That one time . . .

I closed my eyes. I heard babies screaming.

Babies.

Not crying. Not *crying*.

Screaming.

And then . . . and then I realized I'd fallen asleep. I was in a dream. The apartment had blown away around me like bubbles. The sky was candy purple. A breeze drifted by, warm. I lay back on the grass, which grew thicker to cushion me. It felt like flying, but without needing the Binky.

It felt real.

And then Dream Lady hovered over me. She smiled, pursed her lips, and blew me a kiss.

It always started this way. Pretty soon, she would unbutton her silver jumpsuit, but dream-vision would prevent me from seeing her naked. I would still have the *sense* of seeing her naked, though. The pull and the heat.

And she would promise . . .

"Why?" I asked her. "It's almost every night now. Why?"

She toyed with the first button. "You were always my favorite, Baby Blue."

"Don't call me that."

She floated over me, reached out. I hated this part. I hated it. I knew she couldn't actually touch me unless I let her. But her hand came within a millimeter and hovered there, gently glowing.

And I wanted to. I wanted to let her touch me. I wanted to feel the pleasures she'd been promising since I'd hit puberty and she'd made her way back from the Other Side of the Pillow.

"It'll be like nothing you've ever felt before, Tyler," she cooed. "All you have to do is let me. I promise you, it will be *magnificent*."

Oh, and it would be, I knew. All I had to do was say the word, and all the pleasures of the flesh *and beyond* would be mine.

And Dream Lady would return to the Real World.

"No thanks," I told her.

She didn't take it personally. She never did.

Because she knew.

She knew I was only human. And eventually, after night after night after night of trying, she would break me.

It wouldn't even be difficult. I was already so broken, after all.

The Monster Under the Bed

Rain woke me. I'd forgotten to close the window, and it whipped into the living room on a cold wind, spattering me with droplets of icy wetness as I lay groaning on the sofa.

I stumbled to the window, closed it, then staggered off to the bedroom.

I was halfway to the bed when I realized what I was doing. Holy fucking fuck of fucks, *I had almost walked right up to my bed.*

I slipped the Binky into my mouth and shot up into the air, then landed on the bed. And yeah, I sleep with the Binky. Little Tyler, who never needed a pacifier or even a thumb when he was in a crib, now can't get through the night without his Binky.

Nothing else works.

I've tried storing things under there. Tried using a platform with solid sides that go all the way to the floor.

But the fact is, no matter how small the space, there's always room for the Monster Under the Bed.

Power Baby Red

It was still raining the next morning. I flew to Brian's because I had nowhere else to go and because sometimes he had good weed that gave me a decent night's sleep. I was in the market for a decent night's sleep these days.

Brian was out of weed, but his parents were out of town, so it was cool for me to hang. None of the Power Babies' parents are big fans of Blue—they're worried I'm a bad influence. That their precious gravy trains will decide to get emancipated.

Here's a lesson, parents: Don't fuck your kids over, and they won't leave you.

Brian had converted the garage into his own little suite, complete with a bathroom, a kitchenette, and a sofa facing a massive TV. He still had the Rattle—whipped it around in circles from the end of the cool custom chain he'd grafted to its handle. The rumor was that only Brian could hold the Rattle, but that was bullshit we made up to keep people from trying to steal it.

"How you doing, man?" He gave me a big hug, led me to the sofa. I could tell he was already drunk as hell, and it was barely noon.

He offered me a beer, and when I declined, he popped it open and took a deep drink.

I didn't drink. I didn't like drugs at all. I only smoked Brian's weed when I was desperate for a night without Dream Lady threatening me with sexual delights unknown to humankind.

"I'm OK. The usual."

He flopped next to me on the sofa and fired up Netflix.

"Fuck, no, come on . . ."

But he was already queuing up the first episode of *Power Babies!*: "Baby Power!"

"It's funny, man!" he told me, punching my shoulder. "You never developed a sense of humor about it. That's your problem."

I sighed as the show started. That damn jingle. The deep voice narrating our origin story. And then the action started.

On the show, Patty, the owner of our daycare, was a cute twentysomething, not the mid-fifties grimalkin of reality. In real life, Patty had cashed in and was living a pretty sweet retirement in Florida, I had heard.

Everyone had gotten paid. Even me. I just didn't get to keep it.

"See, they had *fun* with it!" Brian was saying, pointing to the screen. "Like we used to. Remember how much *fun* we used to have? Forget the good deeds and the villains. We were three and four, and we just had a blast with those powers. That's what people loved about us."

I relented. The cartoon was almost hypnotically good, I had to admit. "It would have been pretty cool to have a headquarters like in the cartoon," I confessed.

Brian snorted. "Yeah! That's the spirit." He raised his beer bottle. "I still think they should have called it the Crib, not the Cradle."

"We were too white to pull that off."

Brian groaned. "Are you still pissed about the Reed Wilson thing? We didn't *ask* for the powers, man. Dump that white guilt shit."

The more time I spent with Brian, watching him drink himself into a stupor as an animated version of my childhood sang and danced in the background, the more I realized I couldn't stay. After about an hour, I made some excuses and headed for the door.

Brian said nothing, staring at the screen. The grin had slipped off his face. He was slack-jawed, beyond drunk.

I knew this Brian. Knew him too well.

As I opened the door, he called out to me. I turned back.

He spoke without looking over, without turning his attention away from the cartoon.

"Hey, uh, man . . . do you still . . . are you still afraid of . . . you know?"

"Fuck no," I said with derision. "I'm not a baby anymore."

Fear Is Real

But I *was* still scared. With good reason.

I flew to the park. The storm intensified, and the sky went black with rain, pouring down in torrents. In buckets.

Season two, episode twelve: the Power Babies have to stop an actual rain of cats and dogs . . .

Ugh. Never happened.

Or did it? Sometimes I couldn't remember.

But I remembered the fear.

And on top of the fear . . .

All the anger. The recriminations. The self-doubt. The outrage.

I realized I was screaming in the rain, bellowing at the storm clouds. Before I knew what I was doing, I slipped the Binky between my lips and hauled off and punched the nearest tree. Felt nothing. The tree split with a resounding *CRACK* that could have been a sound effect right out of the cartoon.

No one was around. The storm had driven everyone away. So I dropped to my knees and I screamed some more and I cried because it was safe to cry in the rain, where no one could see your tears.

"Tyler," said a soft voice.

I ignored it.

And then there was a hand on my shoulder. A dry hand, despite the rain.

"Tyler, look up at me."

I didn't have to look to know.

It was the Nanny.

The Nanny

The Nanny. From the planet AuPair. Like, are you *kidding* me? It was drivel, and yet it was real. It was my fucking life, and I was supposed to take it seriously.

She looked exactly the same as she had all those years ago, when she'd come to us and changed our lives. In her thirties, with a puckish grin, light green eyes, coal-black hair in tight curls. Wearing a cable-knit sweater, yoga pants, a welter of spangly bracelets on one wrist.

I had only seen her the one time. Only heard her voice once. But I'd never forgotten.

(On the cartoon, she shows up every two or three episodes. Special guest voice: Scarlett Johansson. But in reality, she'd never appeared again.)

"You've changed so much," she said to me. For some reason, I was amazed that the rain did not touch her. I don't know why. "But you're still my special boy."

My tears came again, stronger this time.

"I messed everything up," I told her. "I ruined everything. I was the leader, and now . . . now there's nothing."

"That's not true," she said. She offered me a handkerchief, miraculously dry, and I used it to wipe my eyes. Then she helped me to my feet and led me to a park bench.

It was dry. When I sat on it, the rain just fell *around* me.

I've lived a weird life; this shouldn't have rattled me. It did.

"I guess I'm a big disappointment to you," I told her. "I guess you want this back."

I held out the Binky on my open palm.

Without a word, she folded my fingers over it. "It cannot be taken from you, Tyler. Not even by me. Once given, it is *given*. And no, I am not disappointed in you. Not at all."

I hiccupped something between a laugh and a sob. "Well, you're the first in that line. Because I've let everyone down. Including myself. You know what I dream about?"

She shook her head, pursing her lips.

"You know what I dream about when I'm not being dragged

into some soft-core fantasy by one of my old supervillains? I dream about being normal. I dream that you never came to Patty's Place that day. You went over to, like, KinderGym or something. Grabbed some poor suckers from that place and gave them the powers. And right now, I'd be living at home with my parents and looking at colleges instead of squatting in a miserable little one-bedroom and trying to hustle my next gig."

"That could have happened," she said agreeably.

"Why did you choose us?" I got it out without whining, but the second time I said it, compelled to repeat myself, it *hurt* on the way out. It came out raw and bloody and desperate. "Why us? And why . . ."

I couldn't stop myself.

"Why four white kids? Maybe people would like me more if it didn't look so . . . Why not at least one more girl?"

I didn't really expect her to answer, and for a long time she didn't. She just sat and watched me, her eyes flitting over me. I'd never known if this was her real form or some kind of projection.

"There are many answers to your question, and more than one of them is true. But only one actually matters."

"Don't talk in fucking riddles!"

A mischievous light gleamed in her eyes. "Watch your language, young man. I'm not your mother, but I am twelve thousand years old, and nothing can stop me from putting you over my knee."

I kinda knew she would do it, too. "Sorry, ma'am," I said sheepishly.

"You deserve an answer, Tyler. You've done well."

"Have I?"

"We do as well as we can," she told me. "As well as our limits allow."

I knew what that meant: I was a fuckup, and I'd performed to the limits of my fuckuppery.

"As for why I chose you and your friends . . . well, consider:

"Perhaps I am simply a racist and wanted the power in the hands of whites. I can see that makes you uncomfortable, but you have to consider it.

"Perhaps I had chosen one of you already, but I had to give the powers to a group, a collective. And your society, due to its ingrained systemic racism and classism, had put my chosen child in an environment with no children of color.

"Perhaps it was mere coincidence.

"Perhaps there was a deeper reason. Which you already know. I had a reason for choosing you to receive your gift. You know what I said to you when I gave you the Binky, Tyler. You remember what I told you. Why I was granting you such power."

I nodded. "Yeah. *To stand against evil and bad—*"

She shook her head fiercely. "No. That's from the cartoon. You're confusing your life with your legend. Think, Tyler. Remember."

The Day I Got the Binky

Four of us. Together. Always together.

I arrive first. Daddy drives me in Green Car to Patty's. Patty's my friend. She takes care of all of us. Me and Brian and Jonny and Cordelia and the little babies, too.

Patty makes oatmeal. I sit at the kitchen table and watch, zooming my toy car back and forth.

We eat oatmeal with blueberries. I like when Patty makes it. Daddy doesn't make it the same, so I don't like it at home.

Patty wipes my face. She changes my pull-up. She pats me on the head and kisses my forehead and tells me to go play with my friends.

We go outside. Patty has a fence around the yard so we can play outside without her. We find balls. Throw them.

And then the sun goes dark.

A new light explodes near us.

A woman steps out of the light. Pretty lady. She smiles and tells us she's our Nanny and she's brought us presents from outer space.

We line up. She hands them out. Puts a pacifier in my hand and says:

"Use this power to make the world a better place."

And we try.

It's still raining as I come out of the memory. Only now I'm soaked again, because the Nanny's gone.

I had a reason for choosing you to receive your gift.

You.

Not *all of you.*

Just me.

She had a reason for choosing *me.*

Power Baby Pink

The rain had tapered off by the time I got to Cordy's house. Her parents bought a big house in the suburbs with the option money from the cartoon. The property was big enough that a year ago, they built a separate house for Cordy in the back. The lights were on, so I landed there and knocked.

"You're drenched," she said when she opened the door, then peered up at the clear sky.

"It's raining in the city. Can I come in?"

"Of course."

It was a nice place. Soft couch. Fireplace. She wore the Pin on her sleeve. Never kept it far from her.

I wonder what she dreams about.

Cordelia was always the most reasonable of the four of us. I was the leader, but she probably should have been. On the cartoon, they really played this up, making her so much more mature than the rest of us.

And in real life, it worked out that way, too. She had her shit together the most.

If I could convince her, the others would fall in line.

"I have to talk to you about something. Something important."

She nodded, handed me a dish towel. I dried off as best I could. I didn't want to sit on her pristine couch, so I let her sit and stood near the fire.

"You OK, Ty? You look . . . peaked."

"I haven't been sleeping well. But I . . . I've been thinking."

She smiled at that. A sad sort of smile, the kind I remember my mom making. Back when I talked to my mom.

"Ty, if you need money, I can—"

And the hell of it was, I *did* need money. But that wasn't why I was there.

"I think we have to give up the toys, Cordy."

As soon as I said it, it was like . . . like the first time I put the Binky in my mouth. A rush of power. A blast of cool calm and understanding. I shivered in the heat of the fireplace, but I was completely at peace.

"Give up . . . the toys." She brushed the pads of her fingers against the Pin.

"Yeah. Surrender them. Give them to someone else."

She leaned back. Damn, that sofa looked comfortable. More comfortable than anything I'd experienced in years.

"Why?"

Simple question.

"Because . . . it's time. It's past time. I don't think we were supposed to keep them this long. I'm not even sure we were supposed to have them at all."

"But the Nanny gave them to *us*," she said, puzzled. "They're ours."

"Yeah, and that's why we have to give them up. To balance the scales. To make the world a better place."

With a sigh, she stood, came to me. Cupped one stubbly cheek with her hand. The press tried a few times to imply that we were a couple. Sold a lot of newspapers, but it was never true. She was too sensible, and I was too haunted.

"Ty, it kills me to see you like this. You're not thinking straight. I need you to get some sleep. Real sleep."

I had once made the mistake of telling Cordy about my

dreams. She'd told me that Dream Lady wasn't real. It was all in my head.

And of course, that was exactly the problem—Dream Lady *wasn't* real. It *was* all in my head.

She took her hand away. "Ty. Are you listening to me?"

"Yeah."

"Can you do that? For me? Get some sleep? You can stay here. I have a guest room . . ."

I shook my head violently. I didn't need sleep. I didn't need Dream Lady offering to perform sex acts without name or number on me, if only I'd let her into the real world again.

I *was* thinking straight. My thoughts had never been clearer.

"I'll be OK," I told her, and headed for the door. When I opened it, I saw that the storm had followed me; raindrops pattered onto the cobblestone path that led to Cordy's front door.

She followed me to the door and stood there, hugging herself. "I'm worried about you."

And something long dormant worked its way out onto my tongue. Something I'd thought and held close to my heart for so long. Something I'd never said before.

My voice was hollow and thin in my ears when I spoke.

"You know that time we fought the . . . you know?"

I never had to say its name. None of us did. We knew.

"Yeah?"

"Remember how it was rampaging through Patty's Place? And we were trying to keep it away from the littles?"

The littles. The babies in Patty's care. Soft, helpless dollops of cream and nothing and everything.

"Yeah?"

"Well, you guys were blockading the nap room. But I chased it under Patty's bed, remember?"

"Yeah?"

"I just . . . I was *so close* to it, Cordy." Even now, fourteen years later, I could feel its breath on my neck. The oil-slick probe of its tentacles in my brain. All of its eyes, unblinking, seizing me.

"I was so close, and I wonder if it did something to me, if it lingered, if that's why . . ."

I couldn't go on. God knows I wanted to. I wanted to say it out loud. Wanted someone to hear.

But the look on her face already said so much.

And then she said more, with a moue of patient pity. "Ty, you're looking for an excuse for why your life turned out this way. But it wasn't the Monster or the Nanny or the Binky. Your parents screwed up. You made some bad decisions. It's just *life*, Ty.

"It's just life."

The Gift

So, the problem with my life was life. That was helpful. Fuck you and your ten-grand-a-month endorsement deal from that fucking women's gym chain.

I can't believe she gets paid to do Pilates.

Why can't I get paid to do Pilates?

I looked up at the sky. The storm clouds rolled into position, as though they knew I'd just stepped outside.

Cordy was the mature one. The sensible one.

But I was the leader.

OK, Ty. Lead.

It took me the better part of the night to find Adam. I looked all over when I should have gone straight to City Hall, where a vigil was still in progress, despite the rain. A sea of black umbrellas, slick and spotted. Of course that was where he was.

I alit a block away, put the Binky in my pocket, and walked through the drizzle down to City Hall. Candles guttered and rallied. Someone was murmuring a song.

I found him at the edge of the crowd. Sidled up next to him. "Got a second?"

When he realized it was me, Adam did an actual double-take. I couldn't hold back a small chuckle.

"What the hell?" he whispered. "We're honoring—"

"I know. But this is really important."

I stared straight ahead. I could feel him measuring me with his eyes. Then he tugged at my jacket sleeve, and we walked a few yards away, onto the sidewalk near a street sign.

"What is it?" he asked.

I had prepared something to say, but in that moment, I realized there was no point. I had been three years old, and I'd understood. That's how simple it was.

So I handed him the Binky. "Here."

"Whoa, whoa!" He backed away from me, shaking his head. But I noticed he didn't drop the Binky. "Are you *serious*? What the hell am I supposed to do with this?"

I shrugged. "Make the world a better place. Oh, and you might want to rinse it off first."

He had had the thing halfway to his mouth. Paused. Stared at the Binky in his hand as though it could bite.

"Why me? Because I'm Black and you're full up on white guilt?"

"An alien babysitter handed that to me when I was three years old and never really explained why. So, sure, it's because you're Black and I'm full up on white guilt. That seems like as good a reason as any other and probably better than most."

He had nothing to say to that. I grinned weakly, gave him a little wave, and started to walk uptown, away from the vigil.

"Hey, Pow—Tyler!"

I turned back.

He fidgeted for a moment, passing the Binky from one hand to the other. "I always thought you got it raw with that Reed Wilson thing, man. You were just a baby."

"Thanks."

"Can I give you a lift home?" he asked. And then, as though to assuage any doubts, gestured with the Binky.

"No thanks," I told him. "I'll walk."

A Better Place

That night, I dreamt I was in a cartoon.

This was not a scam by Dream Lady. After so many years and so many dreams, I could always sense her presence. And besides, she was never one for subtlety—subtlety wouldn't get her what she wanted.

This was my own dream.

My own cartoon.

I was the artist and the subject. And I wasn't a baby. I wasn't even a teenager. I was a grown man with a little paunch and my hair thinning a bit.

Overhead, the clouds parted, and I caught sight of a gleaming figure against the sun. It was Adam. Or maybe it was one of Adam's children. I don't know.

I knew one thing for certain, though: I was in a better world.

When I woke up, I lay there for a few moments. Then, very deliberately, I rolled out of bed. I lowered myself until I lay prone and pressed my cheek against the threadbare carpet.

Gazing under the bed.

Nothing there. Nothing but darkness.

And then eyes opened. Too many eyes.

But for the first time in a long time, I was not afraid.

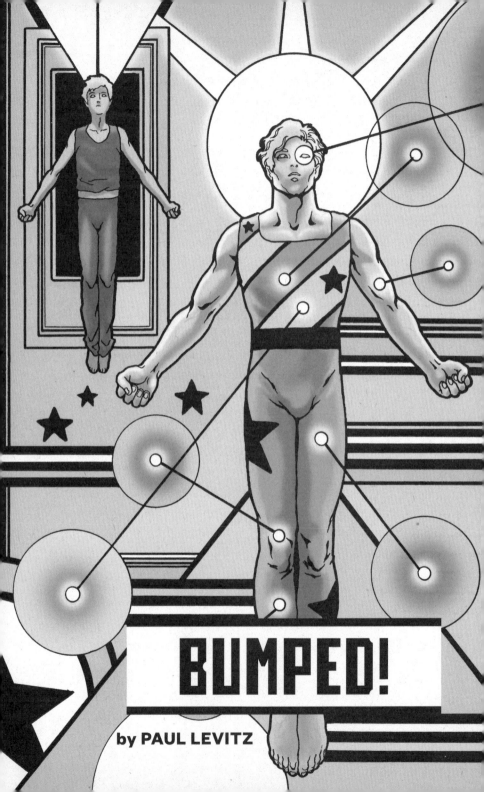

BUMPED!

by PAUL LEVITZ

BACK AT THE BEGINNING OF THE SIXTEENTH
century, when a genius named Erasmus wrote, "In the kingdom
of the blind, the one-eyed man is king," he wasn't just being
wise and witty—turned out he was prescient. Not quite literally, and it took six centuries to get there, but close enough. If
his contemporary Nostradamus had been that clear, we'd have
had quite a guide to the future.

No such luck.

Turned out that the most common side effect of the pollution war of 2132 was a dramatic downturn in most people's
vision; their optic nerves progressively atrophied in response
to one of the nasty chemicals let loose in the atmosphere. It
wasn't quite living in the kingdom of the blind, but it wasn't
just the bastard who designed those pollution bombs who was
shortsighted.

The signage on Main Street was bright and bold, LED
screens and lights shouting out their enticements in a way
their neon ancestors would have rejected as "too gaudy." But
when so many of the shoppers were visually impaired and the
air swirled with gray clouds saturated by ever-so-slowly decaying pollutants, what was a merchant to do? Latter-day Sam
Waltons had tried using loudspeakers to lure in customers, but
the cacophony of invitations just made for an indistinguish-
able roar. Older folks picked their way dimly through the haze,
recognizing their destinations by the familiar colors and pat-
terns more than reading the words on the signs; youngsters
wore shades, polarized to cut the glare to manageable levels.

Garret straightened his glasses, cutting down the polarization so his eyes shone through. It made him look more

grown up, and that was important today. He looked down, doing one last check before it was too late. Not the latest fashion, something the kids would have tossed out as "so yesterday." Probably the oldest thing in his closet that still fit properly, in fact. Luckily, he'd gotten most of his growing done early. It was the right visual effect.

His shoulders filled the shirt out well, and the jacket had padding that made him look older and stronger than he really was. Since he'd cut his hair back when he'd started this hunt, it looked mature. He'd gotten some grief from his friends when he'd chopped his locks, but considering he'd had to do it himself, it hadn't turned out badly. And it felt like that single act of conformity had added at least a year to his apparent age. His face had cleared up, too, at least as much as anyone's could under the constant assault of the chemicals fouling the air. Confidently striding forward, he was sure he could pass.

On he went, past shop windows filled with things that would have made life better, easier . . . or that would've at least brought a brief smile to his mother's face, if he were able to afford any of them as a gift. She'd bought him small birthday presents on this street—some years, anyway—and he really wished he'd been able to reciprocate even once.

He turned into the store that had the small **HELP WANTED—CASHIER** sign glowing in its window, concentrating on his posture. He had been studying people a few years older, trying to make sure he adopted all their mannerisms, all the signals of being mature, capable, ready. Jobs were scarce, and ones that didn't require extensive schooling, experience, or other qualifications he didn't have . . . well, this was a rare opportunity. As long as it didn't require filling out forms he'd have trouble focusing well enough to read.

"About that job," he began, addressing the balding man squinting at him across the information desk.

"Cashier. Minimum wage. Thirty hours a week, shifts on seniority, so you start with lots of nights. Done it before?" His voice sounded like he gargled with the cheap bleach the store sold, and he barely bothered to look at Garret.

"Night work's OK, I don't mind. I've never been a cashier, but I have lots of references—my teachers, my pastor . . ." He reached for the chip in his pocket.

"Waste of time. Everybody's got someone to lie for them. Doesn't matter. Any idiot can do the job, just change the tapes on the scanners and stop anyone who sets off the alarm at the door," the old man growled, but what he said raised Garret's hopes. If experience really didn't count, maybe he *could* get this. "Got your ID?"

Garret had enough self-control not to show it, but his heart started racing. This was the critical moment; he'd spent the last of his cash for the card. Even the hologram looked right. He slid it across the counter.

And as he did, the old man moved faster than Garret imagined he could, stabbing a bioreader needle into the back of Garret's hand. A drop or two of blood welled up, nothing that would hurt him physically, but . . .

"Sixteen? With an ID that says eighteen," he said, tossing the card back at Garret roughly as the bioreader lit up. "Get outta here, kid. Go sign up to be laser bait—army's the only outfit that'll take you underage."

His shoulders slumped, Garret slunk out of the store. Were bioreaders getting so cheap that any little store could afford to use one to check applicants? He'd heard buzz about the new algorithm that read telomeres, but he'd thought it was still something only the fancy labs might have. Or was that the state-of-the-art model that could estimate your years to collapse, and this was a cheaper version that could read your age from your DNA? Did it matter?

"One more fail in a life full of them," he muttered under his breath. "No chance I'll catch a break, earn enough to get bumped, get a place of my own, much less be awarded a repro permit. As if there's a girl who'd want to have my kid. No money. No score on the Q-qualifiers worth a place in tech school or anything . . . gonna end up doing scut work for robots if things keep going like this. Might as well go to the front. At least it won't be boring."

The lights in the street assaulted him as he moved out of the doorway. He probably had only another couple of years before his eyes started getting really bad, but for now, reaching for the polarizing control on his glasses to gray it all down was his best defense. Better. He could squint and see his way through the mists and glows, all big and bright. If only he could see a path to his goal.

Adding frustration to his humiliation, the most sensible route home took him down his personal street of dreams: the blocks crowded with clinics advertising all the ways you could get bumped. Each one was a scruffy or polished purveyor of the minor miracles of modern technology. Want an implant to replace a worn-out body part? Job you're hunting requires you to be able to lift a heavier load? Fix your eyes so you can thread a needle? Every kind of bump that science had squeezed out of genetic manipulation and cyborg technology was available. Mostly risk-free, but that was the only place "free" showed up in the paperwork. The clients didn't come from the public housing where Garret grew up.

At least he didn't have to pass the enlistment office around the corner, with its constant drone cutting through the clamor of the other loudspeakers. "Sign up—see the world through sharp eyes—be the person you *want* to be!" Or, "Special—enlist today, get bumped before you deploy!" If he couldn't get a job, couldn't raise the cash he needed somehow, the only way to get what he wanted might be to enlist. *Laser bait*, the nasty old guy had said. Well, he was honest at least.

Public housing hadn't improved much in the last hundred years or so. It was carbon neutral now, but everything had to be. The steady creep of the shorelines had flooded so much of the old cities that it was never clear whether they should allot more money to building seawalls or retrofitting the world to slow the rise of the temperature. Low-energy systems kept the units at a livable eighty degrees most of the year, and if there wasn't heat in the winter, sometimes forty felt like a nice change.

The rooms were pretty dusty most of the time, but Garret's mother couldn't see well enough for it to bother her anymore. He'd gotten used to it and mostly worked to keep his treasures clean: a couple of shelves of old toys, the books his mother had read to him when he was little and her eyes were stronger, a raggedy teddy bear standing guard over them.

He thought about his mother moving slowly and carefully through the familiar space, rarely going out more than necessary, but her hearing was as sharp as ever, and he knew that the soft beep from the keypad under his fingers was music to her ears.

"You're home, just in time for dinner. I made your favorite . . ."

"I didn't get the job, Mom." The disappointing words fell with a thud to the concrete floor.

"Next one. The next one will work out, Garret. This one's their loss, anyway."

"Maybe."

"Remember when you were little and I'd read to you when you were sad or got hurt? I wish I could do that now."

"So much better than the Wound-Be-Gone goo, Mom. Maybe if I read to you . . ."

"Would you, Garret? That's so sweet."

He picked up one of the dusty books, brushing off the soot, and opened it. The pictures were bright and vivid, almost as he remembered them, but the words . . . They weren't fuzzy when he'd looked at them as a child, just mysterious until he'd learned to sound them out. Had he read the book so many times that he'd worn out the type, or was it just his eyes?

Deep breath. Deep memories. It was there in his head from a thousand bedtimes long ago. He began, "'Dorothy lived in the midst of the great Kansas prairies . . .' This is where I'd always ask you what a prairie was, right, Mom?"

"And I'd tell you I saw a holo about them once at the museum when I was little . . . all tall grass and things growing . . ."

The time passed magically, and even if Garret didn't recall the story perfectly, the sound of his voice was pleasure enough for his mother until she realized how late it had become. She rushed off to serve dinner, embarrassed that she'd let herself be distracted from her responsibilities.

The smell of the spices rising from the soy burger in the microwave was comforting, and the simple dinner was filling. It had been the two of them alone against the tides of the world for as long as he could remember. They commiserated and made unlikely plans late into the night, sharing hopes made futile by mistakes that were made long before either of them was born. Damage to the ecosystem, failure to build an educational system to train people for this century's challenges, and casual disregard for the fate of the working class combined to ensure that most of their dreams were totally out of reach. But come nightfall, the lights automatically began to dim for curfew, and in sleep, dreams could still come, no matter how unlikely.

Morning brought clarity. Not the kind that made the sun peek through the endless smog or sent a breeze to blow it away; the weather predictions had given up offering that kind of optimism when Garret was young. The options now were bleak or bleak with rain. ("Caution, stay inside—acid content today is high!") The clarity was inside him, the sharp kind of vision his eyes denied him but his imagination provided. If there was only one way to his goal, he'd take it.

The streets were quieter in the early morning, when stores kept their lures off to save on power. Only a few people ventured out before the hours when the sun had the best chance of penetrating the clouds. Garret walked steadily, grim resolution all over his face. His mom had still been asleep when he'd left, sparing him a confrontation or the need to lie. The blocks passed swiftly until he was almost there.

But as Garret turned a corner, he saw a bright flash ahead and heard a crack like thunder, but far too close for comfort. A giant electronic sign had shorted out and was wobbling on its mounts, seeming ready to break loose. Below it, a skinny guy was bent over, adjusting the straps of his shoes, oblivious to what was happening above.

Garret took a cautious step forward, squinting to assess if there was a safe path on the far side of the street, when another boom echoed down the street and the sign tottered.

There are moments when you can react without thinking, some deep lizard brain commanding your muscles into motion when there's danger. Garret's adrenaline surged, and he threw caution to the wind . . . and himself across the street.

Tackling the startled man, he sent them flying a few meters seconds before they heard the crash behind them. The falling sign sent glass, metal, and plastic scattering through the air like shrapnel, most of it hitting the street but a few fragments ripping into Garret's back through his clothes.

"What the hell are you—" the man growled, but his voice fell off fast as he looked beyond Garret to the sidewalk, which had been cracked open by the falling sign's impact. "Oh."

"Sorry I couldn't warn you, but I didn't think there was time." Garret stood and started to brush fragments of the sign off his body. His hand came away smeared with blood where one of the metal shards had cut right through his clothes.

"Yeah. Guess I owe you, young man. That could have been bad."

"Glad I was there. Think I better go home, see if I need to hit the clinic." He stared at the sharp metal smeared with his blood.

"I'm an RN. Let me take a quick look." The man began looking over the damage to Garret's back. "Yeah . . . you need to get a fast anti-infect and maybe some quick seal. Come with me. Name's Ben Poindexter."

"You don't need—"

"Shuddup. The doc'll take care of you. She wouldn't have wanted me to call in from an emergency room. We have a full schedule today."

Ben took his hand and steered him down the street to one of the many buildings advertising the services Garret had wished for; bumps of all sorts were on offer. The small, dignified (and very secure to its wall) sign advertised **DOCTOR KATZ—IMPLANTS**. As they walked into the polished white room, the receptionist gasped at Ben's disheveled appearance, then again at the bleeding youngster he steered through the door, and in a minute, they were in an examining room. No explanations were needed.

Everything happened so fast, Garret could barely focus. His jacket and shirt were off, medications were applied that he'd never experienced before, and in what seemed like an instant, he was staring into the mirror at the reflection of his seemingly healed back, only an artificial-looking thin stripe betraying that he'd ever been injured.

The doctor, meticulously arranging her instruments for the autoclave and smiling sweetly, said, "Thanks for saving Ben. He can be cranky, but he's the smoothest operating room nurse I ever had."

Ben did not object; he could have even been smiling.

Garret felt their eyes on him, their attention weighty and unfamiliar. "I just did what anyone—"

"Actually, no," Dr. Katz interrupted. "Most people don't take risks for others. You were brave and decent, and that should be rewarded. We owe you. Is there anything else I can do for you?"

Anything else. She said it so calmly, when she held in her hands the power to do *everything* else. Did she even know? Could she even understand what she could do to and for someone like him?

And it was all there for the asking.

As he slipped his torn jacket back on, Garret leaned forward, blushing, and whispered softly to her, embarrassed in this unprecedented situation. He had always earned his own way. In a sense, maybe he had this time, too. At least enough to ease his conscience and let him ask.

She shook her head softly, sighing, and said, "I wish I could, lad, but—"

He rushed out the door before the rest of the sentence even came out. The whole thing was crazy. Kids from the projects didn't get treated in gleaming doctors' offices, and they certainly didn't get to talk about their fantasies of being bumped with a specialist who probably charged more for the simplest upgrade than his family had earned in a lifetime. He didn't belong there, and he was foolish to have admitted his dream.

Back out on the street, he ran until the red in his cheeks came more from the wind than from embarrassment.

Garret might have felt differently if he'd heard the conversation in the doctor's office later as Ben and Dr. Katz prepared for the next patient. The doctor sat at her desk, gently bowing her head as Ben told her that he'd looked up and down the block and couldn't find the nameless young man.

Dr. Katz sighed. "Maybe I could have gotten Ackert to do it—professional courtesy and all—but it's simply not a bump I ever mastered."

"The kid's just dreaming, Doc. Don't worry about it. He'll be fine."

"Maybe . . ." She shook her head and reached under the ultraviolet light for sterilized tools to use on her next patient. "But if he'd listened for another minute or two . . . we could have changed his life."

I thought it was a miracle. So close. If only that guy had worked for a different doc . . .

The thoughts raced through Garret's mind as fast as the blood surging inside him. He needed to calm down, get his blood pressure back to normal after this roller coaster of a morning. If he showed up like this, he'd lose his last opportunity for sure. *Breathe. Just breathe. Slowly.*

He slowed down, trying to get his body moving at the pace he wanted his corpuscles traveling. There was one peaceful spot he'd loved when he was little, and it drew him like a magnet now. When the water had started to rise and the city retreated, the riverbank had become a strange mixture of what was lost and what nature was reclaiming. Here and there, rooftops of the structures that used to line the grassy verge poked out: the top of a tennis court, part of a pier that had once launched tourist boats, even the bombed-out shell of a sewage treatment plant. But on each one grew sea plants and barnacles, flashes of color against the graying decay. It was a haunting sight, a reminder that the Earth would, in the end, win and claim them all.

Garret remembered it as more vivid than it looked now. Surely the colors had been brighter, the plants more beautiful? Was it the haze of the day hiding them, the mists that had grown thicker in recent years? Or, more likely, was it simply the way his eyes were already failing? Would even this terrifying beauty vanish from his world as the degeneration progressed?

He shook his head, breaking his reverie. When he checked the pulse in his neck, it felt more normal. Bittersweet as the riverbank view was, he was calm now, even clearheaded.

His decision from earlier was the right one, the only one. It was time.

═══════════════════════════════════════

The tests seemed endless and were mostly incomprehensible. In a more primitive time, they might have been perceived merely as evaluations of fine motor skills, then gross. But the algorithms also probed specific prescribed mock movements demonstrating the ability to manipulate the current devices of war, as well as basic measures of intelligence and emotional temperament—surely someone would be needed to supervise the civilians of conquered territory. Some of the tests were physical and hurt, taking samples from every part of his body, or so it felt. There were strange exams in a totally dark room and one requiring him to assemble a complex object in a space overflowing with jarring and unfamiliar noises. There was even a test that simulated working the controls of a vehicle unlike any that Garret had ever encountered in his simple life. But he marched through each in turn, doing his best, refusing to give up on his dream.

At last, there was an end to the endless. He entered a bare room, well lit, with a single chair facing a standing man—an officer, by the look of the metallic pins and symbols on his uniform. "Congratulations, kid. You qualified."

"You mean I can join? I'll get bumped?"

"That's what you came here for, right? You'll be the new-and-improved model when the docs are done with you. We want you well equipped for the war." (He'd be filling out a unit emptied by the casualty rate of 47 percent, but that wasn't a number that anyone was permitted to say out loud.)

"Where do I sign?"

"Sign? You're already sworn in," the officer said as a hologram of Garret saying "I'm here to join up" appeared in a flash of light. "Now, it's off to the medi-corps for you, and when they're done and you've recovered, we'll send you off for training."

—

A timeless time passed. Garret was probed and plumbed, genetically manipulated and magnified, chemically amplified and enabled. When it was done, he stood taller, broader. If this was what it meant to be laser bait, at least no expense had been spared to make him capable of giving as good as he got in battle. He might or might not live to be a hero, but he certainly looked the part.

He returned to the bare room, and the recruiting officer—now he knew how to identify the meaning behind the gleaming decorations—was there to congratulate him. "You look good, kid. You're ready."

And he did look good. It was as though he'd aged years in the weeks he'd been in the system. There was a maturity to his bearing beyond the sheer physical strength that had been squeezed into his genetic code, altering his frame, the texture of his skin, and everything inside. Each soldier was bumped to the limit of their body's capacity for health and strength, for sharpness of the senses, and for the ability to heal from the inevitable injuries. Even if warriors were simply laser bait, it was worth it to build them up so that they were the strongest, fastest, best fighting machines modern science could create. Garret was designed to do the most damage he could before he was brought down.

"Here's the deal. It takes a month for all the fixes to completely settle into your system, so we won't ship you off to training until then. Go home, say what you have to, square up your affairs. You won't see your family or friends again until your enlistment ends—or we send what's left of you back to them."

"Yes, sir." He saluted, for he had learned that much military discipline while they were transitioning him. Questions weren't welcomed, and doubts were to be swallowed faster than pocket rations. He'd become more conscious of the price of his dream every time he looked at the ever-less-familiar face in the mirror, but he had achieved it. He'd been bumped, and he had a month to use it.

He felt different as he walked down the street away from the recruiting office: stronger already, his changing body pressing tightly against his clothes like a child outgrowing a year-old outfit. His senses were getting stronger, too, and the lights that had attracted his attention before now felt like glaring beacons, annoying him.

Garret shaded his eyes, looking away from the advertisements. Adjusting the polarization of his glasses didn't help;

he needed to keep his focus off the lights entirely. And that was when he saw it: In the shadows of an alleyway, huddled between a dumpster and a decaying wall, a man was hitting a struggling young girl.

The autocops who patrolled the area were designed to respond to the shopkeepers' panic buttons or even alerts from personal comps, but the girl obviously couldn't reach hers and wasn't wearing her control pin. Garret was surprised that he could see well enough to notice the absence of the little spot of shiny metal, and he started to reach for his own to make the summons. Then the change in his body chemistry hit him, a burst of hormones urging him to fight or flee. There was no question what his choice would be.

By the time the autocop rolled over to the alley, the girl was blubbering in Garret's arms and her attacker was sprawled unconscious on the ground. Garret's newly issued military ID made the explanations go quickly, and the autocop's scan of the offender's DNA, which showed a deformity of the cingulate cortex section regulating morality, closed the case. Garret was free to go home with the girl's thanks and a commendation being relayed to his new superior officers.

His home looked smaller—so much smaller—when he walked back in. Part of it was his new size, inches of fast forced growth added to his height and shoulders and padding all over from muscles that were still growing in. But part of it was also the way he now saw the world with a broader perspective due to the information loaded into his chip-assisted brain, and with eyes that focused more sharply than an eagle's. Garret's mother seemed so small and fragile, as if she had shrunk and aged while he was being bumped.

"Oh god, Garret, I was so afraid of what they were doing to you. The stories I heard . . . But you look like you're . . . well . . . just different. Older? Stronger? Did it hurt much?"

"Nothing I couldn't handle, Mom. All I had to do was think about what I wanted to do after I was bumped . . . and think about you."

She started to cry then and didn't stop. Garret ignored the dinner she'd prepared, waved aside the idea of seeing his old friends and relatives. He wasn't going to let anything interfere with what he'd wanted to do since he'd first started dreaming of being bumped.

He sat down by the dusty old shelf, saluted the guardian bear, and took down book after book that he and his mother had read together when he was a child. He caressed the covers, connecting with his old friends, his eyes again able to make out the fine type, and he began to softly read to his mother the stories she was no longer able to read herself. They sat there for hours, Garret reading, his mother crying and listening. And he had a small recorder going all the while, so she'd be able to replay all the stories again and again when he went off to war. As they said in the enlistment ads: Mission accomplished.

ABOUT THE AUTHORS

BARRY LYGA

Barry Lyga (editor) has written a metric ton of books. He's an award winner, a *New York Times* bestseller, a "YA rebel author" (thanks, *Kirkus!*), and a guy whose entire life has been spent reading, writing, studying, selling, buying, and otherwise involved in superheroes. Seriously, it's a sickness, people. He can name every member of the Legion of Super-Heroes, their birth names, and their planets of origin. (Yes, he was very popular in high school.) Find him online at barrylyga.com.

COLLEEN DORAN

Colleen Doran (illustrator) is the *New York Times* bestselling artist for Neil Gaiman's *Troll Bridge* and Stan Lee's autobiography *Amazing, Fantastic, Incredible Stan Lee*. Her work for Gaiman's *Snow Glass Apples* won the Bram Stoker Award for Superior Achievement in a Graphic Novel, the Eisner Award for Best Adaptation, and the Ringo Award for Best Graphic Novel. She has won Eisner and Harvey Awards and the International Horror Guild Award. Art from *Troll Bridge* was selected for the Spectrum annual collection featuring the best science fiction and fantasy art of the year. She has illustrated a wide array of projects including *Amazing Spider-Man*, *The Teen Titans*, *Gotham City Garage*, *Captain America*, *Superman*, *Sandman*, and *Guardians of the Galaxy*.

MORGAN BADEN

Morgan Baden's debut young adult novel, *The Hive*, co-written with her husband, Barry Lyga, was named a Best Book of Fall 2019 by *People* magazine and was called a "gripping, tense, action-packed thriller" by *Booklist*. She's also the author of *Daphne and Velma: The Dark Deception* and *Daphne and Velma: Buried Secrets*, and has an established career in corporate communications, including for the world's largest children's book publisher and distributor. Morgan lives in New Jersey with her husband and two children. She once thought the X-Men were aliens, but eventually grew to embrace the world of superheroes. Find her at morganbaden.com.

JOSEPH BRUCHAC

Joseph Bruchac, an enrolled member of the Nulhegan Abenaki Nation, is a traditional storyteller, musician, and writer. For over forty years he has been creating literature and music that reflect his Indigenous heritage and traditions. Joseph is the author of more than 170 books for children and adults in many different genres, and his poems, stories, and essays have been published in hundreds of magazines and anthologies, ranging from *The Magazine of Fantasy and Science Fiction* and *The Paris Review* to *National Geographic* and *Smithsonian Magazine*. He's a master gardener and a martial arts teacher with black belts in Pentjak Silat and Brazilian jiujitsu, and his experiences include three years of teaching in Ghana and eight years of running a college program in a maximum security prison.

ELIZABETH EULBERG

Elizabeth Eulberg is the international bestselling author of over a dozen novels for young readers, including *The Lonely Hearts Club*, *Better Off Friends*, and her latest, *The Best Worst Summer*, as well as the acclaimed middle-grade detective series The Great Shelby Holmes. As a child, Elizabeth spent many hours in the backyard spinning around in hopes of turning into Wonder Woman. She's still waiting . . . and a bit dizzy.

STERLING GATES

Sterling Gates is a *New York Times* bestselling comic book creator and award-winning screenwriter and producer. Gates's critically acclaimed run on *Supergirl* with artist Jamal Igle redefined the character for a new generation and was named one of the "100 Greatest Superhero Comics of All Time" by *The Hollywood Reporter*. Gates's screen credits include The CW's hit TV shows *Supergirl* and *The Flash*, Marvel Animation Studios's *Spider-Man*, Spin Master's *Super Dinosaur*, and the independent superhero film *The Posthuman Project*. He's also a very proud Eagle Scout. You can find him on Twitter at @sterlinggates and at sterlinggates.com.

LAMAR GILES

Lamar Giles writes for teens and adults across multiple genres, with work appearing on numerous Best Of lists each year. He is the author of the acclaimed novels *Fake ID*, *Endangered*,

Overturned, *Spin*, *The Last Last-Day-of-Summer*, *Not So Pure and Simple*, *The Last Mirror on the Left*, and *The Last Chance for Logan County*, as well as numerous pieces of short fiction. He is a founding member of We Need Diverse Books and resides in Virginia with his wife.

VARIAN JOHNSON

Varian Johnson grew up reading comics about superheroes, and now he gets to write about them. He is the author of several novels for children and young adults, including *The Parker Inheritance*, which won a Coretta Scott King Author Honor; the graphic novel *Twins*, illustrated by Shannon Wright, an NPR Best Book; and the graphic novel *Mister Miracle: The Great Escape*, illustrated by Daniel Isles. Varian lives outside of Austin, Texas, with his family and can be found on the web at varianjohnson.com and @varianjohnson.

PAUL LEVITZ

Paul Levitz is a longtime comics fan (*The Comic Reader*), writer (*Legion of Super-Heroes*), editor (*Batman*), executive (former President & Publisher, DC Comics), historian (*Will Eisner: Champion of the Graphic Novel*), and educator. He was inducted into comics' Eisner Hall of Fame in 2019 and has written more than 500 comic stories. "Bumped!" is his first prose fiction. For more info, please visit paullevitz.com.

SARAH MacLEAN

Sarah MacLean wrote her first book on a dare and never looked back. Now a *New York Times*, *Washington Post*, and

USA Today bestseller, she is the author of romance novels that have been translated into more than twenty languages. Sarah is a leading advocate for the romance genre, speaking widely on its place at the nexus of gender and cultural studies, and the cohost of the weekly romance novel podcast *Fated Mates*. A graduate of Smith College and Harvard University, she lives in New York City. Find Sarah at sarahmaclean.net or fatedmates.net.

ANNA-MARIE McLEMORE

Anna-Marie McLemore (they/them) is a queer, Latine, nonbinary author who grew up hearing La Llorona in the Santa Ana winds. Their work has won the Otherwise Award, a Stonewall Honor, and two Northern California Book Awards. Their books include *The Weight of Feathers*, a 2016 William C. Morris YA Debut Award Finalist; *When the Moon Was Ours*, which was longlisted for the National Book Award in Young People's Literature; *Wild Beauty*, a *Kirkus*, *School Library Journal*, and *Booklist* best book of 2017; *Blanca & Roja*, a *New York Times Book Review* Editors' Choice and one of *Time* magazine's 100 Best Fantasy Novels of All Time; *Dark and Deepest Red*, a Winter 2020 Indie Next List title; Junior Library Guild Selection *The Mirror Season*; *Lakelore*; and *Self-Made Boys: A Great Gatsby Remix*.

AXIE OH

Axie Oh is the author of the mecha sci-fi novels *Rebel Seoul* and *Rogue Heart*, the romantic comedy *XOXO*, and the reimagining of a classic Korean folktale, *The Girl Who Fell Beneath the Sea*. She studied Korean history and creative writing as an undergrad at the University of California San Diego and holds an MFA from Lesley University in Writing for Young People. Her passions include K-pop, anime, stationery supplies, and milk tea. She currently resides in Las Vegas, Nevada, with her dog, Toro (named after Totoro).

DANIELLE PAIGE

Danielle Paige is the *New York Times* bestselling author of the Dorothy Must Die series, as well as the Stealing Snow series. In addition to writing young adult books, she works in the television industry, where she's received a Writers Guild of America Award and was nominated for several Daytime Emmys.

MATTHEW PHILLION

Matthew Phillion has been a journalist and filmmaker, and written about everything from health care to cybersecurity, but his heart has always belonged to comics. He wrote his first YA superhero novel, *The Indestructibles*, after giving himself permission to embrace the inner comic book geek he has always been, and his world has been full-time nerdiness ever since. He has expanded the Indestructiverse setting to include five novels and two spinoff series, the Atlantis-based *Echo and the Sea* and the Dungeon Crawlers novellas." He is based in Salem, Massachusetts, where he is either bouncing plot ideas off his rescued terrier or running shared storytelling role-playing games for his friends.